1/18

15/09/2

KT-451-249

EAST FINCHLEY
LIBRARY

e
e
g
y
s
e
s
)
n

n

Please return/renew this item by the
last date shown to avoid a charge.
Books may also be renewed by phone
and Internet. May not be renewed if
required by another reader.

www.libraries.barnet.gov.uk

BARNET
LONDON BOROUGH

30131 05616834 4

LONDON BOROUGH OF BARNET

By the same author:

Humbugs and Heartstrings
Green Beans and Summer Dreams
Mistletoe and Mayhem
Four Weddings and a Fiasco
The Secrets of Ivy Garden

Christmas at the Log Fire Cabin

Catherine Ferguson

avon.

A division of HarperCollins*Publishers*
www.harpercollins.co.uk

This novel is entirely a work of fiction.
The names, characters and incidents portrayed in it are
the work of the author's imagination. Any resemblance to
actual persons, living or dead, events or localities is
entirely coincidental.

AVON

A division of HarperCollins*Publishers*
1 London Bridge Street,
London SE1 9GF

www.harpercollins.co.uk

This paperback edition 2017

2

First published in Great Britain in ebook format by
HarperCollins*Publishers* 2017

Copyright © Catherine Ferguson 2017

Catherine Ferguson asserts the moral right to
be identified as the author of this work

A catalogue record for this book is
available from the British Library

ISBN-13: 978-0-00-827459-7

Typeset in Birka by Palimpsest Book Production Ltd,
Falkirk, Stirlingshire

Printed and bound by CPI Group (UK) Ltd, Croydon, CR0 4YY

All rights reserved. No part of this publication may be
reproduced, stored in a retrieval system, or transmitted,
in any form or by any means, electronic, mechanical,
photocopying, recording or otherwise, without the prior
permission of the publishers.

For Carole. Half-cousin? Or twice-removed? Still not certain. Just really glad you're my cousin!

Prologue

When I woke, I knew – even before I drew back the curtains – that it had snowed overnight.

The light was subtly different and there was an eerie, muffled quality to the early-morning sounds out in the village of Angelford, where the shop-owners were gearing up for another chaotic, till-ringing day of pre-Christmas cheer and gift-buying.

I slipped out of bed and crossed to the window. The snow glittered in the weak early-December sunlight, swathed like a smooth layer of white icing over our tiny front garden, making comical bulbous shapes out of the holly bush and the little rickety gate.

Standing there, I thought of that other Christmas long ago, when I was twelve. Our mad snowball fight. How I'd battled to keep the snowballs coming to defend myself, hurling them too soon in my excitement so that they ended up as little more than puffs of snow rising up into the air. I remember squealing with laughter as icy water leaked down the back of my coat, my hands numb and raw with the cold because, despite Mum's best efforts, I wouldn't wear my gloves.

The snow always brought the memories of that time flooding back.

Not that I ever forgot.

I'd tried to wipe it from my mind. Pretend it didn't matter. But meeting my real dad when I was twelve, only for him to turn his back on me, wasn't exactly the sort of thing you could blot out at will.

I'd spent four days with him that Christmas. Days that were full of kindness and laughter and learning all about exotic Italy, the place where he was born. And how to make the perfect snowball. Alessandro Bianchi made me feel that I was worth knowing. He'd listened intently to the things I told him about my life and laughed at my jokes, such a stark contrast to the way my bullying stepfather, Martin, made me feel. Although it had happened years ago – I was thirty now, all grown up – I could still recall that breathless sense of wonder when Mum told me Alessandro was my real dad.

I'd had a sense that I was on the brink of something really special; that a whole new life was opening up for me...

How wrong I'd been.

My insides clenched and I turned away from the snowy scene.

It never did me any good to think about the time my real dad came to visit; to linger on those few days I spent with him, as Mum stood by, wary and watching, like a hen protecting her chick.

In my hopeful childhood innocence, I'd assumed it would be the start of something real and life-changing. But in the end, those few days of Christmas turned out to be sparkling but transitory, like the snow itself. All too soon they had melted away into nothing...

Chapter 1

When I open the door to my best friend, Erin, she's standing there trying not to smile and give the game away. But I can see by the sparkle in her green eyes that she has news.

She flicks back her long blonde hair as if to build up the drama. Then she whips something from behind her back and pushes it into my hands.

'What's this?' I laugh. It's a beautiful scarlet apron sprigged with a modern design of snow-white Christmas trees. 'For me?'

She nods gleefully. 'For you, Poppy. You're going to need it. Mrs Morelli wants you to cook for her on Saturday night!' Her last few words are more of an excited squeal.

I glance wide-eyed from her to the living-room door. It's open just a crack. 'Are you mad?'

Her face falls a fraction. 'But why not? It's only a dinner party for eight.'

I stare at her in horror. It's all very well cooking for Harrison, and occasionally Erin and Mark as well. I'm never happier than when I'm doing that. But cooking for *eight strangers*?

'Oh God, Erin, you haven't told her I'll do it, have you?' My heart is beating frantically. Partly because cooking for a living would be a dream come true, if I'm honest. But mostly because I know that I could never pull it off in a million years.

Erin grins. 'I might have,' she says coyly, before catching my dismayed expression. 'Hey, don't worry. I just said I'd check with you.'

I breathe out slowly, my hand on my chest.

'But ... oh, Poppy, you're a brilliant cook!' Her face twists into a frown. 'You're wasted at that Pretty Flaming Cheek Hotel.'

'Pretty Flamingo Boutique Hotel,' I remind her tartly, although she knows full well.

I've been a waitress in the restaurant of the Pretty Flamingo Boutique Hotel since I was sixteen and started working shifts at weekends for extra pocket money. Fourteen years later, I'm still there. I used to dream of going to catering college, but it would have meant moving away from home and I knew Mum needed me close by. Working in the next village means it's easy to pop in and check on her in between shifts.

The hotel is owned by Evelyn and David Nutter, a

couple in their fifties, although it's Mrs Nutter who cracks the whip and makes sure to squeeze every last drop of profit from the business. She's always been okay with me, although Erin doesn't agree. She isn't a fan of their hard-nosed approach to business and she thinks the Nutters take me completely for granted.

'You must admit they do have a flaming cheek the way they treat you. You're *always* being leaned on to do extra shifts by that Mrs Nutjob, and you're far too nice to say no!'

I grin at her. 'Erin, I enjoy being a waitress and I'm good at it. And Mrs Nutter is just trying to make the hotel a success so she and Mr Nutter can retire into the sunset.'

Erin grunts. 'I know you're good at your job. I'm not arguing with that.'

'And I'm about to be promoted to restaurant manager, remember?'

'Of course I remember. Mr Hastings is retiring and everyone knows you're the perfect person to step into his shoes.' She tries to look pleased. 'And that's brilliant, of course. It just seemed like fate when Mrs Morelli mentioned she was looking for a caterer.'

Her voice rises when she's excited or agitated. I put my finger to my lips and indicate the living-room door, behind which my boyfriend is sitting on the sofa, poring over numbers on his laptop.

'Sorry,' she murmurs, leaning closer. 'Didn't mean to announce it to the entire universe. Is Harrison in?'

'Yes. Harrison's just back from work,' I tell her in a normal voice, so he knows we're not whispering and plotting. (Hardly necessary, really. When Harrison's looking at numbers, he's in his own little world.) 'I'd invite you in but Harrison's showing me some – erm – financial projections.'

'Oh. Right. Well, marvellous!' She beams, and I can see from her expression that she's already planning a speedy escape. 'I'll leave you to it, then, shall I?'

Erin is thinking of buying a flat with her boyfriend, Mark, and last time she popped by, Harrison helpfully gave her a detailed run-down on the advantages and pitfalls of what every bank in Britain is currently offering in the way of mortgages. Well, it *seemed* like every bank to me. But that's only because I'm not particularly great with numbers.

Harrison is quite the opposite. He's an accountant and currently in line for promotion at the big London firm where he works. He commutes every day from our home in Surrey and will often work late at the office on the nights I'm serving dinner at the hotel.

'Better get home. I've bought oysters and some fizz for tonight,' says Erin, showing me the bottle in her bag.

'Ooh, what's the occasion?'

She gives me a rather lewd wink. 'No occasion. Except getting Mark in a loving mood, if you know what I mean.'

I grin. 'Do I really need to know about this?'

She pulls a face. 'He's been a bit distracted of late. I think they're working him too hard, poor lamb. Feeding each other oysters is sure to get us back on track.'

'They *are* supposed to be an aphrodisiac.'

'Exactly! You should try them on Harrison.'

'Seafood brings him out in a rash. He's more a steak pie man.'

Erin starts slip-sliding up the snowy path. 'I'll let you get back to your financial projections,' she calls. 'You've got a good one there, Poppy. Mark wouldn't know his APR from his VPL.'

I grin. 'Er, neither would I. APR? Um ... Annual Percentage Thingy?'

She nods. 'Annual Percentage Rate.'

'And VPL?' I cast around for possible words. 'Very Preposterous Logarithm?'

She giggles. 'Visible Panty Line, actually.' Closing the gate behind her, she sets off for her flat at the other end of the high street, pausing only to call, 'Think about Mrs Morelli.'

'I don't have to. It's not happening. But thank you for this.' I hold up the Christmas apron. She shakes her head at me with weary affection, and I wave her off.

Erin and I met six years ago when she started weekend-waitressing at The Pretty Flamingo to make extra cash to fund a course in flower arranging. She couldn't stand working for the Nutters so she didn't last long. But she's since found her perfect job working in a florist's in a neighbouring village, and her dream is to one day own her own shop.

When she first arrived at the hotel, I thought she was loud and a bit of a show-off.

Actually, I still think she's loud and a bit of a show-off, but she's also very kind and loyal with a fabulous sense of humour. The day I realised this, was also the day I was almost sacked by Mrs Nutter for breaking a porcelain statue of a flamingo.

I'd been serving a couple at lunch and I'd thought they were acting a bit oddly. They were already drunk when they sat down, and they spent the entire time whispering together, giggling and glancing over at me. My suspicions turned out to be right. At the end of the meal, they left without paying.

Realising what had happened, I dashed out after them, telling my friend and fellow waitress Maxine to let Mr Hastings know. I've no idea what I thought I was going to do – I just knew that I had to do some-thing to stop them. I was racing through reception when my foot caught on a rug and I went flying against a big glass-fronted cabinet.

The cabinet housed the owners' precious 'pretty flamingo' statue, which gave the hotel its name – and when I jarred the cabinet, the flamingo inside toppled over and smashed. (Although at least Mr Hastings was able to catch the car number plate of the couple doing a runner.) Being young and naive, I felt sure I'd be sacked on the spot. But instead, I had the insurance excess docked from my next month's wages.

When she heard about it, Erin was furious on my behalf and marched me along to see Mrs Nutter. Erin explained why she thought the whole thing was very unfair on me, since all I'd been doing was trying to stop the thieves. I don't think the Nutters were used to being challenged by their employees. Next month, the money was returned to me.

Erin and I have been the best of friends ever since.

Now, staring up at the frosty, star-studded night sky, I pause for a moment at the door, hugging myself against the cold. It's only two weeks till Christmas Day and they're predicting we'll have a white Christmas this year.

A little sigh escapes at the memory of that long-ago snowball fight. My feelings about the white stuff are always bittersweet. Which is why it's definitely best not to dwell on it...

Resolutely, I turn my thoughts back to Erin.

Oh God, Mrs Morelli and her dinner party!

A little jolt of panic surges up in my chest. It's lovely

that Erin has such faith in me. And to be fair, it's not just her own opinion of my cooking talents that she's going on. When we went on our cookery course down in Cornwall last year, the tutor, Greg Allan, took me to one side on the last day and said some very complimentary things. I can remember his exact words. 'You've got an incredible flair for combining flavours and textures, Poppy. I think you have real talent as a cook.'

It felt truly amazing, hearing that from an expert. But I'm starting to wish he'd never said it. Erin was with me at the time and, ever since then, she's been dropping 'hints' the size of ten-tonne boulders that I should ditch the waitressing and become a self-employed caterer instead.

But although she knows me as well as anyone alive, what even *Erin* fails to grasp is my lack of faith in myself.

I just can't do it.

I don't mean that I can't cook. Because I know I can. In fact, apart from when I'm waitressing at the hotel – where everything is so very familiar after fourteen years of working there – my own kitchen is the only place I ever feel totally confident. But to set up on my own and take that huge leap into the unknown would take courage and a level of self-belief I simply don't have.

Sure, part of me would love to do it. Every time Erin

mentions my 'cooking enterprise' as she calls it, a little spark of joy, apprehension and excitement leaps inside me. Just for a moment, I think: *maybe I could...*

But then the memory of my stepfather's mocking face slips into my mind. *Let's face it, she's far too timid. She'll never amount to anything.*

Martin lives in Australia now, with his new wife, and all the rows and the horrible tensions of my childhood are just a bitter memory. I should be able to move on but that's easier said than done. I've told myself a million times that it was nothing personal. Martin was just a troubled man with anger issues, who basically couldn't tolerate the fact I was another man's child. But I still can't stop the little voice in my head, nagging me that he was probably right to doubt that I'd ever be a success in life.

Closing the front door, I catch my reflection in the mirror. Flushed cheeks. Dark-brown eyes clouded with memories of the past. Waves of dark glossy hair, almost black, tumbling over my shoulders, so strikingly similar to Alessandro's colouring in the one creased photo I have of my real dad.

'Poppy? Come and look at these financial projections. I think you'll be stunned.'

Harrison's voice brings me back to earth. Thankfully, my lovely boyfriend doesn't have a bee in his bonnet about me changing my career! In fact, I think he'd be happy if I was a waitress at The Pretty Flamingo for the rest of my working life. He loves my food and is always so appreciative. He thinks cooking is a marvellous hobby to have. But as for turning a pastime into a job? Harrison thinks it would be far too risky.

The one time I mentioned it, he gave a sort of worried grimace, checked the time in Hong Kong on his watch and said something about the unrest in the Middle East having an effect on oil prices. I couldn't quite fathom his thought processes, since the only oil I'd be concerned with was of the cooking variety. But I got the gist. Financially, it was too much of a risk in the current climate to start a brand-new venture.

I walk into the living room, and Harrison pats the seat beside him. 'Erin okay?'

'Yes, she's fine. She and Mark are thinking of the Caribbean for their next holiday.'

He winces. 'Currency rate is appalling at the minute. And that's a *fourteen-hour* flight.'

I glance at his handsome profile as he concentrates on the screen. I can't imagine either of these factors putting Erin off her dream of lounging under a palm tree, with Mark on hand to rub in the sun cream. Or me, for that matter. The furthest Harrison and I have been is Bournemouth. He says it's because there are so many places we've yet to discover at home, here in the UK, and I do think he's got a point. But I suspect it's also an excuse because boarding a plane might bring on one of his anxiety attacks. (He gets twitchy when his feet aren't safely on terra firma.)

I'm very proud of Harrison. He has lovely wavy blond hair that makes him look a bit like an artist and he's the most super-logical, intelligent person I've ever met. The thick-rimmed glasses he wears would look geeky on some men, but on Harrison, they look quite sexy. He's also caring and very responsible – the sort of person who doesn't take chances. He actually sits down and *reads* the terms and conditions, instead of flicking over them and assuming everything's in order.

'So, as I was saying before Erin arrived, if you were to transfer your savings into this high-interest account, I think you'd be onto a winner.'

Turning, he catches me stifling a yawn and smiles. 'You don't really care, do you?'

I grin at him. 'Yes, I do. Honestly! But you're so much better at this stuff than I am, so I suppose I just rely on you to tell me what's best.'

He shrugs and runs a hand through his blond waves. 'Well, what I think is best ...' He reaches an arm around my waist and drops a kiss on my neck. 'Come on, wriggle closer,' he murmurs.

I smile and hitch along the sofa, snuggling up to him. Perhaps we'll forget about numbers for a while – a very *long* while.

'That's better,' he says, tapping my back and returning to the laptop. 'You can see the screen properly now. Now, high-interest savings.' He rubs his hands together then peers eagerly at the screen. I study him affectionately, like a mum watching her kid tear the wrapping off a Christmas present.

'Unless –' He turns with a sexy glint in his eye and my spirits rise. 'What do you say to throwing caution completely to the wind?'

'I'm all for that,' I murmur, running my hand along his thigh. *I wonder what he has in mind? Sex on a week night, perhaps?*

He pats my knee and gives me a cheerful wink. 'Brilliant. We'll go for investment funds, then, shall we? Let's live dangerously.'

'Oh. Right.'

After a while, my mind starts to wander.

I keep thinking about Erin planning her romantic night with Mark. Perhaps I should do something similar. Harrison always says sex is best left for weekends when he's got more energy, but I'm sure I can persuade him that a little mid-week spontaneity would be nice.

I spring up off the sofa.

'Where are you off to?'

I wink at him. 'Wait and see.'

Upstairs, I rummage in my underwear drawer and find my one pair of black stockings. I'm out of practise so it takes me the best part of fifteen minutes to get them on smooth and straight. But when I wriggle into the close-fitting little red dress I bought to wear at Harrison's work do last Christmas, I'm feeling really quite sexy. Adjusting my hair, I allow some dark tendrils to fall down, framing my face. A slick of scarlet lipstick and an extra coat of mascara and I'm ready for anything!

I navigate the carpeted stairs carefully in my black patent high heels and strike a pose in the living-room doorway. 'What do you think?'

'About what, Puss?' Harrison is focusing hard on the screen.

'About this dress you chose for me last Christmas?' I experiment with a sexy pout in profile.

'Hm?' he murmurs, still not looking up.

I sigh, feeling a bit of an idiot standing there in my best harlot outfit, knowing I come a poor second to a graphic of the FTSE 100.

'Harrison!'

He glances up at the urgency in my tone. His face relaxes and breaks into a smile. 'Very nice. What's the occasion, Puss?' He pats the seat next to him.

I wince slightly at the pet name, which has only recently come into being, but I'm heartened by his positive response.

'No occasion.' I smile enigmatically and sit down next to him, crossing my legs artfully to reveal just a glimpse of stocking top. 'I'm not at the restaurant tonight, so I thought we could – erm – celebrate.'

'Oh? And what did you have in mind?' He slides his hand up my thigh and waggles his eyebrows suggestively, which for some reason makes me think of Groucho Marx. I shake the image from my head and lean over to kiss him – just as he turns to glance at his watch, which means my mouth totally misses the target.

'The news is on in a minute,' he says cheerfully. 'How about we watch that then nip along the road for a takeaway?' Clocking my lack of enthusiasm, he tucks a loose tendril of hair behind my ears and says, 'Keep that lot on, though. You're looking very sexy, Puss!'

Sighing, I teeter back upstairs and slip into jeans and a jumper. I don't really mind. It'll be another night of falling asleep in front of the telly, but there's something really cosy and intimate about that, isn't there? I'm so lucky to have someone like Harrison in my life.

Chapter 2

'What do you think?' asks Mum, holding out a plastic lemon-squeezer with the sort of feverish excitement she once reserved for Def Leppard concerts.

'It's a plastic lemon-squeezer, Mum.'

She doesn't hear me. She's too busy dropping it in her trolley along with a bright-green loofah in the shape of the Incredible Hulk and a set of labels for jam-making – ooh, where's she off to now? Ah, yes, of course, the washing-up liquid.

I stand there, experiencing a horrible panicky sensation like I always do with Mum, as if my insides are slowly deflating. I wonder if things will ever change. I really should be helping her heft that bargain box of twenty-four 'Skweezee' bottles into her trolley but I can't seem to summon up the energy.

'Right, that should do,' she says, avoiding my eye.

I can't help it. I have to say it. 'You never make jam, Mum, so why the labels?'

'They're marked down. And you should never say never!' She smiles triumphantly and trundles off towards the checkout. My heart gives a painful little squeeze. Mum used to be so vibrant and self-assured when she worked at the hospital. She had an easy way with the staff – firm but always fair seemed to be the general opinion of her. And with her pale-golden hair pushed back in a quirky knot, she managed to be stylish, too – not always easy when you're wearing scrubs. I remember being so proud of her.

Now, the hair that straggles down her back contains a lot more grey strands than golden, but she refuses point-blank to let me organise for a mobile hairdresser to call round and give her a trim.

Back at hers, we lug the spoils out of the boot and I brace myself to face the house. I should be used to it by now, but the impulse to escape is just as strong as ever. When I finally moved out, three years ago, into a little flat of my own nearby, the relief (and the guilt) was enormous.

She unlocks the door and pushes it open to its full extent and we squeeze through the small gap. Manoeuvring the gigantic load of washing-up liquid, I accidentally knock against the hall table and the tower of boxes perched on top tumbles off, spilling their contents everywhere. (A mish-mash of car-boot sale tat, by the looks of things.)

Mum turns and gives me a frosty look. 'Tidy that up, will you, dear?' She pushes on into what used to be the living room but is now just an extension of the chaos in the hallway: boxes and objects piled high, and towers of newspapers everywhere, most of them unread. She has two newspapers delivered every day – one national and one local – and I'm never allowed to throw them out. I used to try sneaking a few old papers in my bag to dispose of at home, but she's no fool, my mum. She's got eyes in the back of her head. So now I've given up. It's not worth the bitterness and the hurt silences.

'Pot noodle?' she shouts from the direction of the kitchen.

'I brought some sandwiches,' I call back, stacking the load of washing-up liquid bottles on top of an identical monster family-pack, bought the last time we were in the shop seven days ago. 'Ham salad. Your favourite.'

'Oh, lovely. Bring them through.'

We eat squashed together on a two-seater sofa, an ancient standard lamp with a fringed green shade towering over us on one side. On the other, a chest of drawers is bumped right up to the sofa, and a laundry basket sits on top, containing a tangle of old electrical leads and dozens of paperback books. Perched at a jaunty angle on this pile, looking sad and slightly cross-eyed, is the largest of Mum's stuffed parrots. This one

– a hideous blue, green and pink thing – is sitting in a cage.

Mum has a thing for exotic birds. She says they make her happy. If it weren't for the man-made chaos in here, you might think she was aiming for a 'tropical rainforest' feel to her décor, in that wherever you are in the house – even sitting on the loo – you're practically guaranteed a sighting of a stuffed parrot.

Mum tucks into the sandwiches with gusto. I'm sure when I'm not there she lives on tea and biscuits and microwave meals. And pot noodles. The oven finally disappeared under piles of junk about two years ago, so now only the kettle and microwave are fully functional. The fridge gave up the ghost about the same time and hasn't been fixed because Mum refuses to have visitors to the house, apart from me (and that's only on the unspoken understanding that I won't criticise her living arrangements) so I try to bring a healthy food parcel every time I visit.

'How did you get that bruise?' I ask, and she glances at a big purple mark on her arm.

'Oh, that.' She shakes her head dismissively and pulls her sleeve right down. 'I was climbing over a pile of bedding and my foot got caught in a duvet, that's all.'

'God, Mum, you have to be careful,' I murmur. 'Anything could happen.'

It's actually my worst nightmare. That Mum's hoarding

might end up being the death of her. That, one day, a pile of boxes will tumble on top of her, or worse, that she might accidentally start a fire that will blaze all the more fiercely as it devours her monstrous, ceiling-high towers of newspapers and medical journals. What if she can't get out of the building fast enough?

But she's immediately on the defensive. 'Oh, rubbish. The place might seem a bit untidy to you but *I'm* the one who lives here. I'm used to it.'

'Yes, but all these newspapers? It's a fire hazard, Mum. And what if a pile of boxes falls on you and you injure yourself and I'm not here to help?'

She laughs and pats my hand. 'Honestly, Poppy, you can be so melodramatic at times. I'm absolutely fine. Now, let's have some tea. And you can tell me all about your new job.'

'I haven't got it yet, Mum.'

'When do you find out?'

'Friday.'

'Well, they'd be stupid not to make you restaurant manager. You know the place inside out.' She takes my hand and squeezes it. 'Who else would do such a good job?'

I smile at her, surprised to find my throat tightening with emotion. Mum's default mode is generally prickly and defensive these days. She's rarely so openly affectionate. 'I hope you're right, Mum.'

She smiles. 'Of course I'm right. You've given everything to that place. It's only what you deserve.' She sets off on a winding assault course to find the kettle, weaving around wobbly landmarks and walking over a rustle of newspapers that haven't yet migrated to one of the towers against the wall.

I stare around me, taking in the full extent of the nightmare. I try not to look, usually, because what tends to happen is, I start noticing things that surely even *Mum* wouldn't be sad parting with. (Most of it is useless tat, to my eyes anyway, but stuff like the growing stack of washed-out tin cans she's keeping 'just in case they come in handy'? I mean, really? So then I'll start hinting about possibly disposing of them to make space for other things, at which point a heart-twisting mix of seething anger and tearful vulnerability will appear on Mum's face, and I'll know to stop because I've gone too far. Then I drive home feeling sad, guilty and utterly frustrated because I've racked my brains and I really don't know what to do to help her.

The one time I gently suggested she might want to speak to someone about her collecting (I wouldn't dare call it hoarding), she stormed away into the bathroom – the only room with an operational door to slam – then wouldn't take my phone calls for a week. She apologised eventually but I haven't dared be so direct with her since.

Mum was a doctor specialising in cardiology before she and Martin divorced and she went to pieces.

The only hearts she's interested in these days are the cheap, ornamental kind with cute slogans on them.

Harrison and Mum tend to give each other a wide berth these days. He and I had a shouting match over Mum – the only heated argument we've ever had – when he said wasn't it time I took the situation in hand and cleared out all the clutter myself instead of letting her fester her days away in such a hell-hole? I couldn't make him understand that Mum has always had a will of iron and that if she digs her heels in over something, there is no one on this earth – not even me (*especially* not me) – who can shift her.

She was pregnant with me when she started her medical degree, and it's a mark of her steely determination that she gave birth during the Easter holidays and was back at uni along with all her classmates when the new term began. Despite baby me keeping her up at night, she still managed to pass her exams that first year with flying colours.

I don't know how she did it without any help and precious little sleep. I always imagine her sitting in a little pool of light at the kitchen table, poring over her medical books at some deathly hour of the night, flicking the pages over with one hand while managing to soothe and feed me at the same time. Having a tiny baby to take care of was never going to stop Donna Patterson, as she was then, in her quest to become a doctor.

When I was one, Mum fell in love with Martin Ainsworth, her next-door neighbour. At least, I think she loved him. She must have, in the beginning. But I can only really remember the rows.

Until I was twelve, I assumed he was my dad because neither he nor Mum ever told me any different. I couldn't understand why we didn't have the close sort of relationship my friends had with their dads. I was desperate for his approval but I never quite managed to please him and I thought it was because I wasn't bright enough or funny enough or well behaved enough. There were times when I almost managed to convince myself that it was just the type of person he was – always harshly critical of everyone – because he was like that a lot of the time with Mum, too. She could never do anything right, either.

But deep down, I always knew it was my fault he didn't love me enough.

When I found out – at the age of twelve – that he wasn't actually my biological dad, a lot of things that puzzled me about him finally made sense. I wasn't his real daughter and he must have resented me being there, particularly because I ate up so much of Mum's time and love.

Mum fell to pieces after he left and they divorced, which surprised me. I thought she'd much prefer the peace that reigned in the house once he'd gone. I certainly did. When Martin was there, it sometimes felt like we were inhabiting a war zone, never quite certain from one moment to the next what was about to rain down on our heads. Not literally. Martin was never physically abusive. But emotional abuse, I discovered, can feel just as wounding.

When he'd gone and it was just Mum and me, I could finally relax.

It was alien to me at first. I marvelled at the peace, picturing the inside of my head as smooth and silky soft, like the new lilac throw on my bed, instead of the jumble of painful chaos it contained when Martin lived with us.

Being older now, and having had time to reflect, I can see that he struggled right from the start, bringing up another man's child. He was a jealous sort of person anyway, and I was a constant reminder to him of Mum's first love. It was never going to be a solid basis for a harmonious family life.

That Christmas when I turned twelve, Martin was working away and I met my real dad, although I didn't realise at the time that this was who he was.

Christmas that year was wonderful.

No arguments. No stern expectations. No worrying

that I was doing things wrong and would upset Martin and ruin Christmas. We just had a fun time, me and Alessandro, doing lots of silly and exciting festive things. Mum said she was pleased I had a good time but she hung back from joining in. I have a clear memory of her standing with her arms folded in the doorway, biting her lower lip, watching as Alessandro and I hammed it up in the kitchen, singing along to Slade as we cooked Christmas dinner together.

Even now, looking back, I get a lump in my throat, remembering how hopeful and excited I was to discover that this fun-loving, kind, affectionate man was actually my real dad. This was how my life was supposed to be. This was how it *would* be from now on! Of course, he had to return to Italy because that was where he lived. But he would come back to see me, I was certain of that.

I don't think Mum was planning on telling me he was my biological dad. When he came that Christmas, she introduced him as a friend from university, but after he'd gone, I kept badgering her about him, asking lots of questions. Even at that young age, I could feel the tension between them and sensed there was something more to their relationship than just friends.

I was also puzzled by the feeling that I'd met Alessandro once before. When Mum introduced him, I thought I recognised his face, although I couldn't for the life of me remember where I'd seen him. When I mentioned this to Mum later, she said I couldn't possibly have met him before because he lived in Italy; he must just remind me of someone because that sometimes happened. It still nagged at me, though.

Eventually, Mum just came out with it and told me he was my biological dad and that she'd got pregnant when she was on her gap year in Naples. That, of course, produced a flood of questions from me, along the lines of why didn't they stay together and why did my dad wait so long to come and meet me? I could tell Mum wasn't comfortable revisiting the past, so eventually I stopped asking questions and just accepted what she kept telling me – that she and Alessandro were both so career driven, it could never have worked between them, and that while Martin might not be my biological dad, in every other way, he was. He'd been there for me all my life – all those years Alessandro was absent. Very gently, she told me I shouldn't count on seeing Alessandro again. He had a life in Italy and who knew when or if he would return to England? I think she just wanted to protect me from being hurt.

But deep down, I knew different. We'd had such a brilliant time together. Of course Alessandro would want to come back and see me.

For a full year, I looked forward to Christmas with a lightness of spirit and a happiness in my heart that

I'd never felt before, convinced he would return. I knew without doubt that we'd have an even better time than the previous year. I was going to let him read the Christmas diary I'd written about the amazing time we'd spent together, and I'd saved up lots of funny stories during the year to make him laugh.

I was so naive.

I learned a cruel lesson that year. Daydreaming can be so dangerous when the reality turns out to be heart-breakingly different to what you imagine.

Alessandro never did come back for me.

'Tea?'

I look up, dazed. Mum is holding out a mug.

Deftly whisking away the tears, I paste on a smile, hardening my heart to the memories, as I always do.

Mum frowns. 'What's wrong?' She's immediately on the defensive, thinking she's upset me. 'I'm going to have a bit of a tidy-up tomorrow, so you don't need to worry about me.'

I shake my head and take a gulp of hot tea that burns my mouth. 'Good, good.' These days, I go along with her pretence that she's going to get around to clearing up the place. I know she won't. And that's why I will keep coming round every day. To make sure she hasn't toppled the huge stack of medical books piled up on the side table, knocking herself unconscious with *The Oxford Handbook of Clinical Diagnosis*. (It gives me nightmares, that tower of hardback books, but Mum point-blank refuses to move them, saying that she might need them for reference.) Or that she hasn't accidentally set one of her revolting stuffed parrots on fire. Actually, that would probably be a *good* thing.

If I don't laugh about it, there's a danger I might start weeping and never be able to stop.

I take a deep breath and change the subject. 'We'll need to talk about Christmas Day. When I should collect you and bring you over to ours.'

It's going to be just Mum and me this Christmas. Harrison's dad died earlier this year and his mum lives in Spain, so Harrison is flying over to join her for the festive season. It'll be strange not to be together on Christmas Day.

Mum waves her hand. 'Oh, there's plenty of time for that,' she says, even though there really isn't. I know she finds the festive season hard. I suspect that if she had her way, she'd elect to stay here with her pot noodles for company. She hates thinking she's a burden to me. But I'd never want to spend Christmas without her.

I feel suddenly overwhelmed with sadness. If I were ever granted a wish by some passing fairy godmother, it would be this: Please help Mum to move on with her life the way Martin has…

*

On the short drive home, I think about relationships and how it's so difficult to know if you've met the right one for you. Mum thought she had, but how wrong she was.

I'm happy with Harrison, and I know the feeling is mutual. We're quite different in many ways but they do say that opposites attract, don't they?

Everyone should have a hobby, and Harrison is fascinated by Britain's industrial heritage. He reads weighty tomes on the subject (weighty in the physical sense, as well as the intellectual – they're the sort of books that come in really handy if a door needs wedging open). And he particularly enjoys photographing manhole covers. He says there's a wealth of fascinating history right under our feet that people don't even notice.

I must admit, it took me a while to get my head round his passion for manhole covers. But after a weekend in London dedicated to showing me many fine examples of cast-iron street furniture, I can sort of see why he's interested. (Well, actually, I still struggle. I'd rather have gone to Madame Tussauds, to be honest. But that's just me. Embarrassingly lacking in intellect. We did have a brilliant full English next morning, though.)

To be fair, it's not *just* manholes. Harrison will also drive a fair few miles to see a good coal-hole cover, and the occasional drain grating. At first, I thought it was a really weird hobby to have. But I've been online and it absolutely isn't! You'd never believe it but there's actually a whole army of 'gridders', as they call themselves.

This morning, over breakfast, he was telling me that he'd heard about a particularly fine specimen of drain cover in cast iron somewhere along Ribblesham High Street. (Interestingly, not all drain covers are made of cast iron. Concrete is also used. And it's a little-known fact that manhole covers date back to the era of ancient Rome, which is obviously a very long time ago. I know these things now.)

Another interesting fact is that Harrison and I actually *met* over a drain cover. It's true! Mum's bungalow is built on the site of an old ironworks and, would you believe, there's a manhole cover almost right outside her house that has the name of the ironworks company on it. I'd never really noticed it before. Until the day Harrison was there, taking photos of it from dozens of different angles.

It was a boiling-hot afternoon in July last year. I'd nipped over to see Mum in between shifts, only to find her in despair over a blocked toilet. We tried pouring bleach down and waiting before flushing, but that had no effect. Mum was almost in tears because she knew what was coming. I was going to have to call a tradesman.

'It's fine,' she said, pleadingly. 'I read somewhere

baking soda can work wonders. I'll see if I can find some.' She went off to perform the hoarder's equivalent of finding a needle in a haystack, and I stared after her in despair.

'Mum, you have to get it sorted properly. You can't live with a blocked toilet. I'm going to phone a plumber.'

'No! I won't let you!' She beetled back and made a grab for my phone. It fell to the ground, smashing the screen, and I had to bite my lip to stop myself yelling at her. I couldn't leave Mum without sorting out the damn toilet, but how could I do that without a plumber? And now my phone was broken!

The burden of caring for Mum was suddenly too much. I escaped outside on the pretext of looking for something in the garage, and leaned against the wall, taking big gulps of fresh air and trying to calm down so that I could try to address the problem logically.

That's when I noticed a youngish, fair-haired man, with dark-rimmed glasses and what looked like a camera, peering intently at the ground just beyond Mum's front gate. Wondering if he was okay, I went over to investigate.

He looked up and I thought how handsome he was.

'Do you live here?' he asked, gazing at the house as if it was a palace.

'No. But my mum does.'

'Wow. Does she know she has a piece of social history

right outside her front gate?' He pointed at the circular piece of metal, with a design on it, set into the pavement. 'Look at that. A Victorian coal-hole cover, made by a foundry that doesn't exist any more. Amazing!'

'Gosh. Now that I know it's a piece of Victorian history, I'll take more notice of it in future!'

He smiled, showing lovely white teeth.

I took out my hanky to dab my wet mascara.

'Are you all right?' He seemed genuinely concerned, so I ended up telling him all about Mum's blocked toilet and how she hated having tradesmen in because then they'd see the state of the house.

'I know a bit about plumbing,' he said. 'Would you like me to have a look?'

I was so relieved, I actually laughed. 'Would you? I'd be so grateful. If I can't fix it, she'll have to come and stay with me tonight.'

'Oh, well, in that case, we'd definitely better do something!'

We laughed at his joke and went inside, and I distracted Mum in the kitchen by making tea, while Harrison burrowed his way through to the bathroom. He took the piles of junk in his stride, and not once did he turn back to me to roll his eyes or give me a funny look.

Twenty minutes later, after he'd poured a whole bottle of shampoo down the toilet, followed by a bucket of hot water, Mum was smiling with relief that her loo was flushing properly again, and offering him tea.

His name was Harrison, and Mum seemed amazed to learn that she had a piece of social history right outside her front gate.

I swear it was fate at work that day. I mean, what are the chances of there being a manhole cover *right outside Mum's house* that Harrison just happened to be photographing at the *exact time* I was inside having a complete meltdown over Mum? Often, we'll be talking fondly about the unexpectedness of our first meeting, and Harrison will heave a sigh, abandoning himself to sentimental reminiscences. 'Remember that manhole cover!' he'll say.

And I'll smile and recall how he rode to my rescue. I'd been at my very lowest ebb that day, desperately scared about Mum's future and feeling so alone. But Harrison turned things around.

It's something I'll never, ever forget.

Chapter 3

When I arrive back from Mum's, Harrison is still out, so I decide to make a start on the mince pies I've offered to bake for his office party on Friday.

He's been making a big effort lately to show that he's worthy of a promotion at work, and he's hoping to impress his sweet-toothed boss with my special Christmassy pies. They have a deliciously rich and crumbly orange-and-cinnamon pastry, and I add apple brandy to the filling to make them extra indulgent. I doubt my festive snacks alone will land him the job he's after, but it's lovely that Harrison considers my baking worth showing off.

Thinking about Harrison's hopes of promotion reminds me that in a few days' time, I'll find out if I'm to be The Pretty Flamingo's new restaurant manager! A bolt of nerves and excitement surges through me. Everyone seems to think I'm the obvious candidate and I know Mr Hastings, the retiring restaurant manager, likes and trusts me. The fact that I've worked through every Christmas period for the past six years is sure to count in my favour. Plus the fact that I'm always happy to work extra shifts when they're short-staffed. If I get the promotion, Erin might stop badgering me to leave and take up cooking for a living!

But perhaps they won't think I'm good enough.

Instantly, I'm back in that kitchen doorway, a miserable ten-year-old, overhearing a bitter-sounding Martin muttering to Mum, 'Let's face it, she's far too timid. She'll never amount to anything.'

Something inside me dies but I brush the feeling away, as I always do, telling myself I don't care. If I get the job, great. If I don't, it really doesn't matter.

The message light is flashing on the landline in the living room. Pressing the 'play' button on the speaker, I head through to the kitchen, already rolling my sleeves up to start baking and expecting to hear Harrison telling me when he'll be home.

I stop in the doorway.

Unless he's caught a horrible cold that's deepened his voice and added a barrowload of gravel to it, that's definitely not Harrison. Maybe it's a friend of his or one of his colleagues. I hurry back into the living room, just as the stranger's deep voice rumbles, 'pulling out your heart by its bootstraps. But enough of that ...'

Intrigued, I hit 'play' to hear the message from the beginning.

Hi Clemmy, it's Jed Turner. Have to say it was amazing seeing you on Saturday night. Can't believe it's been so long since our legendary holiday in France. And by the way, you never spoke truer words than when you said about love reaching into your chest and pulling out your heart by its bootstraps. (A throaty chuckle here.) But on to cheerier matters. I'm calling to invite you to spend Christmas in the country. Log fire, hot tub and an entire forest of fir trees. How could you refuse? Phone me to say yes.

I stand there, staring at the phone, the cogs of my brain whirring madly.

Who on earth is Jed Turner? And who, for that matter, is Clemmy? It must be a wrong number. All the same, I listen to the message again, although it's more out of curiosity than anything else.

Jed Turner has a deliciously deep voice. *Someone's* obviously had their heart broken with all that bootstrap talk! I wonder if it's him?

I listen to it twice more, shaking my head at the weirdness of the message landing on our phone, and wondering vaguely where this amazing place is with its log fire and hot tub. Somewhere quite palatial, by the sounds of things.

I feel a bit guilty, as if I'm eavesdropping: It should be Clemmy listening to the message, not me. But that's silly – there's nothing I can do about it. Presumably when Jed doesn't hear back, he'll phone her again and, this time, he'll get the number right.

But I need to get on. I have mince pies to bake!

I wash my hands and gather my equipment and ingredients, all the while mulling distractedly over the phone message.

What is the relationship between Jed Turner and Clemmy? They'd been on a 'legendary' holiday to France, but that seemed to be a while ago. Were they boyfriend and girlfriend when they jetted off together? Describing a holiday as 'legendary' means it was obviously pretty special in some way. Maybe they had stupendous sex for the first time in their lives, or maybe they had a mad, passionate fling but were forced to go their separate ways at the end of their magical holiday, or maybe I should stop dreaming up these ridiculously romantic scenarios because the reality is probably very different. It's just that having heard Jed Turner's rumbling and seductively deep voice for myself, it's little wonder my imagination is running riot.

I stop and stare into my bowl. *What am I doing?* The recipe calls for 200 grams of plain flour, but I've somehow carefully measured out the same weight in granulated sugar instead! I never usually get it wrong. What's going on?

It's that phone message.

It's thrown me because I really don't know what to do about it. Obviously, Jed is keen to get together with Clemmy, and inviting her to spend Christmas with him is a pretty bold move. But Clemmy didn't receive the message. *I* did. And how sad is that? What if they never get a chance to meet up and possibly reignite their passion? All because Jed Turner punched in the wrong digits?

I need to get his number on 'call return' and phone him to tell him about his mistake.

Oh, shit!

Glancing down, I grimace at the greyish lump of dough in my hands.

What's the golden rule of making perfect pastry? *Use a light touch!* But for the past few minutes, I've been pummelling the pastry to within an inch of its life, squeezing and mangling it like I'm trying to hand-wash a stubborn stain from a favourite cardy. I stare into the bowl in dismay. Forget 'light and flaky'. These mince pies will be hard enough to substitute as balls at Wimbledon.

An hour later, I'm just cracking a tooth on one, trying it fresh from the oven, when I realise I've got a text from Harrison, sent half an hour ago.

Getting five-o'clock back. Will phone when on train.

I smile affectionately. Harrison's texts are always brief and to the point, with no emoticon extras, but I'm used to that. It's just him.

I glance at my watch. It's five-fifteen. Panic surges within me.

Oh God, what if he phones me on the landline?

Dropping the mince-pie disaster, I race through to the living room and snatch up the phone before Harrison's call can wipe the last 'call return' number. Dialling 1471, I carefully note down the digits on a nearby piece of paper, noticing that it's a local call.

Then I study the number thoughtfully.

Jed Turner sounds like a perfectly nice man and I'm sure he would welcome my call. But something is stopping me phoning him, and I'm not really sure what it is.

Carefully, I fold up the paper and slip it into my jeans pocket. I'll phone Jed Turner when I've got more time.

I definitely will...

Chapter 4

'Time for a coffee at your place?' I call after Erin as we battle our way through the crowds to the main exit of Bradbury's department store. With less than a fortnight to go until the big day, Christmas-shopping madness in Angelford is reaching fever pitch.

Erin turns and signals happily with her thumb over the heads of several shoppers, totally oblivious to the fact she just almost put a man's eye out. Wincing, I weave my way through the throng and join her outside on the pavement. After the warm fug of the centrally heated store, the frozen air makes me gasp. We huddle into our coats, hands deep in our pockets, and start walking along to Erin's flat.

'So, anyway,' she says, finishing a 'bad break-up' story she was telling me in the perfume department before we got separated in the crowd. 'He was the one who *waited till after midnight* so he didn't have to break up with me on my birthday! Can you believe that?'

I roll my eyes at such idiocy and hunch up my shoulders for warmth.

Erin can relate all these bad break-up stories with a big smile on her face for one very good reason: Mark. Since they met over a year ago, she and Mark have been totally inseparable. They truly are two halves that make up a whole. Same daft sense of humour. Same weird obsession with zombie films. And completely besotted with each other.

I'm so pleased for her because her romantic life before she met him was a non-stop disaster. She seemed to be forever falling heavily for a guy, then finding she'd picked the only bloke in the room with a weird hang-up.

'He wasn't as bizarre as the freckle guy, though,' I remind her.

She snorts. 'Yeah. That was weird. He said he never went out with freckled girls but he'd make an exception because he thought he might be falling in love with me.'

'Then he dumped you two weeks later because he tried – he *really tried* – but he just couldn't get past the freckles!'

'Mark loves my freckles.' She beams, and I smile back at her, not even minding that she sounds unashamedly smug. Erin *so* deserves happiness in love for once.

She's been out with some real horrors, who took advantage of her trusting nature (and in one case took her jewellery box as well). But she always bounced back and never once wavered from her conviction that 'the one' for her was out there somewhere.

I so admire this inner strength of hers. I'd have been a basket case if Revolting Ronnie had scarpered with *my* mum's ruby dress ring. But then, I am – as Erin continually points out – a bit inexperienced when it comes to dating. I've had boyfriends, of course, because I do like men. Trouble is, until I met Harrison, I never trusted them to stick around. And so, of course, they never did.

Erin is a true romantic at heart, and she adores her little one-bed flat with its cute Romeo and Juliet-style balcony. It's on the first floor of a rather stylish, modern block built of mellow red brick. A little sign declaring 'Home is where the heart is' hangs, quirkily lopsided, from the wrought-iron balcony railings and there's just about enough room for one person and a plant to sit out and enjoy the view over the park opposite.

It's nearly four and already dark – Christmas lights flash all along the high street – by the time we climb the stairs to her flat on the first floor. I collapse onto her lovely, squashy sofa while Erin goes off to put the kettle on.

'If Harrison were to propose, where would you like it to be?' she calls through from the kitchen.

I laugh. 'We've only known each other eighteen

months. I doubt he'll be suggesting marriage any time soon.'

'Oh, you never know. But supposing he did, where would you choose?'

'Ooh, erm … in Tiffany's on Fifth Avenue, then we could choose the ring there! What about you?'

'Not sure.'

'Top of the Eiffel Tower?' I suggest, grinning, as she comes through with the coffee.

'Nah! Mark's terrified of heights so that would be no good.'

'Of course. I'd forgotten about that.'

She smiles affectionately. 'He doesn't even like stepping out onto my balcony, bless him. Speaking of which, how do you fancy having coffee out there, looking at the Christmas lights?'

I laugh. 'Go on, then. If we must.'

Erin takes every opportunity she can to sit out on her little balcony and I don't blame her. It's got a great view over the high street and the park. Trouble is, it's bloody parky out there at this time of year.

In the end, we compromise, drinking our coffee inside, then shrugging on our coats and going out to lean on the rail and gaze out over the festive rush hour.

'What's all this talk about proposals, anyway?' I ask. 'Are you psyching yourself up to ask Mark to marry you?'

'*He* should be so lucky!' she retorts, sounding surprisingly bitter.

'Everything okay?' I ask.

'Yeah, fine.' She sighs and stares moodily over the park.

I glance at her profile, wondering what's wrong. She's been complaining recently that Mark is taking her for granted. But that probably just means he's started buying her flowers once a fortnight, instead of every week. I can totally understand her nervousness, though, after all the bad luck she's had with men in the past.

'If Harrison ever proposed, it would probably be over a manhole cover because that's how we met,' I say, to try and cheer her up.

She laughs. 'Very romantic.'

'It would be romantic wherever it was.' I shrug. 'I wouldn't need a three-ring circus. Just me and the man I love.'

'Aw, you put me to shame, missus. I'd definitely need the full works. I'd want to feel like he'd been planning it for weeks and that he hadn't just got drunk and grabbed for a makeshift ring!'

'What are you two doing for Christmas?'

She's back to looking gloomy. 'Nothing. I wanted to go away, just the two of us, but Mark says he can't afford it so that's that.'

'Did I hear my name mentioned?' calls the man

himself, and Erin spins round.

'How long have you been there?' she laughs, going inside to say hello.

'Long enough to hear you describe me as mean,' he growls, grabbing her and pulling her in for a kiss.

I smile to myself. From where I'm standing, I really don't think Erin has anything to worry about. Mark seems just as crazy about her as ever.

Chapter 5

'Problem customer!' murmurs my colleague, Maxine, halfway through our Friday-lunchtime shift.

'Really?' My heart sinks. I'm so tired. This afternoon, I'll find out who will be the new restaurant manager, and I've been up half the night feeling anxious about it. I've been trying to throw myself into my work, as if it's just another shift, but as my meeting with Mr Hastings at three-thirty creeps nearer, my stomach is growing more and more jittery by the minute.

The last thing I need is a tricky diner using up my last reserves of strength.

Maxine flicks her eyes across the room and I peer over, pretending that I'm checking to make sure everything is looking as it should.

'She's complained about everything from the temperature in the room to the flowers on her table not being entirely fresh – and that's even before she's started eating!'

As we look on surreptitiously, the woman summons eighteen-year-old Ellie with one imperious finger raised in the air. It's Ellie's first week in the job and she's quite shy and terrified of making mistakes. (I can *so* empathise with her. I was just like her when I started.)

Ellie darts forward helpfully.

It's clear that something else is wrong. The woman is frowning and speaking rapidly, and as we watch, Ellie's face falls.

I catch her in the kitchen and it's obvious from the tension in her face, she's desperately trying to hold it together.

'What's wrong?' I ask.

Ellie swallows and looks down. 'She said I must be stupid because I didn't bother to find out the soup of the day before I came on shift.'

'Right. I'll handle her.' I walk calmly back into the restaurant, only to be immediately summoned by our difficult diner. Pasting on my best polite and helpful smile, I walk over to her table. 'Can I help?'

She looks at me frostily. 'I certainly hope so. This fish is staring at me.'

'I beg your pardon, madam?' Feeling slightly wrong-footed, I glance at the contents of her plate.

'The mackerel. It's staring at me. I don't like it. It's putting me off my lunch.'

'I'm *so sorry*.' Carefully, I turn the plate a half-circle. 'Is that better?'

'Are you being funny?' She peers at me suspiciously.

'No. Definitely not. I just thought if the fish wasn't facing you ...'

'Yes, but I'll still know they're there, won't I?' she snaps. 'The eyes.'

'Of course, madam. Would you like me to take it away and remove the head for you?'

'But then it won't be a "whole mackerel". It'll be a "headless mackerel", which isn't quite the same thing, is it?'

'Um ... no, I suppose it isn't.' It's an effort to keep my tone upbeat. What on earth is she talking about?

'I want a "whole mackerel", like it states on the menu.'

I clear my throat, stalling for time. I've had tricky customers to deal with before, but this one takes the biscuit. I get the sneaky feeling she's being deliberately awkward just to see how I'll react. I don't mind her leading *me* a dance, but upsetting Ellie by calling her stupid has made me really annoyed. But I persevere with the polite and attentive manner. 'What would you like me to do, madam?'

'Sort it out!' she snaps. 'Stop that fish staring at me!'

A wave of disbelief and exhaustion washes over me and I almost laugh at the ridiculousness of it all. Nothing I do for this diner will be right. Suddenly, tiredness takes over and I do what I never, ever do with customers as a rule.

I resort to sarcasm.

My smile is bright and cheery. 'Right, well, if you don't want me to take the rude little chap away, perhaps we could make him a teeny-tiny little blindfold? Out of a basil leaf? Or maybe two slices of lemon tied together with a sliver of anchovy?'

If looks could kill, there'd be *two* corpses on her plate. She looks as if steam is about to rush out of her ears as she comes to the boil. I take a deep breath.

Remember, the customer is king.

'Sorry, madam. What I meant to say is, do please choose another dish. There'll be no charge, obviously.' I keep my tone polite and respectful. Although what I'd really like to do is pick up the mackerel, wave its glassy eyes in her face and make ghostly 'Woooo!' noises. But that would be silly.

She rises to her feet, glaring at me as if I'm something nasty sticking to the bottom of her shoe. 'No, thank you. I've lost my appetite.' And with that, she picks up her bag and walks out.

Maxine is making *what was that all about?* faces at me. I shrug, just grateful that the woman's gone. (I was only half-joking with the blindfold suggestion. How on earth do you stop a fish staring at you?)

At last, my shift comes to an end. I keep glancing at

my watch, waiting for three-thirty, and as Maxine passes me, she presses my shoulder. 'You'll be fine. Don't worry. Everyone knows you'll make a great restaurant manager.'

I smile at her, a lovely feeling of belonging rippling through me, taking the edge off my anxiety. I'm part of a team here and it's good to know my colleagues like and value me. That's why I can't imagine ever working anywhere else.

It's true that when Erin was trying to persuade me to cook for Mrs Morelli, a little spark of excitement kept firing off within me. Even while I was telling her that she was mad to think I could carry it off, a part of my brain was racing away, imagining what I'd cook and even thinking that I'd need a name for my business. Just for a moment, I knew how it would feel to spend my days dreaming up menus, earning a living from something I really loved doing.

But I'd never have the confidence to do it. Far better to stick to what I know, rising to the challenge of filling Mr Hastings' shoes.

The butterflies in my stomach take flight as I walk upstairs to Mr Hastings' office.

'Ah, Poppy. Come in, come in.' He sits down at his desk and ushers me to the chair opposite. He's a tall, elegant man with stylish glasses and rather beautiful hands. I watch him as he plays with his pen, turning it over and over in his fingers. He seems distracted. I suppose that after so many years of loyal service here, retiring must feel a little bittersweet.

'I can't believe this is my last day,' he says, looking up. 'And now I must reveal my successor.'

'It's the start of an exciting new chapter in your life,' I murmur. 'Time for that cruise!' He and his wife have been planning a round-the-world trip on his retirement for ages.

'Yes!' The smile doesn't quite reach his eyes. My heart goes out to him. Perhaps he's having second thoughts about leaving. 'So, Poppy, you're senior waitress here, and I have to say, you're liked and respected by absolutely everyone here, including the owners who, as you know, gave me the job of supplying them with candidates for the post I'm vacating. And you were at the top of my list, Poppy. Make no mistake about that.' He gives me a brief but warm smile. 'You've made yourself indispensable here with your brilliant way with people, your calm manner and your endless loyalty and hard work.'

My heart is beating really fast at his praise. 'Thank you, Mr Hastings. That means such a lot to me. I'll make sure I do you proud and prove your faith in me was justified.' I smile broadly at him, as I feel around in my bag for the box of muffins I baked last night to celebrate the appointment and thank him for his support.

He doesn't smile back. If anything, he looks a touch awkward. To my surprise, he suddenly rakes both hands through his normally immaculate hair, leaving it sticking up comically on one side. Then he starts playing with his pen again.

Feeling faintly alarmed, I wait for him to acknowledge my little speech. I practised it last night when I couldn't sleep. It seemed to go okay, I thought, except I forgot to add the last bit, about being honoured and delighted...

There's a knock on the door and Mr Hastings looks about to call for whoever it is to come in, but then he changes his mind, rises and goes to open the door himself, so I quickly take the opportunity to say what I was going to say.

'Mr Hastings, I would just like to thank you for believing in me. And I'd like you to know that I'd be absolutely delighted and very honoured to—'

A familiar figure walks into the room, stopping me in my tracks.

What's she doing here? It's the fish-eye-hating customer from earlier. Don't say she's actually bringing her complaints to Mr Hastings?

She glances at me in surprise. 'So sorry. I didn't mean to interrupt. I'm Mimi Blenkinsop, the new restaurant manager.'

I glance wide-eyed at Mr Hastings, who's standing there, frozen to the spot, looking extremely uncomfortable. He nods at me in a resigned way. 'Mimi, this is Poppy, our senior waitress.'

Mimi Blenkinsop says brightly, 'Ah, yes. You were saying something, Poppy, just as I came in and interrupted you?'

I shake my head, feigning bemusement. 'Was I? I really don't remember.'

'Don't you?' She cocks her head to the side and quotes me word for word: 'I'd be absolutely delighted and very honoured to – ?'

My face is the colour of a humiliated tomato. She's not going to let up until I say something.

'Ah, yes, of course. I remember now,' I say, stalling for time. 'I'd be absolutely delighted and very honoured to – ' The aroma of cake drifts up from my lap and tickles my nose. 'I'd be very honoured to – um – offer you both a muffin to celebrate!'

I open the plastic container and plonk two cakes on the desk, leaving a trail of crumbs over a pile of papers in my clumsiness. Hurriedly attempting to brush them off, I manage to dislodge the top sheet, which drifts to the floor. Bending down to retrieve it, my own name leaps out at me. The sheet contains a list of possible candidates, and loopy handwriting alongside my name says: *Obliging girl but far too timid. We need someone with spunk!*

I try to get the lid back on the cake box, but my fingers are trembling so much, it takes ages, and all the time, I can feel Mimi Blenkinsop's eyes boring holes in me. Much like the mackerel eyes terrorised *her*. At last, the lid on, I force a desperate smile and flee from the room, clutching the rest of the muffins to my chest.

*

An hour after my humiliation in Mr Hastings' office, I'm slumped in the corner of the window seat in the living room at home, staring bleakly out at the darkening sky. To say I feel sunk in gloom would be an understatement.

Obliging girl but far too timid.

The words keep running through my head, taunting me. So much for being nice, obliging and conscientious because, clearly, it doesn't get you anywhere! My insides clench with despair. Martin was right. I'm never going to shine.

I've given the hotel fourteen years of loyal service, yet Mrs Nutter still decided to hire that horrible woman instead of me. The worst thing of all is, she'll be my boss! I have a horrible feeling that Mimi Blenkinsop is going to go out of her way to make my life hell.

I should never have believed the people at work when they said my promotion was in the bag. What hurts most of all is that Mrs Nutter didn't think I was up to the job. After all those years of working the entire festive season without a single complaint, I'm passed over for

Mimi Bloody Blenkinsop!

After I left Mr Hastings' office, Mimi caught up with me as I was hurrying through the reception area. 'Poppy! I look forward to having you on my team!' I was pretty sure she emphasised '*my* team'. She smirked and said something about testing out the staff in restaurants she visits, to see how helpful they are. 'You did very well, up until the sarcasm about the blindfold.'

'Gee, thanks.' By then, I was so pissed off, I really didn't care that I was being rude to my future boss. I just wanted to go home.

Now, slouched down in the window seat, I eat two of my sad, white-chocolate-and-raspberry muffins without really tasting them, the self-pitying thoughts coming thick and fast. I'm totally useless. What an idiot, imagining I was actually going to be promoted! And I can't really blame the Nutters for not giving me the job because it's probably obvious to anyone with half a brain that I just don't have the leadership qualities required. I'm much too timid. Not like Mimi Blenkinsop, who'll barge her way through any opposition to get to where she wants to be in life.

I don't like Mimi. But I could probably learn a hell of a lot from her.

I could get some *spunk*, for a start!

This makes me smile wearily. I get up slowly and walk through to the kitchen. There's nothing wrong with being just an ordinary waitress. Who needs promotion anyway? Harrison won't be in the slightest bit bothered that I didn't get the manager job – except perhaps to feel a bit indignant on my behalf.

The thought of Harrison warms my heart. He loves me unconditionally and I feel so safe and secure with him. I decide to get my recipe books out and cook something delicious for when he comes in later. Thankfully, it's my night off, so I don't have to go back to the restaurant tonight and cope with everyone's sympathy. I couldn't bear that. Not right now.

As always, thumbing through my books and planning a menu chills me out and the memory of Mimi Blenkinsop's smirk begins to fade.

When the doorbell rings, I walk through to the hallway, still drooling over a full-colour photo of tagliatelle with pesto and courgettes.

When I open the door, Erin is standing there with a big grin, holding up a bottle of prosecco. 'Surprise!'

'Oh. What's this for?'

'Your promotion?' From her expression – a half-frown – I can tell she's already realising she's got a bit ahead of herself. 'Yes? No?'

I shake my head. 'No. But who cares?' I force a smile. 'I'm cooking tagliatelle tonight!'

'Yum. Can I come in?'

I grin at her. 'Yes, as long as you bring *that*.' I point to the bottle.

It's open in a trice and we make short work of it, with Erin lounging at the table while I cook the pasta dish, make garlic bread, and bring her up to date on my horrendous day. Later, after we've eaten and I've kept some to heat up for Harrison later, I fetch another bottle from the fridge, sloshing more prosecco into our glasses as Erin spins the open Italian cookbook round to face her.

'You know what? That witch, Mimi, has done you a big favour.'

'Has she? How on earth do you make that out? She *stole my job*!' I'm sounding loud, even to myself, and stabbing the air with my finger, having drunk far more than I'm used to. But I'm feeling *a hundred* times better!

'Yes, but I bet she can't cook like you can. I bet she can't make the most *amazing* Italian food like we've just eaten. I bet she'd be sick as a chip if you did a dinner party for Mrs Morelli and it was so great everyone in the surrounding area wanted to hire you!'

'Ha! Sick as a chip! You're right! I'll show her. Mimi Bloody Fish Eye Blenkinsop!'

'You will?'

'Why not?' I fling my arms into a dramatic shrug and knock the prosecco bottle over, which makes me

60

giggle uncontrollably. I'm all fired up. Ready to prove Martin and Mimi wrong. I have talent! I can cook amazing food! And I should stop being timid about it!

Chapter 6

'Shall I tell her you'll do it?' asks Erin, when she eventually stumbles out into the cold night air around eight.

'Sure.' I beam at her. 'I'm going to be a cook!'

'You are, love. I'm going to phone Mrs Morelli now.'

My eyes open wide in alarm. 'Now?'

'Let's strike while the iron's hot,' says Erin firmly. 'You're on the brink of a new adventure. And it's long overdue, if you don't mind me saying.'

The words 'long overdue' trigger a vague memory in my hazy, alcohol-soaked brain. I stab the air. 'Need to phone that man. Tell him he got the wrong number.'

'What man?'

'Jedward.' I giggle.

'*Who?*'

'He's called Jed Turner. Incredibly sexy voice. Invited me for Christmas.'

Erin's eyes open wide.

'Except it wasn't me he was inviting to share his hot tub. It was Clemmy. He thinks he left the message on her phone so I need to let him know.'

'Oh.' Erin peers at me curiously. 'I hope you did the "last-number redial" thing?'

'Course I did. I'm not stupid. I put it in the pocket of my jeans and ... oh bugger, they're probably in the wash!'

Laughing at my panic, Erin hurries off into the cold night while I charge upstairs to investigate the jeans situation. Luckily, they're in the wash-basket and the phone number is still in the pocket. Carefully, I deposit the slip of paper in my bedside table for safety then go down to the kitchen to start clearing up.

My phone rings half an hour later. It's Erin and she sounds excited.

'Poppy?'

'Yes?'

'Get that Christmas apron ironed!'

'What do you mean?' I've actually stopped breathing.

'I just popped in to tell Mrs Morelli you're free on Saturday night after all, and guess what? She's really pleased because the other caterers were going to charge an arm and a leg. You're on!'

'So the only reason I got the job is because I'm *cheap*?' I squeak with fake indignation as my heart bumps around madly in my chest.

She snorts. 'Well, it had to come in handy eventually.'

After she's gone, I collapse onto the sofa to catch up on the soaps, but I find I'm staring at the TV without taking anything in. Rita could be suggesting a threesome to Norris and Ken Barlow and I wouldn't even notice.

What a difference a day makes.

It began with hope, veered into total and utter humiliation at the hands of Spunky Mimi Blenkinsop, then did a smart about-turn and morphed into a landmark watershed day in my life. I'm going to be a caterer! In business for myself! There will be no more 'far too timid'. There will be 'astonishingly brave' instead. And I'm going to start right now by getting that number and phoning Jed Turner.

No shilly-shallying. I'm just going to do it!

Smiling, I push myself off the sofa, stagger slightly to the right and nearly cannon into a nest of tables. It takes a while to remember where I put the piece of paper but eventually, I'm dialling the number.

Someone picks up.

'Hello, Jed Turner?'

'Er, hi!' It's definitely him. I'd recognise those deep, velvety tones anywhere. 'I hope you don't mind me phoning. I – um – just wanted to let you know that I can't stay at yours for Christmas, even though it sounds lovely what with the hot tub and the log fire and everything.'

There's a brief pause.

'Shit, sorry,' he says. 'You're obviously not Clemmy.'

'No, 'fraid not. I'm Poppy. You got the wrong woman.'

'Ah, well.' He gives a throaty chuckle. 'That sounds like the story of my life right there.'

I laugh. 'It's like that, is it?'

'Sadly, Poppy, it is. But things can only get better.' He doesn't seem sad. In fact, he sounds quite cheerful about it.

'Very true,' I agree, thinking of Clemmy, who he'd seemed pretty keen on.

Clemmy is such a pretty name.

'So, Poppy, I'm really glad you phoned me.'

'It was no problem at all.'

'If I hadn't discovered the mistake, my carefully laid plans for a merry Christmas would have gone right up in smoke. I must have hit a wrong digit. Did I get the area code right, at least? Are you in Surrey?'

'I am. I live in Angelford?'

'Ah, yes. In that case you're very close to my uncle's holiday home. Which is where we'll be for Christmas. Lovely area.'

'Yes, I suppose it is. It's just when you live in a place, you quite often don't appreciate its beauty as much as other folk.'

'That's true. Do you think that also applies to people living within spitting distance of the Eiffel Tower? Or over the road from the Grand Canal in Venice?'

'Over the water, you mean.'

He laughs at my very feeble joke. 'You've got an exceptional café in Angelford, if I remember rightly. Best chocolate-fudge brownies in the world. Am I right or am I right?'

'You're right. We do. Although, can I suggest you try the raspberry-cream-and-white-chocolate cheesecakes next time?'

'I'll make sure I do that.' I can hear the smile in his voice. 'Then we can compare notes.'

'You won't regret it. I tried to make them myself but nothing tops their version.'

'Are you a good cook, then?'

'Er, not bad, I suppose. The kitchen's my favourite room in the house.'

'Yes? What sort of things do you make?'

I smile, wondering if he's just being polite. But I don't think he is. He sounds genuinely interested.

'Everything, but Italian food is my speciality.'

'Can you make pasta from scratch? And tiramisu?'

'I can. Actually, I'm making tiramisu for a special dinner party,' I say, deciding on the spot that this is what I'll make for Mrs Morelli's dessert.

'My mouth's watering. This sounds like it's far more than just a hobby, if you don't mind me saying. Are you a chef?'

His question stops me in my tracks. I'm not a chef. But if Erin has her way, I'll certainly be cooking for a living. The pints of prosecco I've drunk make me bold. I take a deep breath. 'Actually, I'm a caterer, specialising in Italian food. I do private dinner parties.'

My heart gives an odd little thump. Just saying those words makes me feel like a different person. More confident and self-assured, somehow.

'Sounds amazing. Are you working tonight?'

'Er, no, not tonight.' Suddenly I feel like a fraud. I'm very glad Jed Turner can't see the burning heat creeping into my face. 'My – um – next engagement is on Saturday.' Why am I trying to impress a man I don't even know?

'Looking forward to it?'

'Yes! At least, I think so.'

He laughs. 'You don't sound sure.'

'I'm just a bit nervous, that's all,' I confess. 'The woman I'm cooking for was born in Italy.'

'Ah, so there's that extra pressure to deliver genuine Italian flavours,' he murmurs, hitting the nail right on the head.

'Absolutely!'

'Well, you sound very passionate when you talk about cooking and that's a great sign. I'm sure you'll impress on Saturday.'

'Thank you.' My face flushes even redder with pleasure.

'I'll keep your number,' he chuckles. 'Just in case I ever have an Italian-food emergency. I live over the border in West Sussex, but an emergency is an emergency.'

'Especially if Italian food is involved.'

'Well, exactly. Getting spaghetti hoops out of the can without a decent tin opener can be a real challenge for a bloke like me.'

'I just happen to have a range of *excellent* can openers.'

'I'll bear that in mind, Poppy.'

There's a brief pause and I rack my brains for something to say. It's been such fun talking to Jed Turner...

'So are you going to call Clemmy?' The question escapes before I can stop myself. I close my eyes, feeling like a right idiot.

'Er, yes. I definitely will.'

'I hope she accepts your invitation after all this palaver.'

He laughs. 'I have a feeling she will. She's a lovely girl. Cute and adorably accident-prone. She just needs to believe in herself a bit more.'

'Oh?' It sounds like he likes Clemmy a *lot*.

'Yeah. She was bullied at school for having blazing red hair and being on the plump side, and these things stick.'

'Kids can be horrible. Does she live in Surrey as well?'

'Yes. She doesn't have a car so she can meet me off

the London train in Easingwold and I'll whisk her over to join the gang at Westbury Edge.'

My heart snags.

Westbury Edge?

I swallow hard. An image of the lake in the tiny hamlet of Westbury Edge flashes into my head, with the little whitewashed cottage on its shores mirrored perfectly in the glasslike surface of the water. It's eighteen years since I was last in that cottage – but it's burned on my brain as if it all happened only a week ago...

'Poppy? Are you still there?' Jed Turner asks.

'Yes! Sorry, the connection's not great,' I say, crossing my fingers and hoping he doesn't think I'm completely weird. 'You – er – work in London, then?'

'Yes. It's been crazy lately, but I'm leaving at lunchtime on the nineteenth of December. So, come hell or high water, I'll be on that two p.m. train heading home for the Christmas holidays!'

'Sounds good.' My legs are still shaking from hearing the name Westbury Edge after all this time. I grasp the arm of a chair and sit down.

'It'll just be great to relax. But what about you? This is probably the busiest time of year for a caterer?'

'Er, usually. But this year, it's not too busy at all.' *I'm actually not lying!*

'Good. Well ... I hope you have a very merry Christmas.'

'Thank you. And I hope you make the two p.m. train.'

He laughs. 'You bet your life I will! Bye, Poppy. Good luck on Saturday.'

*

Erin is practically as thrilled as I am at the prospect of my first proper catering job, and I love her for that. But bearing in mind his aversion to financial risk, I'm not quite so sure what Harrison's reaction will be.

I'll have to reassure him that it's just a one-off, and I'm not going to do anything rash like hand in my notice at the hotel.

I might have been feeling all bold and daring with Erin the other night, fuelled by pints of prosecco, but in the cold light of day, I'm realising that my dream of becoming a full-time self-employed caterer is likely to remain just that. A lovely fantasy.

When I finally break the news to Harrison about Saturday night, I'm really surprised at his response.

'Good for you.' He pats me enthusiastically on the back. 'Really well done, Puss.'

'Thank you.' I smile happily, cheeks flushing.

He beams at me. 'It's worked out very nicely.'

'Oh?'

'Yes. I've actually been invited to a meeting of grid enthusiasts on Saturday night.'

I arrange my face into a pleased expression, which I hope hides my bafflement. 'Gosh. That's wonderful.'

He nods cheerfully. 'They're the Drain Cover Enthusiasts, Southern Division, to give them their exact title. If you're going to be out, I'll tell them I can be there.'

'That's great! Gosh, I never realised there were enough – er – drain-cover enthusiasts to make up a whole division.'

'Ah, yes. Well, you'd be surprised!' he calls as he disappears upstairs.

Chapter 7

The day of the dinner party dawns, and I'm so busy running through my lists and doing the prep with Erin as my right-hand woman that I barely have time to be nervous.

I know I am, though, because I'm unable to eat a thing. Except frequently tasting the food for tonight, of course. You must taste. All the time. It's the only way to know if you've got the seasoning absolutely spot on. And seasoning is paramount in the perfect savoury dish.

It all goes swimmingly – especially the main course. I've been unable to source the casserole steak I wanted, so at the last minute, I change my carefully made plan and opt for a slow-cooked version instead. Good decision, as it turns out. The meat melts off the bone and is so good, it's worthy of being written into my diary of champion recipes!

Afterwards, I drive Erin home and we sit outside her

flat for a long time, totally exhausted but high on the triumph that was the evening. Mrs Morelli was full of praise and vowed to tell all her friends and neighbours.

'Are you sure you don't want to come in?' says Erin. 'I could open a bottle of fizz. We really should toast your very first success.'

'Oh, thank you, but I don't think I could get up the stairs, I'm so knackered.' I smile at her, feeling tears prick unexpectedly at my lids. 'I couldn't have done this without you, Erin. You've no idea how much your support and your enthusiasm means to me.'

'Don't be daft. I'm your friend. That's what friends do.'

I shake my head. 'Not everyone. I *love* that you're so excited for me, and that you mean every word of it. At the risk of sounding sentimental, you really are special. Mark is a lucky man.'

She colours up with pleasure. 'Aw, shucks. Okay then, I'm brilliant.'

'You are. And I couldn't be more delighted that things are working out for you and Mark. If anyone deserves to be happy, it's you, Erin.'

Now it's her turn to have suspiciously shiny eyes.

We hug tightly and she gets out.

'This is just the first triumph of many!' she says, and I smile at her, wishing it could be true.

I drive home, eager to see Harrison and tell him all

about my night. He's in the kitchen making coffee, and pops his head round the living-room door.

'Hey, it's my own personal Nigella!' he jokes. 'Want one?' He holds up the coffee jar.

'Yes, please.' I flake out happily on the sofa and call through, 'How was your night?'

'Brilliant. They're a really great group of guys.'

'No females, then?'

'No. Why don't you come along to the next meeting and redress the balance slightly?'

'Er, maybe.' *Is he serious? Surely not.*

I always think it's good for couples to have separate hobbies. It gives them more to talk about. But on the other hand, it would be nice to share our hobbies, too. I'm always wanting him to join me in the kitchen on a normal night, because the idea of couples chatting about their day in the cosiness of the kitchen as they chop vegetables, and perhaps open a bottle of wine and share a kiss or two, sounds heavenly to me. But Harrison always says the kitchen is my domain, just as the car maintenance is his. I don't think he means it in a sexist way. It's more a compliment, really, implying that my cooking is so much better than his.

He comes into the room and holds out my coffee. 'I wasn't being serious, you know, about you coming along to the next one.' He smiles and sits down beside me. 'You'd be bored stiff in under three minutes, I reckon.'

I smile at him. 'You might be right.'

He springs up and puts on my favourite CD, then settles back on the sofa, pulling me into his side and sipping from his mug. We listen to the music for a while in silence and I snuggle into Harrison, thinking about my wonderful night and how lucky I am. If I could stop yawning, I'd tell him all about the slow-cooked beef and how pleased Mrs Morelli was with the dinner, but to be frank, it's lovely just nestling here in companionable silence.

Before long, I hear a tiny snorting noise and turn to see Harrison's head is thrown back. His mouth is open and he's snoring gently. I nudge him and whisper, 'Time for bed?'

He comes to and gives a huge yawn. 'Yes. Bed,' he agrees, standing up and holding out his hand to me.

'You go. I'll be up in a minute,' I tell him.

'Okay, Puss. Don't be long.'

'Mrs Morelli was really pleased,' I tell him as he heads for the door.

'Who?'

'Mrs Morelli – you know, the woman I cooked for.'

'Oh. Yes, of course. Well, that's brilliant.'

I smile excitedly. 'I know. It couldn't have gone any better, really, despite the problem I had with the terrible cut of meat. I ended up having to slow cook—'

His phone buzzes with a message.

'Sorry, Puss.' He glances at me apologetically and wanders out, studying his text. 'You can tell me all about it in the morning,' he calls from halfway up the stairs.

I sit there, staring at the blank screen of the TV. After all the excitement of the night, it would have been lovely if Harrison had wanted to toast my success.

No wonder I'm feeling a bit deflated.

*

Next morning, I'm making toast while Harrison does his morning vanishing act behind *The Financial Times*, when the landline rings.

I dive on the phone, assuming it's Erin calling to see how I'm feeling after last night.

It's a man's voice.

'Hi, Poppy. I hope you don't mind me phoning, but I was just wondering how last night went?'

For a second, I'm thrown. But not for long. That deep voice with a hint of gravel is unmistakeable.

'It's Jed. The total stranger who invited you for Christmas by mistake?'

'Jed. Hi. Um – it went brilliantly, thanks.'

'Was the customer happy?'

I smile. 'She was over the moon and her guests couldn't stop complimenting the tiramisu.'

There's a rustle as Harrison pops his head round the newspaper and gives me a 'who's that?' look.

'Sorry, I've got to go,' I tell Jed. 'But thanks so much for calling.'

'No problem. I'm just glad it went well. Have you got a name for the business, by the way?'

'Well, not really. Although, my friend Erin thinks she's come up with a corker.'

'Which is?'

I close my eyes and smile as I say it. 'Diner Might.'

There's a brief silence, then the sound of hearty laughter. 'Diner Might. Dynamite. I like it. Although maybe not quite the sophistication you're aiming for?'

'That's just what I thought. Any suggestions gratefully received.'

'Right, I'm on it.'

'Is Clemmy coming for Christmas?' I ask on impulse, not caring that Harrison is listening.

'Yes, she is.' Jed sounds surprised that I should ask. 'I'm meeting her when I get off the train at Easingwold on the nineteenth.'

'The two p.m. train?' I smile, recalling how adamant he was about leaving London promptly for the holidays.

He gives a throaty chuckle. 'On the dot. She's cut off her long red hair, apparently, so I've told her she has to wear a carnation otherwise I might not recognise the new sophisticated Clemmy.'

I laugh, feeling the tiniest bit deflated, which is strange. Although, on reflection, it's probably because, while Jed and Clemmy will be enjoying their Christmas together, Harrison will be away in Spain and it'll just be me and Mum rubbing along together.

'It sounds like you're going to have a lovely Christmas.'

'It'll certainly be interesting,' he says dryly. 'What with Uncle Bob bringing his new woman and her two teenage kids, and my workaholic brother forced to tear himself away from his natural habitat to join us.'

'Natural habitat?' I'm intrigued.

'Ryan's a financial trader in the City of London. He does nothing but work and date ravishing blondes. And he hates the countryside.'

'Ooh, yes. Well, anything could happen.'

He groans. 'Precisely.'

There's a brief pause. Then he says, 'Bye then, Poppy. It's been nice chatting.'

'Who was that?' asks Harrison as I sit down at the table and start buttering my toast.

Breezily, I say, 'Oh, just a friend wanting to know how last night went.' It comes out a little more snippily than I intended.

Completely oblivious, Harrison smiles and puts his paper down. 'And how *did* it go, Puss? You haven't actually told me.'

I plaster on a smile. 'It went really well, thanks. Can

you pass the marmalade, please?'

He settles back behind his newspaper, then pops his head round again a second later. 'Dynamite? What was that about?'

I shake my head and smile, thinking about how hilarious Jed found the name. I did tell Harrison about Erin's daft suggestion, but he's obviously forgotten all about it.

'It's nothing,' I tell him. 'Do you want some more toast?'

Chapter 8

It's the night before Harrison leaves for Spain, and I'm keen to talk to him about my future plans. Ever since Mimi took over from Mr Hastings as restaurant manager, my morale has been on the floor, and the idea of catering dinner parties is becoming more and more attractive by the day.

I make him his favourite steak pie, and afterwards, we settle down cosily on the sofa.

'You know how I went on that cookery course with Erin?' I begin, feeling actually rather nervous. And excited. 'Well, I haven't mentioned this, but I was talking to the tutor and he said there was a big demand for companies catering for events and private dinner parties. And he – well, he actually reckoned I've got what it takes. To cook for people.' Even talking about it makes my heart skip along a little bit faster.

Harrison's eyes widen. 'I thought you'd given up that idea.'

'Well, I never really considered it seriously. But after cooking for Mrs Morelli, I've realised I can actually do it. So what do you think?'

'Well, your food is fabulous, there's no doubt about that.' He stares at me intently and I can almost hear the cogs whirring as he weighs everything up. 'Do you know, Poppy,' he says at last. 'I think you're talented and clever enough to achieve anything you set your mind to.'

'You think so?' I flush with pleasure. I'm always amazed to hear Harrison say things like this about me. A part of me is even starting to believe that what he says is true.

He kisses my forehead. 'I certainly do, you clever little Puss.'

'So do you think I could actually run a successful catering business?'

Harrison stares down at the floor, an intense look on his face. He's obviously considering the idea very carefully indeed, and my heart lifts. It's so lovely having Harrison on my side, backing me in everything I do.

'I honestly think I could do it, you know?' With Harrison's support, I really feel I can. 'I mean, obviously I couldn't give up work straight away. I'd have to build up the business slowly, then—'

'There's a snag in this carpet. Look.' He points, still staring down, clearly not having heard a word I was saying. 'I thought I was seeing things for a minute. I think we'll go for quality over price next time.' He looks up and smiles. 'You were saying, Puss?'

'The catering business,' I repeat, a touch frostily. 'Do you think I could do it?'

He pulls me closer and nuzzles my neck. 'Oh, there'll be plenty more chances to show off your talent for cooking, don't you worry about that. Mum's coming over from Spain at Easter, remember? She'll be thoroughly impressed. As long as you avoid sprouts and beans of all varieties.' He shrugs. 'Flatulence. Cabbage is okay, though. As long as it's red.' Absently, he massages my waist while keeping one eye on the TV.

I pull away and arrange myself so that I can look at him in the eye. 'The thing is, Harrison, that's not really the point.' He turns in surprise at the unusual sharpness of my tone, and I smile to show I'm not really cross with him. 'I don't want to "show off" my cooking. I want to explore the possibility of turning cooking into a business.' I'm surprising myself here, never mind Harrison, but it suddenly seems really important that I convince him I'm seriously considering Erin's idea.

'The tutor at the course said I could do it, and I think he might be right. I've got a little money saved up, so it's not as if I wouldn't be able to pay my way ...'

He nods slowly, and I wait on tenterhooks, subconsciously preparing myself for the put-down.

She's far too timid. She'll never amount to anything.

'You know what, Puss? It's time.'

I look at him quizzically.

He smiles. 'It's time you gave up your job at the hotel.'

There's a beat of silence.

'Sorry?' I must have misheard him.

'Give up your job,' he repeats, taking my hand. 'They obviously don't appreciate you. I was going to suggest it, actually.'

I stare at him in astonishment. 'You were?'

'Yes.' He smiles and pulls me towards him again, and I melt into his kiss, my head reeling happily. I should have known my lovely, caring boyfriend would be one step ahead of me. My brain is racing. What a difference a day makes! *Me*, planning a possible *business*? Perhaps Mimi Blenkinsop has actually done me a favour.

'We could continue this upstairs,' I suggest coyly.

He frowns at his watch.

'You've got a full twenty minutes before the news comes on,' I point out.

He smiles sheepishly. 'You know me too well.'

'News junkie! Honestly, I swear you'd get the shakes if you ever missed the late bulletin.' I smile impishly and start tickling him.

I can usually tease him out of his serious moods, and tickling is very good for that. There's a particular spot on Harrison's side that's guaranteed to render him utterly helpless, like right now. It makes me giggle to see him so vulnerable. It's quite sexy, actually, despite the peculiar brays of laughter that my tickling produces, which make him sound like a donkey gasping for breath.

We end up in bed, and it's lovely. I even help him when he puts the second condom on over the first. (Harrison believes firmly that the arrival of children should be scrupulously timetabled, just like everything else in life. And until babies are on the agenda, why take a risk when it's well documented that condoms can tear?)

As he takes his shower, I linger in bed, marvelling at myself for daring to think about stepping out of my comfort zone and giving up my job. I never thought Harrison would be so relaxed about the idea. But it was he who suggested it! Maybe we're rubbing off on each other. Perhaps, under my influence, Harrison's losing his need to plan everything to the nth degree. Loosening up a bit...

He knows how passionate I am about cooking and he's always saying how much he enjoys my experiments in the kitchen. So, I guess he's finally realising, as I think I am, that it might be the right move for me. Of course, there's a lot to be said for erring on the side of caution – but on the other hand, if you don't try, how will you ever know what you might have achieved if you'd been that little bit braver?

I'm in my absolute element when I'm dreaming up a new menu, sourcing the best ingredients from the market (you can tell a perfect, ripe tomato just by breathing in its wonderful aroma), and getting happily steamy in the kitchen. And tasting. Always tasting, adjusting the seasoning, and tasting some more. (It's a wonder I'm not the size of a modest detached house. Mind you, Harrison did once slap my bum playfully and remark that he liked his women 'well upholstered', so I guess I'm not a slender studio apartment either.)

If I had my way, I'd spend most of my life in the kitchen. And I love creating Italian dishes best of all.

Not that everything I attempt is a success.

On my second date with Harrison, I tried to impress him with slow-cooked lamb's liver and braised cabbage because he'd mentioned he liked traditional British food. I should have stuck to shepherd's pie. It was definitely not my finest hour. The cabbage made my little flat smell like a hospital, and the liver – after stewing in the slow cooker for a full eight hours – basically disintegrated to a thick, brown mush, leaving us with a sort of warm offal smoothie. Luckily I had the number of an excellent local curry house to hand.

I was seriously amazed when next morning, as I sprayed air freshener around to banish the evidence of the liver-and-cabbage disaster, Harrison phoned to say he'd had a great time and did I want to go on another date?

I've come on *a lot* since then. It sounds corny, but the cookery course really lit the fire in me. I'd been making my own pasta for a long time and perfecting sauces to match the different pasta shapes. But on the course, I learned how to refine and combine flavours to incredible effect, using lots of fresh herbs to lift a dish to a whole new level. (The effect of adding fresh basil to a homemade tomato and mozzarella sauce was a real turning point for me. *The flavour!*)

I also learned that the trick to producing dishes that people get excited over and demand the recipe for, is to create the sort of food you're genuinely passionate about.

Stretching out my arms and legs, I glance lazily around the room, which has only recently been decorated, revelling in having the whole bed to myself for a while. When we rented this house three months ago, we decided to decorate, and Harrison left the colour scheme entirely up to me, saying that a 'woman's eye' was always so much better than a man's. I laughed fondly at his slightly old-fashioned view, and dived into the task of choosing paint shades and wallpaper. I'd never lived with a guy before and it felt like a big adventure.

I'd had my doubts before I agreed to move in with Harrison.

It wasn't that I thought we wouldn't be compatible.

It was just that I'd lived at Mum's until I was twenty-seven and I knew only too well how claustrophobic it could be, putting up with someone else's clutter and having barely any space to call your own.

I eventually got over my guilt at the prospect of leaving Mum, and moved into a little flat of my own, just along the road from her. I loved that flat. It was small but wonderfully airy and uncluttered. Minimalist, I suppose you'd call it. I felt I could finally breathe. And I did, that first evening when the removal men had gone. Long, restorative breaths, looking out over the village green at dusk and revelling in the nerve-tingling feeling of freedom and endless possibility. It felt quite surreal to be able to walk from one room to another without the elaborate ducking and twisting for fear of knocking anything over.

When, a year later, Harrison asked me to move in with him, I was a bit nervous at first. I loved having my own space at last. Did I really want to give it up? But I felt better after Harrison assured me that he also hated clutter and ornaments everywhere. (I was grateful for his diplomacy. 'Clutter' was a huge understatement in describing the state of Mum's bungalow.) And while his reasons for wanting to cohabit with me weren't the most romantic in the world, I could see that his idea of pooling our resources and sharing the bills made a great deal of practical sense. (Erin chortled a bit when

I told her about his clever spreadsheet detailing hot-water usage, but even she had to agree that I'd be better off financially.)

Harrison emerges from the bathroom with a towel around his waist and I beckon him over to the bed with a saucy smile. He pulls on his boxers and jeans then sits down on the bed without fastening them and looks down at me, his eyes crinkling in a smile.

Sitting up, I hold the duvet around me and run my hand admiringly over the smooth skin of his back. 'So, you really think I should take the bull by the horns and just do it?'

'Give up the restaurant? Yes, of course. They don't appreciate you anyway.' He smiles and leans down to kiss me. 'Not like I do.'

My heart expands with love. 'I'm so glad you think that. I mean, obviously I'd start small. And I won't be earning a great deal at the beginning but I've got savings, so—'

He shakes his head. 'Don't worry about that. We'll easily manage.'

I sink back onto the pillows happily. I can't believe he's being so supportive! But I should have realised he would be. I don't know why I doubted it. We're a team now and that's what partners do – they root for each other.

'When I get my promotion, it will mean a big step

up in salary,' he says. 'So, the fact is, we'll *more* than manage. In fact, you won't need to work at all.' He beams at me as if this will be music to my ears. 'You can just stay at home. Look after the house.' He winks, getting to his feet. 'And me.'

He zips up his jeans, picks his shirt up off the floor and walks out, just as the music downstairs announces the early-evening news.

My mouth opens but nothing comes out.

A minute later, I scramble into my dressing gown and follow him downstairs. This is far more important than the news.

Blood is rushing through my veins, urging me on. I'm normally so mild-mannered, any sort of confrontation makes me feel physically sick, even if I'm only an observer. But having my hopes and wishes discarded so easily by Harrison – with no attempt by him to understand what they actually mean to me – has really touched a nerve.

I don't yet know if I have the courage to branch out in a new direction, but it suddenly seems massively important that I let Harrison know where I stand on the subject. I'm not quite sure where meek and mild Poppy has disappeared to, but something deep inside is urging me on and it's not the steak pie I had for dinner!

'Harrison? Question: what about *my* career?' I stand

squarely between him and the TV. I might sound calm but my whole body is shaking.

He looks taken aback by my directness and I almost feel guilty. But irritation is expanding inside me. *Why is it okay for Harrison to be focused on his brilliant future career at the accountancy firm, but not me?*

'You can still do your cookery thing,' he says magnanimously, trying to peer around me at the TV. 'If you really want to.'

Suddenly, I'm doing a petulant little dance, moving from side to side, so he can't see the newscaster. Eventually, he gives up and sits back, looking mildly puzzled.

I take a shaky breath, hoping to quell the nausea. 'I *want* to work, Harrison. I'm not the type to be a lady of leisure. And you know what cooking means to me. I really think I need to do this. If I'm brave enough.'

'And so you can,' he soothes. 'A little job here and there?' He winks. 'As long as you'll still be here most nights cooking up a storm for when I come in exhausted from work. You look after me so beautifully, Puss.'

A little job here and there? Is he actually listening to a word I'm saying?'

'Harrison, If you cared enough, you'd realise this is important to me. If the course tutor thinks I can do it, then why not? Perhaps I really can make a proper career out of cooking.'

There's a tense silence.

Harrison, I can tell, is bemused by my taking a stand. I'm actually quite shocked myself. And I'm determined not to back down like I usually do.

He sighs and gets up off the sofa. 'Okay, okay. Maybe you can.' His voice is gentle, if a little patronising, but I decide to ignore that. He pulls me into his arms. 'Just as long as you don't go rushing into something you'll regret,' he murmurs, close to my ear.

'What do you mean?' My voice is muffled by his sweater.

'Well, what you have to realise is that, long-term, working full-time probably won't be possible. That's all I'm saying.'

I pull away and stare up at him.

Why won't it be possible?

Am I missing something here? He's not making any sense.

He shrugs. 'When the children arrive ...'

'Children?' Confused, I turn and glance out of the window, half-expecting to see a school bus park up outside and a load of kids pile out.

'Yes. The children *we'll* have.'

He takes my hand. 'I can't believe you think I don't care enough about you, Puss. I care very much indeed. In fact, I'll prove it. I've been thinking about this for a while. Since last Tuesday, in fact.' He stares into space, his brow faintly knotted. 'No, it was Wednesday. The day the Footsie plummeted five hundred points.' He shakes his head. 'Anyway, that's not the point. Obviously, I would have preferred to wait for a more romantic setting, but since you seem to need reassurance that I'm here for you –'

Abruptly, he falls to one knee, still grasping my hand, and for a second, I think he must have spotted another snag in the carpet.

Then my heart starts to gallop like a husky across the snow as I realise what's about to happen.

Harrison clears his throat.

'Poppy Valentina Ainsworth, will you marry me?'

Chapter 9

My head is whirling; it's all so totally unexpected. *Harrison wants to marry me!*

Then an awful thought hits me. What if I've misunderstood? What if he's playing some kind of weird 'joke'? But why would he be? Isn't that just my insecurity coming out?

He's still down on one knee, staring solemnly up at me and, to be fair, he doesn't look as if he's joking.

My heart melts. 'Oh, Harrison. You really want to marry me?'

'Yes, Puss. I do,' he says earnestly, before shifting gingerly from one knee to the other.

This brings a big lump to my throat. Harrison loves me enough to want to spend the rest of his life with me!

'Are you sure?' The words are out of my mouth before I can stop them.

He looks bemused. 'Of course I'm sure.'

'Yes. Sorry. Yes. I'm just being daft. I expect it's the shock. I mean, the *wonderful surprise*!'

I draw his hand to my lips and kiss it tenderly. 'I just want to be sure *you're* sure. Before I say ... *yes!*'

He adjusts his position. 'Listen, would you mind terribly if I stood up? My knees are aching.'

'Oh, of course.' I help him to his feet, wondering if he heard what I just said. I think I just agreed to walk down the aisle with him! Visions of white dresses and flower-filled churches dance through my head. I'll be able to design and make my own wedding cake! Chocolate, maybe? A fruit cake? Or maybe a cupcake tower? Everyone loves those, although I've heard they're quite complicated to assemble—

'Poppy?'

Harrison is looking at me quizzically.

'Sorry. I was far away there.' I hug him round the waist, and he kisses my forehead and pulls me so close I can barely breathe, which is lovely. We stay like that for a moment, as I concentrate on squeezing air into my flattened lungs. I don't want to spoil the moment! It feels amazing, wrapped in the arms of the man I love. The man who wants to marry me!

'Harrison?'

'Yes, Puss?'

I pull back, gazing at him lovingly with teary eyes. 'I haven't given you a proper answer yet. So, here goes: I would absolutely *love* to—'

Startled, I find a finger placed gently but firmly over my lips.

Harrison is shaking his head.

'No?' I'm confused. Has he changed his mind already? And if so, will this qualify as the shortest engagement in history?

'Don't give me your answer yet,' he instructs softly.

'But I already did.'

'Did you?'

'Yes. I said "yes". But your knees were acting up so maybe you didn't hear me?'

As romantic proposals go, this one isn't going so great. But it's not as if we're in the movies or something where proposals are sure to go as planned.

Harrison takes my face in his hands and smiles at me.

Perhaps he's going to ask me again and we'll do it *properly* this time. 'Are your knees okay?'

'Fine now, thanks. But listen, Poppy. I have a question for you.'

I smile indulgently at him. I think I *realised* that!

Harrison squeezes my hands gently, and I prepare to be swept away.

'You remember when I advised you on which life-insurance policy to take out?'

Life-insurance policy?

Well, yes, I do recall that. How could I forget? I spent an entire evening looking at small print. Reading clauses and sub-clauses and sub-sub-clauses. But I didn't complain because I knew Harrison was only being super-cautious because he cared about me.

'I remember.'

'Do you recall there was what's called a "cooling-off period"?'

'Ye-es. They gave me thirty days to change my mind, so I'd be sure it was the right policy for me.'

He smiles. 'Exactly. So I was thinking that *we* should have a cooling-off period.'

'Really?' I can't help feeling dismayed.

It must have shown on my face because he's quick to reassure me. 'I want to marry you, Poppy. Of course I do. But you know "spontaneous" isn't exactly my middle name and, to that end, I've actually been doing some research.'

'Research?' I can't help feeling wary. I honestly never knew proposals could be so complicated.

'Yes. And according to my findings, a cooling-off period would increase the probability of us staying together over the long term by 7.94%.' He says the numbers in a punchy, pleased sort of way, then stands back, awaiting my response.

'Gosh. 7.94%. Wow.' I'm not sure what I think about this. It seems quite a paltry result for a lot of bothersome waiting.

'I know. Odds like that are worth working for, don't you think?'

A thought occurs. 'Do we have to wait thirty days?'

'No, no.' Harrison smiles fondly. 'We don't want it to be like a *business* agreement. That would be a bit odd.'

I laugh, relieved. 'So how long?'

'Well, I'm off to Spain to visit Mother tomorrow, which is the nineteenth of December and I'm back on New Year's Eve. So that's twelve days.'

'The Twelve Days of Christmas!' I exclaim in delight. Now, that sounds like it's meant to be!

Harrison frowns. 'Well, strictly speaking, the twelve days of Christmas start with Christmas Day, or in some traditions, the day after, on St Stephen's Day. So really—'

'Yes, yes. I suppose I just meant ... it could be *our* Twelve Days of Christmas!'

'Whatever you'd like, Puss.' He gives me a teasing look. 'And I expect you'd like an engagement ring?'

I smile shyly. 'Well, if you insist.'

He nods. 'After the cooling-off period, obviously. Are there any elastic knee bandages in the first-aid kit?'

*

Next morning, I wake to find Harrison already up and packing a case for his flight to Spain later that day.

'Tea, sleepyhead?' He looks up from folding a jumper

and I struggle up, yawning. 'Yes, please.'

It's only when he's left the room that it suddenly hits me.

I'm engaged!

Well, *almost* engaged. I sink back against the pillows to contemplate this stunning turn of events. I can't quite believe it, to be honest. Harrison is so cautious by nature, I suppose I'd assumed he might never want to take a chance on us. Because marriage is a gamble. But it seems he considers me worth taking a punt on!

A warm feeling floods through me. Then I remember our 'cooling-off period' and my enthusiasm wanes ever so slightly. But it's just twelve short days. Not long at all, really. And if it's important to Harrison, I owe it to him to take it seriously.

I reach into a bedside drawer for a pen and a note-book, and after a moment's thought, I write:

Twelve days till I'm engaged! Harrison is caring, handsome and very intelligent. Plus he's a great judge of character because he wants to marry me! (That was a joke. Obviously.) He also makes me smile. A lot. And I feel so lucky we found each other. I know Erin probably thinks Harrison is a bit boring and that our life together is rather dull. But what she doesn't get is that I actually think 'ordinary' is great! I used to pray for 'ordinary' when Martin was living with me and Mum. Life then was the very opposite of boring – but in a bad, energy-sapping way. Mum and I were forever walking on eggshells in our own house because we never knew when Martin was going to erupt next. By comparison, life with Harrison is calm and peaceful, and I'm allowed to be me. If that's 'dull', I'm all for it!

*

Later, I drive Harrison to the airport.

'Give your mum my love,' I tell him, snuggling close for one last time before he sets off through the security channels.

He kisses me deeply, surprising me and making me almost want to beg him to stay and take a later flight. 'Behave yourself, Puss.' He smiles, tapping the tip of my nose. 'And remember – you have Twelve Days of Christmas to decide whether you want to make me the happiest man alive!'

I smile up at him a little awkwardly, wishing I could just say, right then and there, 'Of *course* I'll marry you, Harrison! Why would I need twelve days to decide?'

But I'm sure he's right.

With Harrison deposited in a different country, we'll both have loads of time to think and when I finally say 'yes', I'll be even more certain than I am now that it's the right thing to do. I just have to hope that Harrison doesn't change his mind in the meantime!

As I drive through the outskirts of Easingwold on the way home from the airport, I'm still smiling at the thought of Harrison's passionate kiss. He must feel he's really going to miss me. And I'll miss him, too. The house will be weirdly empty without his laptop on the sofa, and financial papers on every available surface. It will be sad, too, having the bed all to myself, with no Harrison to snuggle up to on these cold, Christmassy winter nights.

Still, it's probably for the best that it won't be the three of us on Christmas Day. Harrison would just start trying to urge Mum to clear out her house, like he did last year when I brought her over. He blundered right in, not quite realising how super-sensitive Mum is on the subject, and told her she'd feel so much better if she had a good old sort out. I sat there, making meaningful expressions at him, but he just carried on extolling the virtues of a tidy house equalling a tidy mind.

Mum kept quiet but I could feel her defences getting higher and more battle-worthy by the minute. And when Harrison made the grave error of referring to her 'collections' as 'junk', I had to close my eyes against the image of her hurling boiling oil over the ramparts. Later, as we washed up together, she had a few stern words with me about Harrison's lack of sensitivity, then she clammed up completely for the rest of the day.

Driving along, I'm just about to turn into a road that's a shortcut home, past a little row of shops and offices, when I spot a familiar figure coming out of a hairdresser's called 'A Cut Above'.

It's Erin's Mark.

I slow down, ready to wave cheerily at him. But he hasn't noticed me.

As I grin inanely in his direction, he looks both ways, up and down the street, then digs his hands in his pocket, hunches his shoulders and walks swiftly away in the direction of the town centre.

Funny. I was sure Mark used the same hairdresser's as Erin, in the centre of Easingwold…

Then, as the traffic slows almost to a standstill, I catch sight of a sign in the window above the hairdresser's. I gaze up at the first-floor windows, just as the motorist behind hoots to tell me to hurry up. And just before I put my foot down and accelerate away, I catch the lettering on a placard there.

Mariella's Matching Agency.

Odd, I think to myself, for two reasons. Firstly, I didn't think old-fashioned, traditional agencies like that existed anymore. I suppose I assumed they were all online now. And secondly, what on earth was Mark doing there?

I shake my head. He must have come out of the hairdresser's. Erin loves her Groupon bargains. I can just imagine her telling Mark to get a cheap haircut to swell their mortgage deposit!

Driving on, I indicate to turn left at the next roundabout, heading for home. A sign for Easingwold railway station points straight on. I slow down, my mind ticking over, glancing at the clock on the dashboard. It's nearly three p.m.

Shall I do it?

My heart starts pounding in my chest. All day, I've been daring myself—

Another toot from the driver behind.

Oh God, why not? Let's live dangerously!

I click off the indicator before speeding up a little to appease the motorist at my rear, then slow down for the roundabout and take the railway-station exit. I've really no idea why I'm doing it and I have a sneaky feeling that nothing good will come of it, but all day it's been lodged in my head that Clemmy will be meeting Jed off the train that leaves London at two p.m. I've checked the timetable and it's due to arrive into Easingwold soon after three.

I know it sounds daft but, without my intervention, this lovely romantic meeting on the station platform might not even be happening. Call it friendly interest, or blatant curiosity, but I need to be there to see their reunion. Make sure it all goes off without a hitch.

Chapter 10

I drive stealthily into the car park, trying to act as normally as possible. I know it's silly – neither Jed nor Clemmy would know me from Mary Poppins – but my heart is in my mouth all the same. The last thing I need is to be spotted spying on them!

Parking up, I lean over and fumble around in the glovebox, emerging with an ancient pair of sunglasses with gigantic round frames, popular around the turn of the century. I put them on and, instantly, the icy gloom of the December afternoon switches to dead of night. I can barely see out through the windscreen but at least I'll be able to go incognito.

Getting out of the car, I head for the arrivals board and – lifting the glasses so I can actually read it – I see that the London train is indeed due to arrive at a few minutes past three. I make my way over to platform two and take cover behind a concrete pillar.

People are gathering on the platform, heads turned,

watching for the train to arrive. A man with a briefcase and grey frizzy hair keeps peering at me, clearly wondering why I'm loitering behind the pillar looking so furtive and wearing weird sunglasses as if I've just had an eyelift, so, eventually, I partially sidle out and remove the glasses, trying to look cool, as if I'm meeting someone off the train.

Then a girl hurries onto the platform, out of breath. She's dressed in a beautiful jade-green coat with black buttons, a pair of elegant black heels and a black hat, but she manages to ruin the sophisticated effect by tripping over her own feet. She just manages to stay upright but her hat slips to reveal a glossy mane of shoulder length flame-coloured hair.

Red hair.

Adorably accident-prone.

Clemmy?

It must be her.

I whip the glasses back on so I can study her surreptitiously.

The girl who's won Jed's heart is rather voluptuous, with large eyes and a sweet, open face. Her newly shorn hairstyle frames her face, and she's practically spilling out of the coat's deep V-shaped neckline.

She's frowning slightly as if she's nervous. Then she spots the shelter of my pillar and dives over, standing next to me and enveloping me in a little cloud of floral perfume. As I cast a sideways glance at her, she digs around in her black, snakeskin-look handbag and pulls out a mirror, then checks her reflection anxiously.

She must really like Jed to be so nervous.

Satisfied, she puts the mirror back and peers out along the platform. But the train hasn't arrived, so Jed can't be here yet. Then she takes a deep breath and tries to loop her bag over her arm. But she fumbles and it slides to the floor, scattering the contents far and wide. We both stare at it for a second then she looks at me, aghast, before starting to gather everything up. Smiling in sympathy, I bend to help, scooping up a lipstick, a mini pack of tampons and some loose change.

'Thank you,' she says breathlessly as I hand them over. 'I'm all fingers and thumbs today. That's what love will do to you, I suppose.'

My heart pings. *She's in love with him! And I helped to make this happen!*

I laugh nervously. 'I suppose it will. Are you – um – meeting someone here?'

My question brings a glow of colour to her peachy complexion, and her eyes light up in a smile, a perfect dimple studding each cheek. She nods. 'He's over there. Thanks again. It was really kind of you.' She presses my arm and hurries away, along the platform. I watch her, puzzled. Maybe Jed caught a different train. Escaped from the office earlier than expected.

Clemmy half-runs towards her target, weaving among the crowd, and at one point, she almost stumbles into someone's case. After apologising profusely to the owner, she carries on at a fast walk, shaking her glossy hair as she prepares to meet her love.

I peer with interest at Jed Turner. He's medium height with a stocky build, a handsome, clean-shaven face, and close-cropped blond hair. Clemmy looks so pleased to see him. She's chattering nineteen to the dozen, hands flying around, while Jed stands there looking, if I'm honest, slightly bemused. And not like I imagined at all. I can see from Clemmy's body language that she likes this man. A *lot*.

I'm puzzled by Jed, though. He sounded so warm and friendly when I spoke to him on the phone. But, in person, he looks rather stiff and detached. It's funny how you can hear a voice and instantly you have an image in your mind of what that person might look like. Apparently, I got it wrong on this occasion. Jed doesn't look anything like his voice.

Then the tannoy crackles into action, announcing the arrival of the London train. At which point Jed and Clemmy both turn and look along the tracks.

The train glides to a halt and people are alighting with bags and children and dogs, and there's temporary mayhem. Then, as the crowds start to disperse, I suddenly spot the person Clemmy and Jed appear to have been waiting for. Clemmy is waving energetically at a man in a dark-grey suit, who has just alighted from the train at the opposite end of the platform.

He's very tall with broad shoulders and thick, chestnut hair that curls on the collar of his white shirt. Striding along the platform towards Clemmy, his long powerful-looking legs make easy work of the distance. Reunited with his friends, he starts talking animatedly – standing a head taller than Jed – perhaps telling a funny story about something that happened on his journey. Clemmy, looking flushed, is smiling up at him with unconcealed delight, while Jed stands silently beside her, hands thrust deep in his pockets.

All three glance towards the exit and start walking along the platform. Then, as I stand there gawping at them, half-hidden by the pillar like a trainee spy, Clemmy suddenly looks across at me and our eyes meet.

Shit!

And now they're walking over and Clemmy is smiling and saying something about me and they're all looking over.

I stand there, a grin frozen on my face.

Bloody hell, if I have to speak to Clemmy, Jed will recognise my voice and think it's really strange that I just happen to be on the platform, hiding behind a pillar, at the exact moment the two p.m. London train arrives into Easingwold Station.

We are now approaching Stalker City. Stalker City next stop.

Oh God, but it's going to look really strange if I suddenly turn round and beetle off.

So, I smile in their general direction then glance at my watch and mime a Big Shock. As in: *Crikey, I'm late for that thing*! Making a clown face at Clemmy to convey my meaning, I scuttle off towards the exit.

But, in my rush to get away, I manage to take the wrong route, then have to double back on myself to locate the actual exit. Panicking, I search the crowd around me. There's no sign of them. So I'll just bomb along here and slip through the barrier, and—

'Hello there!' says a cheery voice. 'Thank you *so much* for rescuing me earlier.' With a sinking heart, I turn round and there's Clemmy, beaming at me with those friendly dimples.

'I'm pretty accident-prone,' she says. 'But I'm not usually in the habit of throwing my tampons all over the place.'

I laugh. 'Hey, I was pleased to help.' I glance anxiously behind her. Her two companions are bringing up the rear and I'm getting palpitations at the thought of Jed recognising my voice.

'Actually.' I lean in with a confidential whisper. 'I've got this weird, er, tonsil ailment thing.' I touch my throat and swallow painfully. 'Trying not to talk.'

'Oh, you poor thing.' Clemmy's face is a picture of concern. 'That's awful. Are you taking anything?'

I nod. 'Antibiotics.' Jed and the other man are almost upon us, so I whisper, 'Better go. Nice to meet you, though.'

Clemmy takes my arm. 'Listen, my gran always swears by lemon and honey in a glass of hot water for sore throats, with a slug of whisky if you have any kicking around.'

'Fab! Thank you.' I stick up my thumb and edge away. 'I'll give it a go.'

'But you have to drink it really slowly – oh, Jed, Ryan.' She turns and greets them, and my smile freezes. Again. 'This lady helped me rescue my handbag contents. Long story.' She frowns. 'Oh, but I don't even know your name.'

All three are looking at me expectantly.

Panicking, I touch my throat (actually, 'grab' would be nearer the mark) and Clemmy says, 'Oh sorry, you can't speak, can you?'

I swallow and wince dramatically for good measure.

She turns to the other two. 'Horrible tonsil thing.'

They nod in sympathy and I whisper, 'It's Pamela. My name's Pamela.'

She holds out her hand and we shake. 'Pleased to meet you, Pamela.' Her smile is so warm and genuine. I feel terrible for lying to her.

I smile back, whispering hoarsely, 'And you too, Clemmy.'

She blinks in confusion.

Shit! Bugger! I'm not supposed to know her name!

Then I spy a visitor's badge on her blouse under the green coat. I point at it and her face clears. I raise my hand and smile at them, walking backwards and doing another Oscar-worthy throat clearing as if I might be about to croak my last.

'Poppy Ainsworth? Is that really you?' booms a voice at my shoulder a second later, and I spin round to see an old 'frenemy' from school who I haven't clapped eyes on in years. We were friends until she copped off with my boyfriend, Leslie. We were only ten, mind you. I really should have got over it by now.

'Heather Connelly, hi!' I greet her, rather too loudly. Wincing, I glance back at Clemmy, who's looking understandably confused at the sudden name change. Luckily, Jed has taken a call on his mobile and definitely didn't hear me.

My shoulders sink with relief and I prepare to swap stories about school days.

'Are you all right?' Heather asks, her beady eyes scouring my face for signs of how I've aged in the past decade or so. 'You look a bit flushed.'

'Yeah. Bit of a tricky situation there, actually,' I confide in a low tone, keeping an eye on Jed. He's still busy on his phone, thankfully. 'Some people I wanted to avoid.' I laugh awkwardly. 'If you know what I mean.'

'People like me, you mean?' says a voice right behind me. A deep, velvety voice with a hint of gravel that I'd recognise anywhere...

Jed?

But isn't that Jed over there, talking into his mobile?

I spin round and find myself staring up into the amused face of the much taller man with chestnut hair who got off the train.

Chapter 11

'Poppy? The very woman behind *Diner Might?*' He smiles, looking amazed. As in, *What are the chances of us meeting like this?*

I groan inwardly.

Honestly, Jed Turner, you have no idea!

'Er, yes, that's me.' My brain is still trying to catch up. This must be him. He certainly sounds like Jed. And he obviously recognised *my* voice.

But why, then, did Clemmy practically dive on the other man with such enthusiasm? And who *is* the other man?

'So not Pamela, then?' He looks confused, as well he might.

I swallow. 'Er, no. Well, yes, actually. It's – erm – my middle name, which I sometimes use ...' I trail off, my face scorched with embarrassment.

'Poppy Pamela,' Jed murmurs, solemnly weighing it up. 'Interesting.'

He grins at me, his eyes twinkling, and I have a terrible feeling he's seen right through my pathetic attempt at hiding my identity from him. Oh God, he must realise I'm there to spy on him!

'Anyway, it's nice to meet the entrepreneur in person, whatever you want to call yourself.' He holds out his hand.

Dazed, I offer up my paw and he envelops it in a cool, strong grip.

'It's Poppy,' I tell him firmly. 'Definitely Poppy.'

He nods. Then he glances behind him. 'I'd introduce you to my brother, Ryan, but he seems to be occupied.'

We both look over at the man Clemmy was so pleased to see. He's frowning into his mobile phone, deep in conversation, and Clemmy is standing nearby, looking a bit like a fish out of water, waiting for him to finish.

'So that's your *brother*?' I murmur, gazing at Ryan with interest. There's a definite likeness around the mouth, but in terms of colouring and stature, they're very different. Ryan is blond, slim and medium-height, while his darker-haired brother, Jed, is much taller and rangier, with a powerful build.

Jed grins. 'Ryan hates the countryside. It took all my powers of persuasion to get him to spend Christmas in a log cabin in the middle of nowhere.'

'It sounds heavenly to me.'

He studies me with a slightly bemused look on his

face, as if he's still trying to work out whether bumping into each other was by coincidence or design. 'So, Poppy. How's the throat now?'

Oh God, I've been forgetting to whisper!

'Erm, well it's ...' Gingerly, I 'try out' my voice. 'Gosh, d'you know it actually seems a bit better now.' Fire flames in my cheeks at being found out. But by the look on his face, he wasn't in the least bit fooled anyway.

'Good. Good. I've been trying to think of a name for your cooking enterprise.'

'You have?'

'Yeah, it's pretty good, actually. You could call it 'Cordon Blur' with a logo of your van hurtling at top speed to the diner's rescue. So fast, you're just a blur?'

I open my eyes wide. Is he serious? He *looks* serious. His lips twitch. 'Only joking.'

Heather, who I've quite forgotten about, clears her throat pointedly. I turn and she's waggling her eyebrows and making signs that she wants an introduction. I think of Leslie and decide she can dream on.

'Anyway, nice to see you again, Heather.' I beam. 'But I'm afraid I really must dash.'

'Oh. Well, cheerio, then.' She looks none too pleased at being so abruptly dismissed. 'Nice glasses!' she calls back with a sneer.

Oh, shit! I'd forgotten I was wearing them. I've been vaguely assuming there was a thunderstorm brewing outside.

I whip them off and sneak a sideways glance at Jed.

'Bad hangover?' he remarks casually, as we head for the exit.

'What? Oh, the glasses. Yes. Er, very bad.'

'Celebrating after your successful night last Saturday?'

I smile at him, flattered he should have remembered. 'Something like that.'

'It's a small world, isn't it?'

'Sorry?'

'I mean, what an amazing coincidence that we should meet like this,' he points out. 'Were you seeing someone off on the train?'

I glance at him, uncertainly. I thought he'd rumbled me straight away. But perhaps he does, after all, think our meeting was entirely accidental. 'Yes! I *was* seeing someone off ...'

He looks at me interestedly, as if expecting more, so I swallow and cross my fingers behind my back. 'Yes, it was my – erm – Great Aunt Lucinda, actually.' I shrug. 'She was staying for a few days.'

'Did she travel far?'

'Er, yes, *Leeds*. She – um – lives in Leeds. With her cocker spaniel. Called – erm –' I glance around for inspiration. 'Costa!'

He grins knowingly. 'As in Costa Coffee?'

'No.' I adopt a haughty tone. 'As in *Costas*. He's Greek. The dog.'

I fumble in my handbag to hide my desperate blushes. Of *course* he knows I'm fibbing. And now I've just gone and made an even bigger plonker of myself.

'Actually, I'm glad I bumped into you,' Jed says smoothly, stopping at the entrance, presumably to wait for his friends to catch up. 'I was going to phone you anyway.'

'You were?' I stare up at him, surprise at this mixed with relief that the subject of Costas the Greek dog appears to have been dropped from the agenda.

He nods. 'I – um – find myself in a bit of a knotty predicament which I was hoping you might be able to help with. You see, I rashly agreed to host the family Christmas at my uncle's holiday home, on the under-standing that his caterers would be available to do the honours for us over the festive season.'

'But that's not going to happen?' I ask, not quite sure I like where this is leading.

He shakes his head. 'What I hadn't banked on was Uncle Bob meeting a woman called Gloria during a business trip to Newcastle, and falling madly in love at first sight. And subsequently forgetting – in his lovesick delirium – to engage the caterers for the Christmas period.' He grins. 'They're off to cook for a client in Barbados over the festive period and who can blame them?'

'So you're stuck with no one to cook for you?' My

heart is cantering about like a frisky thoroughbred. 'And I'm guessing it's impossible to engage a caterer this close to Christmas?'

He answers with a rueful nod.

'Couldn't you all just pitch in and do it yourselves?'

He laughs heartily at this by way of an answer, clutching his hand to his chest for emphasis.

'Right.' I nod understandingly.

Suddenly serious, he locks his green eyes onto mine. 'I was actually going to ask if you'd consider doing it?'

For a moment, the world stands still. I'm staring up into the depths of Jed Turner's intense gaze, feeling weirdly mesmerised. It must be the total shock I'm feeling at his sudden request. I open my mouth but nothing comes out.

'You don't need to decide now,' he says swiftly. 'I realise you'll have to talk it over with your other half because obviously cooking for us would mess with your own Christmas plans.'

I swallow and finally manage to speak. 'Well, actually, Harrison – my, erm, boyfriend – is away for Christmas. At his mum's in Spain.'

Jed nods. 'Very nice. Lucky Harrison. But still, you shouldn't agree to do it out of politeness. I *will* manage. If I have to.' He pretends to wail into his coat sleeve, which I – and several passing women – find very funny. 'Incidentally, the place we're going to is called the Log

Fire Cabin and it's pretty special. Not that I'm trying to influence you in any way, shape or form.'

My heart revs up from a canter to a full-blown gallop. I can't do it. *Can I?* Just the thought of it terrifies me. So why on earth am I giving him hope that I might say yes?

I take a deep breath. I'll just say to him, 'No, sorry. Now that I think about it, I'm all booked up this Christmas.'

But weirdly, my mouth seems to have other ideas because, instead, what comes out of it is far less decisive. 'I might be able to help you out but I'll have to check my diary. Can I let you know later on today?'

Jed's face breaks into a warm smile that reveals beautifully even white teeth, and crinkles up his green eyes as he gazes at me with undisguised relief. This is a worry, to be truthful. Have I somehow implied that I'll definitely do it?

My heart is banging, and excitement is whipping my poor brain into frenzied overdrive. My head might very well explode as a result, and it would probably serve me right (although I'm not sure what for). Perhaps I'm channelling my inner Erin: maybe that's where this sudden bravery is coming from. How else to explain the sneaky desire I'm feeling to just say 'yes' to Jed Turner?

Of course, the fact that my cooking at Mrs Morelli's

was such a great success has boosted my confidence. I've proved I can do it – and do it surprisingly well – so why not spread my wings a little further? It's such an amazing opportunity. I don't even have to worry that I'll be spoiling Harrison's Christmas because he won't even be here.

Then I think of Mum. I'll be spending Christmas Day with her and the last thing I want to do is let her down. My brain whizzes round a bit more as I frantically work out the logistics. As long as I'm hired to cook only Christmas dinner on the big day, I'd still have plenty of time to spend at home with Mum. We could still open presents together in the morning, and then have our Christmas lunch, just the two of us, before I nipped off to cook the Log Fire Cabin Christmas dinner in the evening.

But what about Erin? I'll need her help. What if she has plans with Mark that she can't alter?

But she *will* help. Of course she will. She's lovely and I'll bribe her if necessary. A romantic weekend away for her and Mark in the New Year – if only she'll be my right-hand woman!

We've stopped by the station entrance, waiting for Ryan to finish his phone conversation and come over with Clemmy.

I smile shyly up at Jed, who's looking incredibly relieved. It seems faintly odd that a big man like him

– he's well over six feet with a powerful body and an equally powerful presence – should be practically wiping the sweat off his brow at such a close shave, saved by me at the final hour from a near calamity on the cooking front! I can't disappoint him now, can I?

'So you'll do it? If your diary's clear?' he asks.

I smile, feeling suddenly certain. 'I will.'

'That's brilliant, Poppy.'

His voice is so smooth and velvety. Jed Turner could audition to be the host on a late-night radio show.

He gives me a lopsided grin. 'I was trying to act cool about the situation. But the thought of all that cooking was making me want to head for the nearest airport, to be honest.'

'So, is that all I'd be doing? Cooking on Christmas Day?'

His look turns apologetic. 'Well, I'd hoped for a little more than that. The gang arrives on the twenty-second of December and they'll be staying right through until the second of January.'

I gulp. That's a lot of catering. 'And I'd be cooking for how many?'

He narrows his eyes, thinking. 'Me, Ryan, Clemmy, Uncle Bob, his new girlfriend Gloria plus her two teenage kids. That makes seven.'

'And would you be wanting all meals?'

He looks at me thoughtfully. 'That would depend on

you, really. As I said, the last thing I want to do is screw up your Christmas. Perhaps just dinner each night?'

'And maybe a cake for afternoon tea each day?'

'Sounds perfect.'

'Well, whatever you need, I'm sure I can manage. You're the client.' Jed Turner has no idea that underneath my calm exterior, I'm running round in circles going *waaaaah!*

Then another horrible thought crashes me back down to earth.

What about my waitressing duties at the hotel? They'd never give me time off so near to Christmas.

That's that, then. I can't do it. I shouldn't have promised until I'd thought it through properly. There's just something about Jed Turner that seems to make me act out of character. Yes, I'll blame him. It's definitely his fault.

I wonder if I could make dinner in between my shifts and get Erin to serve it in the evening?

But, even as I'm thinking this, I know it could never work. So many things could go wrong and I wouldn't be there, at the Log Fire Cabin, to sort them out. It wouldn't be fair on Erin to leave her with the nerve-racking task of making sure the food was presented well before getting it to the table. *Oh God, what do I do?*

Mimi will laugh in my face if I ask for time off this close to Christmas.

I'm going to have to beg. Not a pleasant thought. But I'm definitely a bit braver these days, so maybe I'll just have to do it!

'Are you okay?' Jed frowns.

The panic must be showing on my face.

I paste on a smile. 'Oh, yes. Just thinking hard. Planning menus in my head already!'

'That's the spirit!' He grins. 'And, between you and me, Uncle Bob is currently on the lookout for a talented, reliable caterer to cover business lunches at his architect's firm.'

'He is?'

Jed nods. 'He's not particularly impressed with the current lot.'

'Gosh. Right.'

'He's a bit of a foodie, though, is Uncle Bob, so you might have to pull out all the stops to impress him.'

Me? Providing fancy business lunches for a man who's a connoisseur of food? I almost laugh out loud at the very idea. My childhood stammer would return with a vengeance.

But instead, I give Jed a pert look. 'I *always* pull out all the stops – even if I'm *not* trying to impress Uncle Bob!'

As soon as I've said it, I feel like biting my tongue off. I shouldn't be cheeking a potential client, even if it was only meant as a joke. I don't know what's come over me.

But Jed gives me a disarmingly sheepish smile. 'Sorry. Of course. I'm sure you do. And that's why I'm asking you to save our Christmas.' He puts his hands together and groans, '*Please* save our Christmas, Poppy! It's the season of goodwill to all men, and I'm a man.'

Oh, you certainly are!

The thought that whizzes through my head is so unexpected, I actually feel myself blushing. I didn't mean it in a sexual way. It's just he *is* big and, standing next to him, with his broad shoulders and long, athletic-looking legs, I feel so very dainty by comparison. It's an unusual sensation. I feel ultra-feminine, somehow.

'Sorry, I shouldn't be putting pressure on you to agree,' Jed says, clearly misinterpreting my awkward silence and red face. 'It's not fair of me.'

I shake my head. 'No, it's fine. And actually, I'd love to cook for you. I'm just trying to work out the practicalities.' I'd better not mention that I'm also working as a waitress because he might think I'm just an amateur. Oh God, and he'd be right!

Straightening up, I tell myself: I *am* a cook. And I'm a good one, too!

'Listen, why don't I take you over to see the Log Fire Cabin just now?' Jed indicates the car park. 'Then you can decide.' He grins mischievously. 'I'm hoping the charm of the place will make up your mind for you.'

'Okay.' I smile up at him, thinking: *never mind the charm of the Log Fire Cabin! The man himself is doing a pretty good job of charming me!*

I glance at my watch. Right now, Harrison will be settling himself into his plane seat (on the aisle because looking at clouds from above makes him feel sick). He'll be buckling his belt and studying the safety leaflet, before settling down to read the book I gave him as a parting gift to take his mind off flying. It's on the subject of mathematical probability, so he's sure to be engrossed the whole flight.

I feel a sudden pang of sadness that I'm not sitting beside him, reading my own book and looking forward to enjoying the festivities together. We'll have to make up for it *next* Christmas. But it will be strange without him, however busy I might turn out to be—

'If you haven't got time now ...' Jed is speaking, pulling me back to the present.

'No, I have.' I smile confidently at him, slipping into professional mode. 'There's no time like the present. Let's do it!'

He leads me to his car, Ryan and Clemmy following a little way behind. Clemmy is chatting away happily, doing most of the talking, I notice. Jed opens the passenger door for me.

I hesitate. 'Won't Clemmy want to sit in the front?' I

don't want to usurp her place.

He grins. 'She won't mind. She can chat up my brother in the back.'

'Oh. Right.' I slip into the seat and he closes the door for me then nips round and slides into the driver's seat. His words strike me as being far too close to the truth for comfort. I glance at him anxiously. He obviously has no idea that Clemmy – the girl he's decided that he wants to spend Christmas with – is clearly enamoured with Ryan.

As I fumble with the seat belt, Jed leans across to help me. His arm accidentally brushes my thigh and I have to stop myself leaping away, it feels so strange. I force myself to breathe slowly while he reaches round for the belt slot. His thick, chestnut hair is inches away and he smells gorgeous. The citrus, slightly peppery scent makes me feel sort of spacey and a bit light-headed.

'Okay?' he murmurs, clicking the seat belt in place, and I feel a flutter of breath on my neck that does very weird things to my insides.

I smile stiffly. 'Great, thanks.' It's a relief when he's back on his own side.

The back door opens and, when I turn, Clemmy's getting in.

'Do you mind scooting along?' she asks with a radiant smile, and Ryan stops fumbling for the seatbelt, glances up at her, and moves to allow her in the same side.

'This is cosy,' she laughs.

Jed turns. 'Poppy has *almost* agreed to cook for us over the holiday.' He gives me a lazy smile and my heart does a little flip. 'So, please be nice to her.'

'Oh, fantastic!' Clemmy's obvious delight makes me even more determined to organise it somehow. She peers at me. 'Poppy, is it? I thought you said Pamela.'

'Middle name,' says Jed, tipping me a sly wink, which I pretend I haven't noticed.

'Ah. Right.' Thankfully, Clemmy seems satisfied by this half-explanation. 'Well, anyway, Poppy, I was just saying to Ryan, the last time the three of us spent more than an evening together was on a family camping holiday in France when we were teenagers!'

'Really?' That must be the *legendary* holiday Jed mentioned in his phone message.

Jed laughs. 'God, yes. La Rochelle. You were appalled at the unisex toilets, remember?'

Clemmy giggles. 'I'd forgotten about that. I was a bit of a prude back then. You were really gentlemanly, Ryan. You used to go in and check the loos for men, to make sure the coast was clear for me. Do you remember?'

'Did I?' Ryan sounds vague.

'Yes, you did,' says Jed. 'Clemmy, I seem to remember my football-mad kid brother used to duck out of knock-abouts on the beach on the pretext of a sprained ankle, just so he could spend time with you.' He grins slyly at his brother in the rearview mirror. 'Ring any bells, Ryan?'

I turn and smile at Ryan and catch Clemmy digging him delightedly in the ribs.

Ryan looks awkward. 'Did I? I don't remember.'

There's a brief, rather awkward silence.

Then Clemmy says, 'So where *is* this place? I can't wait to see it. The Log Fire Cabin! I *adore* the name. Doesn't it conjure up the most wonderful Christmassy scenes? Of course, if your Uncle Bob designed it, it *must* be incredible!'

Jed grins at her in his mirror. 'With some help from me, I'll have you know.'

'Oh, really? It was a joint project?'

He shakes his head. 'I had nothing to do with the log cabin. That's Uncle Bob's baby. But I designed the summer house he added a few years later.'

I glance with interest at Jed. He's an architect, too, then.

'That's some spacious summer house,' remarks Ryan. 'More like a studio flat.'

'Yes, and that's where you and I will likely be sleeping this holiday, I'm afraid.' Jed grins and turns to me. 'The cabin's pretty spacious itself, but it only has four bedrooms, and we have seven people to accommodate.'

'It sounds like a magical setting,' says Clemmy. 'Right on the lakeside.'

Butterflies flutter in my stomach. *Right on the lakeside?* Oh God, I think I know where the Log Fire Cabin might be. But a second later, I tell myself not to be so silly. It can't possibly be there. I mean, what are the chances?

Ryan is silent in the back and Jed is concentrating on the road. Clemmy is chattering away about the friends she's going to be visiting the next day in Easingwold, but I'm not really paying attention. The closer we get to the Log Fire Cabin, along roads that are bringing the memories flooding back, the more my insides are churning.

When we motor through the little village of Westbury Edge, then turn down a bumpy, potholed road that tests the car's suspension to the limit, my fears are finally realised.

The road, not much more than a track, leads to Shimmer Glass Lake. And from memory, nestling on the southern shore is a pretty little whitewashed cottage that was once a B&B.

I sway from side to side, the bumpy track aggravating my slight nausea.

I last saw it eighteen years ago. Christmas at Shimmer Glass Lake was magical. Mum's stubborn determination not to enjoy herself was the only thing to mar a perfect four days. I'd thought it was the start of a whole new chapter in my life. But as quickly as my hopes surged up, they crumbled away to dust.

Suddenly, I'm wishing I could change my mind and tell Jed to drive me back to my car, which is parked at the station. I have a sudden yearning to be away from this place and all the memories. I want to be at home with Harrison, going through our lovely familiar routine. But of course that's not possible. Harrison will probably be flying over the English Channel by now.

'Here we are,' says Jed, and I suddenly realise we've turned off the track earlier than I expected, down a little dip into a spacious parking area, and the Log Fire Cabin is right there ahead of us.

It's built from wood, but this is clearly no ordinary log cabin. Standing among the trees, it's a large, modern structure with lots of tall windows to let in the light. A breathtakingly stylish piece of modern architecture. And yet it tones in so beautifully with the surrounding trees, it almost seems an integral part of the forest.

We get out of the car and Clemmy gives a little sigh of wonder. 'Ooh, it's gorgeous. I didn't know what to expect when you said "log fire cabin". I guess I was picturing something the three bears might live in. A bit rustic. But this is incredible.'

I nod. 'I can just see it featured in a fancy homes magazine.'

'I know. I can't wait to see the log fire.' Clemmy rubs her hands together. 'It's all so romantic!'

'Glad you approve.' Jed's voice rumbles, right at my shoulder. 'You okay, Ryan? You're not saying much.'

'Yeah, fine. I can think of more exciting places to spend Christmas, to be honest. I'm not exactly a fan of getting back to nature in the middle of nowhere. It's far too quiet out here.'

Clemmy nudges him. 'Don't be such a grumpy guts, Ryan. You'll love it once you settle in. And I'm sure the food will be spectacular if Poppy's cooking for us.' She beams at me. 'Your throat seems a bit better.'

'Er, *much* better, thanks,' I assure her, deliberately avoiding Jed's eye.

I love Clemmy already. She's so warm and friendly and genuine.

Jed leads us through to a well-proportioned and deceptively spacious kitchen. A feeble winter sun has broken through the clouds and is filtering through the huge floor-to-ceiling windows, which look down to the lake at the back of the house. Smart, shaker-style units and stainless-steel appliances are ranged along two sides of the room, and a cosy breakfast bar, with great views over the lake, effectively divides the space into a working kitchen area and a place for relaxing, with a squashy, cushion-strewn sofa and a coffee table.

It's light and airy, with big glass patio doors by the

sofa overlooking the lake, but at the same time it's incredibly cosy with its lamps and subtle, under-unit lighting.

'Wow. What a lovely space,' I murmur, running my hand admiringly over the gorgeous grained wood of the island worktop, with copper pans suspended above it. 'A cook could be very happy in here.'

Jed spins round. 'Is that an actual commitment?'

I cock my head on one side, thinking, as everyone – even Ryan – looks at me expectantly. 'Do you know what? I think it is.'

Clemmy gives a little cheer. 'That's fab, Poppy! I can't wait to taste your food.'

Even Ryan raises a smile. 'Thank God. You'd have all been in the shit if you were relying on my cooking skills. I make a mean full English, though.'

'We'll hold you to that, mate,' grins Jed, switching on the kettle and opening cupboards.

My heart is racing. I can't believe I've just agreed to cook for this family for twelve whole days! Only time will tell if grabbing the opportunity was the right thing to do. Or if I've bitten off more than I can chew.

But for now, it feels right, somehow, like an adventure. The start of something brand new.

Of course, the whole thing is far from straightforward. I feel a bit bad that I haven't had a chance to talk it over with Harrison first. And I'm dreading having to ask Mimi for time off over the festive period. My next shift is tomorrow tonight, so I'll sort it out then. My stomach turns over queasily at the thought.

Clemmy does a happy little twirl in front of the sparkling lake view and declares, 'This is going to be the best Christmas ever!'

I push the thought of Mimi from my mind and smile to myself, hoping that maybe – just maybe – Clemmy might be right.

Chapter 12

Jed takes us all on a tour of Uncle Bob's holiday home, and Clemmy and I agree that the inside of the Log Fire Cabin is just as spectacular as the outside.

There's a cosy living room, all velvety drapes, squashy sofas and plush rugs in autumnal, russet shades. Set back from the seating area, by the patio doors, is a beautiful, high-gloss, white baby grand piano that makes me think wistfully of everyone gathered round singing Christmas carols. The focal point of the room is a traditional dark-red-brick fireplace with a deep mantelpiece festooned with church candles. A wicker basket full of logs sits all ready on the hearth, and instantly I'm imagining a glowing fire crackling in the grate when the curtains are drawn in the evenings, and white fairy lights strung around the candles on the mantelpiece, with perhaps some festive pine branches giving off a lovely Christmassy scent.

Right now, the curtains are pulled back, affording

views over the terrace and hot tub, and beyond that, to the expanse of well-cultivated grass that rolls gently down to the lake. At one end of the room is an alcove containing a long, solid-wood dining table with pretty, fabric-swagged chairs. Leaving the living room, we all follow Jed up the beautiful wooden staircase, its banisters polished to highlight the grain.

'That's Uncle Bob's room,' Jed says, pointing to a door at the furthest end of the first-floor landing.' He turns to Clemmy. 'Feel free to choose whichever bedroom you'd like. Uncle Bob, Gloria and her two kids won't be arriving until the day after tomorrow.'

I watch Clemmy, as she starts excitedly opening doors and peering into bedrooms. Is Jed hoping she'll end the holiday sleeping in *his* room? It's all very puzzling. Jed likes Clemmy. But Clemmy seems to like Ryan – despite the fact that Ryan himself has barely said two words to her. Or to anyone, for that matter.

But maybe Clemmy is just really friendly with everyone? Including Ryan? I hope that's the case because otherwise, it seems like Jed might have some serious competition for Clemmy's affections.

'Do you want to come downstairs and we can talk food?' Jed asks me.

I follow him down to the small landing and we stand in front of the big picture window there that affords a spectacular view. I gaze at the sweep of snow-covered grass and the fir trees leading down to the lake. The choppy surface of the water sparkles in the winter sun.

'It's so lovely here.' I smile shyly at Jed.

'Uncle Bob did a good job.'

'And you're an architect, too?'

He nods. 'I'm employed by a big company based in London at the moment but the dream is to work for myself one day.'

We pop our heads round the living-room door again and I admire the elegant, understated nature of the furniture and the splashes of bold colour in the art on the walls. Then something strikes me. 'It's lovely but it's not very Christmassy, is it?'

Jed frowns. 'We've got a Christmas tree.'

'Ooh, lovely.'

'It's spectacular.' He ushers me into the kitchen and points at a straggly little excuse for a fake tree on the breakfast bar. It's almost bald, having lost most of its tinsel. 'No expense spared. What do you think?'

I laugh. 'Not a lot.'

His lips twist into a rueful smile. 'It was all I could find. I'm not big on decking the halls. I wouldn't know where to start.'

I glance through the patio doors and my eye catches the group of fir trees to the right of the house. 'You've got all the decorations you could ever need right out there. We could bring in branches and fir cones and sprigs of holly, and twine them all the way up the banisters.' I look out into the hall, imagining how beautifully festive it could look.

Jed shoots me a querying look. 'Is that an offer of help?'

'Yes. I mean, no. Sorry, I was just getting carried away.' I feel myself colour up in confusion. What on earth am I thinking, advising the client on how he can improve the look of the house? I'm not usually that forward.

'Don't apologise. To tell you the truth, I'd be delighted if you'd help. What about tomorrow? Are you free? Could you do an extra day for us?'

My mind goes into instant overdrive. I'm off during the day tomorrow, so that's no problem. What I'll do after that, I still have to work out.

'So, what do you think?' Jed asks, arms folded, leaning his shoulder against the big stainless-steel fridge as he studies me.

My eyes meet his. 'I love putting up Christmas decorations. It would be a pleasure.'

'That's brilliant.' He breaks into a slow smile, his green eyes crinkling at the corners.

We spend the next ten minutes talking about menus, and he says that his Uncle Bob will love Christmas with an Italian flavour.

'Does he know Italian cuisine?' I ask, a little alarmed.

'He's eaten all over the world in the best restaurants,

and he has a brilliant Thai chef to cook for him at home. He could probably be a food critic if he wanted to be.'

I swallow. 'Gosh.'

'I haven't put you off the idea, have I?'

'No, it's fine,' I lie, smiling brightly. 'I do like a challenge!'

Jed chuckles. 'I have a feeling Bob will like you.'

He takes me through the French doors out to the patio and we walk across the grass, past the hot tub which is currently covered over, down to the lakeside. I find myself transfixed by the little whitewashed cottage on the opposite side of the lake. It looks rundown and sad, the windows bare. My heart squeezes painfully.

It was a little B&B last time I saw it; the place Alessandro stayed when he came to visit all those years ago. But I recently read that the owners went through an acrimonious divorce and it lay empty for years before eventually being sold to a small hotel chain. The company planned to develop it into a luxury country hideaway hotel, but then shortly after buying the property, they went bankrupt. So the cottage is still here, looking in urgent need of a buyer to lavish it with love and attention.

Jed is also gazing over at the far shore. 'When the sky is clear, the landscape behind us is reflected in the lake. A perfect mirror image.'

I nod, remembering. 'Shimmer Glass Lake. You get the best view of it from over that side. I think I have a photograph somewhere.'

I know I have a photograph. It's hidden away inside my little red notebook.

Jed looks at me in surprise. 'You've been here before?'

My heart lurches uncomfortably, but I force a bright smile. 'Yes. We – I swam in the lake one New Year's Day, actually. When I was just a kid.'

'Of course.' He nods. 'I'd forgotten about the New Year Plunge. They usually get quite a turnout, don't they? Perhaps all of Uncle Bob's house guests should take part this year.'

I grimace at the thought.

Jed grins. 'We could have a prize for the person who manages to get Ryan to loosen up a bit and dive in.'

*

Erin's response that evening when I reveal the exciting news that I'm going to be cooking for seven at the Log Fire Cabin is to squeal. Very loudly.

This would be fine. Except we're in the village pub, and several tables of people we vaguely know turn to peer over at the two hooligans currently lowering the tone of the place.

Erin is oblivious. 'Have you got enough recipes for that length of time?'

I laugh. 'I wouldn't be much of a caterer if I couldn't vary the menu for a fortnight.'

'Will it be all meals? From breakfast right through to after-dinner coffee?'

I shake my head. 'Jed and I agreed that I'd provide a three-course dinner each evening and bake a cake every day for tea.'

'Jed and I?' She raises an eyebrow. 'Jed as in Mr Sexy Voice?'

I flush at her expression, wishing I'd never mentioned the message he left on my landline by mistake. 'He's the one who's hosting Christmas, yes. At his uncle's holiday home. You should see it, Erin.' I plunge into a description of the cabin to get her off the subject.

She beams at me.

'Well, you *will* see it,' I add. 'If Mark doesn't mind you helping me?'

The light in her eyes dims a little. 'I don't think he will. Mind, I mean.'

'Didn't you two have things planned, then?'

She shakes her head. 'Not really. I wanted to go away for a few days over Christmas, just the two of us, but Mark was distinctly lukewarm about the idea. Last Christmas, he was almost as excited as me to be spending it together. I don't know what's happened.'

I shrug. 'Maybe he just fancies chilling out at home with you?'

'I suppose.'

'Hey, what's this?' I laugh. 'Usually you're love's young dream, you two. I never get tired of telling people how you waited such a long time for the perfect man to come along. But come along, he did!'

She grunts but I can tell she's pleased. Then she shrugs. 'It's just a feeling I get. I honestly think the "honeymoon period" is over,' she says, doing quotes in the air. 'We don't seem to have as much fun as we used to, and Mark is always having to stay late at work these days, to finish something or other. I keep telling him he needs to play as well as work, but he just shrugs it off and says it won't be for long.'

'He's probably tired if he's working so hard. The Christmas break will do him the world of good.'

'I hope so.'

An image of Mark emerging from the matching agency doorway flashes into my mind, but I brush it away.

'Did he get his hair cut the other day?' I ask on impulse.

'No. Why?'

'Oh, nothing. I just thought I saw him coming out of a hairdresser's, that's all, but it obviously can't have been him.' To cheer her up, I add, 'But listen, about the honeymoon period being over – every couple gets to that stage eventually, don't they? However loved up they are at the start? I think Harrison and I got to that stage about three days after we met.'

Erin bursts out laughing. 'Poppy Valentina Ainsworth! Poor Harrison. What a terrible thing to say.'

'No, it's not,' I protest, at the same time feeling a touch guilty. 'I just mean that Harrison and I have never really gone in for the hearts-and-flowers sort of romance that you guys do. We're both far too practical for that.'

Erin looks gloomy again. 'I don't like practical. Hearts and flowers suit me just fine.' She grabs my hand. 'Oh, Poppy, what if Mark's going off me?' The look in her eyes is pure anguish.

'Don't be ridiculous, Erin. Mark absolutely *adores* you. You don't need flowers as well.'

'I suppose.' She laughs. 'God, listen to me. I'm sounding more grouchy than Ebenezer Scrooge.' She bangs the table. 'I need my sparkly reindeer antlers and a glass of Auntie Noreen's horrible eggnog to get me in the Christmas spirit!'

*

It feels strange having the whole king-size bed to myself tonight. I prop up the pillow, intending to read, but find myself thinking about Harrison, wondering what the temperature is in Spain, and thinking how pleased his mum will be to have him with her. He doesn't believe in phoning long-distance. I keep telling him that these days, it's included in your phone package, but I don't think he quite believes it. He's adamant that a brief text is all you need.

Harrison's texts are always short and to the point, but I'm used to that now. At first, I used to send him long, chatty messages and end up asking something like: 'Do you fancy the cinema on Saturday?' He'd send back a one-word answer – 'yes' or 'no' – and I'd be a bit disappointed. But now I just figure it's part of his charm.

So far, I've had the following text: *Flight fine, Mother okay. Will text tomorrow. Love, Harrison xx*

I sent one back, although I debated for a long time whether to mention the job at the Log Fire Cabin. In the end, I thought it was a bit too complicated to explain in a text, so I just sent a message saying I was missing him. I'll phone him soon to tell him about the new catering job. Otherwise, if I don't and he happens to phone me one evening (stranger things have happened!), he'll wonder where on earth I am, out so late.

My mind is still buzzing too much from the events of the day to fall asleep immediately, so I lie there thinking about lurking at the station that morning, hoping to get a look at Jed and Clemmy, and the embarrassment of being totally rumbled by Jed. But I'm glad I went because otherwise, I might never have landed such an exciting new job over the Christmas holidays.

The only thing that slightly spooks me is the location of the Log Fire Cabin. I can't believe it's situated right across the lake from the cottage where Alessandro stayed. I mean, what are the chances?

He let me down big time by never returning, and throughout the years since, I've resolutely turned my back on all the memories I once cherished. I thought I'd succeeded in almost blocking them out – until an incredible twist of fate led me back to the lake today.

Now, lying here in the dark, I'm powerless to stop the memories of that long-ago Christmas tumbling back into my head.

I stare into the blackness, listening to a smatter of hail rattling at the window, my thoughts drifting to the old cardboard box that I haven't opened in years but that I know is somewhere at the back of my wardrobe, buried under a heap of shoes and scarves. I know I should leave it well alone. But some stronger impulse is urging me to take a look ... just a little look. *What harm can it do?*

I climb out of bed and open the wardrobe. Then I fumble around in the depths of it until my hands close round the box. Drawing it out, I kneel down and set the box on the floor in front of me, staring at it. My heart is in my mouth. How mad it is that an old Clarks' shoebox, tatty around the edges now, should fill me with such trepidation.

I draw a deep breath and tell myself not to be so ridiculous. What is there to be scared of? Only my feelings. And they're bound to have faded in strength during the years since I last looked in the box.

But what if they haven't?

On an impulse, I shove the box back in the wardrobe and slam the door.

In bed, I lie on my side staring at the wall. I told Harrison about my real dad but he thinks I should leave things be because otherwise, I might be disappointed all over again. I wish it were that simple, though.

For a long time, during my teens and early twenties, I had fantasies about going in search of my real dad and actually finding him. Mum would never talk about him, except to say that she had no contact details for where he was living. She would get quite agitated when I asked about him and I realised she didn't want to build my hopes up that I'd ever find him again. I guess she felt guilty that in choosing to bring me up alone, she'd deprived me of my real dad, and she didn't want me pining for someone who was quite possibly lost to me forever. With no address or phone number, she couldn't contact him even if she wanted to.

But secretly, I could never quite give up on him. I

had only one clue as to Alessandro's possible whereabouts - and it wasn't much. I remembered him talking fondly about the beautiful Island of Capri, off the coast of Italy near Naples, and how he wanted to live and work there some day.

That was how I found myself travelling to Italy with my friend, Clare, on my first holiday abroad without Mum, at the age of eighteen. We booked a holiday to Sorrento and, even as we left the travel agent's, I was already planning to find out about organised trips from our hotel across to the island.

It had all felt so unreal when the plane touched down in Italy. This was the country where my roots lay – and where my real dad presumably still lived.

Later in the week, when we finally set foot on Capri, a place so close to Alessandro's heart, my stomach was churning – and not because of seasickness. It felt wonderful to be there, but terrifying at the same time. I walked around with Clare in a dream. I already knew so much about the island, I could probably have given guided tours! When we ordered lunch at a little pavement café overlooking the harbour, I sat watching the passers-by, unable to eat a thing, I felt so on edge and excited. *What if he walked right past our table? I hadn't seen him since I was twelve. Would I recognise him?*

Then my eye caught a street-food vendor, pitched just a short distance away. He was tall and slim with dark, curly hair, and there was a definite similarity. I showed Clare the photo and she wasn't so sure. But I sat there, watching him, growing more and more convinced that it was him. Alessandro was passionate about food – it made perfect sense that he'd be selling his homemade delicacies on Capri, the place he loved.

I wanted so badly to walk over there and ask him if his name was Alessandro Bianchi. But the thought of finding that it wasn't him was almost too much to bear. Eventually, Clare went over to talk to him, while I sat there, feeling sick, my heart drumming so loudly I thought all the people in the café would hear it.

As I watched, Clare engaged him in conversation. He was smiling and chatting, and my heart rose in expectation. How amazing if, after all this time, it really was him.

Clare turned and pointed at me and my heart lifted. He looked over and I prepared to smile and wave. But then I saw the puzzled look on his face and the slow shake of his head.

The rest of the holiday is a blur.

I'd been a fool to think that my fantasy of finding him was ever going to be that easy. I hardened my heart after that. No more searching for a father I barely knew and who clearly wasn't in the slightest bit curious about his long-lost daughter.

Now, I dash away a tear, wishing Harrison were here

to give me one of his lovely bear hugs.

I can't avoid the little cottage across the lake with all its memories, but I mustn't allow myself to get distracted and take my eye off the ball. The food I produce at the Log Fire Cabin needs to be the best I've ever conjured up.

I will *not* allow the ghosts of the past to sabotage my new future...

Chapter 13

As soon as I wake, I remember Harrison's cooling-off period and I lie there thinking of other qualities about my soon-to-be fiancé which make me keen to marry him. After a while, I grab my notebook and write:

Eleven days until I'm engaged! Harrison is one of the most genuine, straightforward people I know. He never plays games and he's not in the least bit pretentious. What you see is what you get and there's something very reassuring about that. He'll talk to people about his manhole-cover passion without being in the least worried that they'll think he's boring and that it's a bit of a weird hobby to have. He never pretends to be someone he isn't.

Thinking of his honesty makes me feel a bit bad. I'm going back to the Log Fire Cabin this morning to help Jed decorate the house – but I still haven't told Harrison about it. It's not that I don't want to tell him. It's just that it's a bit difficult putting everything in a text. I'll phone him later instead, and we can chat.

*

I arrive at the Log Fire Cabin just before ten, my mind buzzing with ideas for turning the place into a Christmassy winter wonderland.

Jed greets me at the door, looking slightly the worse for wear in worn jeans and a T-shirt. I suspect the bottle of Laphroaig single-malt whisky Ryan brought with him yesterday might have something to do with it.

'We had a lot of catching up to do last night. Haven't seen my brother properly since the summer.' He grins sheepishly, then half-yawns and stretches out his big, well-toned arms, revealing a flash of washboard-taut stomach as his T-shirt rides up.

I swallow hard and fix my eyes on his face, stepping over the threshold to the scent of frying bacon. 'You've managed breakfast, then.'

'Oh, yes. Bacon and eggs. Hit the spot beautifully.'

'So, Ryan came up trumps with the full English breakfast?'

He laughs. 'Sadly not. He's probably going to need at least a week to acclimatise to rural life here. Apparently the dead silence kept him awake all night. He could barely manage a coffee this morning.'

I follow Jed into the kitchen, trying not to notice the way the pale, worn denim of his jeans hugs his rear end just perfectly. 'How's Clemmy?'

'Fine.' He turns and my eyes flick upwards, guiltily. 'She stuck to wine and soda, wise girl. She was up, bright-eyed and bushy-tailed by nine, singing the score of *Oklahoma* while crisping the bacon. Great singer, actually. Ryan's borrowed my car and driven her into Easingwold to meet friends for the day, so we have the place to ourselves. Now, first things first. Coffee?' He grabs a mug from the dresser.

'Great, thanks.'

While Jed is busy, I stare out through the patio doors. It's a cold, blue-skied day, very still, not a ripple on the lake. The cottage on the opposite shore is reflected perfectly in the water, along with the snow-covered fir trees that flank it on either side. The forecasters were right about the weather. We've been plunged into a cold snap. More snow fell overnight, making the scene I'm gazing at look just like a Christmas card.

'Take a seat.' Jed indicates the breakfast-bar stools and I choose the one nearest the window so I can angle it with my back to the cottage. He passes me coffee and a jug of milk. 'Hope you're feeling creative.' He grins, perching beside me with his own mug.

Even sitting down, he towers over me, long thighs splaying out as he relaxes on the stool, broad chest and muscular arms lightly tanned against the pale blue of his T-shirt. He rakes back his untamed, morning-after-the-night-before hair and I notice strands of gold and copper in its chestnut depths. He reminds me of a beautiful tiger, although hopefully, as my client, he won't be quite so savage.

It slightly worries me that he's invited Clemmy for Christmas, because from what I've seen of her reaction to the two brothers, she seems more into Ryan than Jed. But it's definitely not my place to say anything. Instead, I start outlining my decorating ideas.

I'm aware of Jed's eyes on me as I reach for the milk. He fills the space beside me with his solid presence and masculine scent, making me feel oddly self-conscious, and I end up fumbling with the jug, slopping some of the contents onto the table. Mumbling apologies, I whip out a paper hanky and start wiping up the milk. So much for making a good first impression!

'Don't worry,' murmurs Jed. He takes the sodden little bundle from me and his fingers touch mine. A little tingle runs all the way up my arm and I watch in a slight daze as he levers himself off the stool and strolls over to drop the hanky in the bin. He soaks a dishcloth under the tap and wrings it out while I try hard not to check out his back view again. When he turns, I flick my eyes to the window and frown, craning my neck as if I've spotted a rare bird in the trees or something.

'Anything wrong?' he asks, giving the surface a quick but thorough wipe.

'No, no. Just – erm – admiring the wildlife.' I crane

my neck a little more, wondering what the hell is wrong with me. I don't usually have any trouble appearing businesslike in a work situation, so why am I feeling so ridiculously jumpy today? As if I'm all fingers and thumbs?

He sits back down, folds his arms and leans casually over to look out himself, and I catch a whiff of his deliciously spicy aftershave.

'I doubt there's much life – wild or otherwise – in late December,' he says.

I feel myself blushing. Is he teasing me? I'm not sure because he then says, 'I saw a robin or two yesterday, mind you. Although it might well have been the same one, popping up in different places.' We grin at the idea. 'So, tell me what you want me to do, Poppy. I'm entirely in your hands.' He holds his arms wide and smiles disarmingly.

'Oh. Right.' This flusters me even more until I realise a second later that of course he's referring to my festive plans for the house.

Awkwardly, I launch headlong into a list of ideas I've had for Christmas decorations.

'Well, for a start, I thought we could bring in loads of branches and fir cones and sprigs of holly and wind them all the way up the handrail of the central staircase?' I use my hands to illustrate, choosing to avoid his eye for some reason. 'Then obviously we need a proper Christmas tree. I've been buying baubles for years. I absolutely love them. Especially if they're Italian. So, I brought loads of them over for you to use here. I won't be spending much time at home over the holidays, so it's no problem if you'd like to borrow them.' I paste on a bright smile and glance at him. 'They're in the boot of my car if you'd like me to fetch them.'

He nods and continues watching me calmly, arms folded, a hint of a smile on his lips. I've got a funny feeling that he finds me rather entertaining, although I can't imagine why. I'm trying my very best to be businesslike.

'As for the Christmas tree,' I sweep on, 'I was wondering if we could dig one up. You've certainly got plenty to choose from out there. And then afterwards, you can obviously plant it back in the ground for next year.'

'Great minds,' he remarks.

'Sorry?'

He shrugs his big shoulders. 'Great minds think alike. After you inspired me yesterday with your plans to transform the place, I went out and chose a well-proportioned tree and dug it up. It's in a pot in the shed awaiting your attention.'

'Oh, wow. Fab! That sounds absolutely perfect.' I cringe inwardly as the words leave my mouth. I don't usually gush like that. *What's wrong with me?*

'Right. Shall we go and have a look? See if it meets with your approval?' There's an amused glint in his eye.

I fix on a smile and drain my mug to hide my blushes. 'Great. Lead on.'

We put on outdoor gear and leave by the back door. A path takes us around the side of the house to a substantial wooden shed, set back from the lake and half-hidden by a little copse of trees. Jed asks what my original plans were for Christmas and I tell him about Harrison and how he's in Spain visiting his mum for the festive period.

'Ah yes, of course.' He opens the shed door and ushers me in. 'What about your parents?'

'I'll be spending some of Christmas Day with Mum, but my dad is ... well, he's not here.' I trail off awkwardly, shivering slightly in the freezing shed.

He nods slowly. 'Neither is mine. He died a few years ago.'

'Oh, my dad's not dead.' It's out of my mouth before I have time to think. 'At least, I don't think he is.'

Jed frowns. 'Don't you see him, then?'

'I've only met him once.' I smile sadly. 'When I was twelve. Mum was a single parent. He lived in Naples when she met him, and was working in the kitchens at one of the big five-star hotels, although he had dreams of becoming a chef. But I've no idea where he is now.'

I can't believe I'm telling Jed Turner all of this. I don't

usually talk about Alessandro to anyone. I suppose I feel I can trust Jed, even though I barely know him.

'Do you want to find him?' he asks softly.

I swallow hard. 'I tell myself I'm not bothered, but –' I lift my shoulders a fraction, and when he nods, I know I don't need to say any more.

Forcing a smile, I point at the big, beautifully proportioned Christmas tree that's leaning against the shed wall, giving off the most glorious scent. 'Wow! That's gorgeous!'

'Glad you approve.' Jed smiles. 'So you don't mind spending part of your precious Christmas holidays with the weird Willinghams and their extended family and friends, then?'

'No, not at all.' I'm about to add, 'I've never done anything on this scale before so it's all quite exciting.' But I stop myself in time. He doesn't have to know that I have practically no experience whatsoever. He might not have hired me if he'd realised this was only my second real catering job!

Jed picks up a cardboard box that's lying by the tree and rootles around in it. He brings out a big bundle of fairy lights, all wound round each other.

'The annual puzzle,' he remarks, pulling a comical face. 'How many festive revellers does it take to untangle the Christmas lights?'

I laugh. 'Just one if that person has a logical brain

and the patience of three saints.'

'Perhaps two sets of hands would make light work of it.' He grins. 'Let's take them inside and separate them where it's warmer. These are all Uncle Bob's decorations,' he adds, placing the box he's holding on top of two more, and hoisting them all up together. 'He looked them out for me last time he was here for the weekend.'

We end up taking four boxes full of promising decorations back into the house. Then we return for the tree, deciding the best place for it is in an alcove in the living room, by one of the big windows overlooking the lake. I bring in my box of baubles from the car and Jed peers inside and draws out a Santa on a sleigh.

'More than anything else,' he remarks, hunkering down to hunt in the box, 'Christmas decorations bring back memories of your childhood. Don't you think?' He dangles a scarlet bauble looped with gold ribbon from one long finger, and we watch as it twirls around, catching the light from a nearby lamp.

I smile wistfully. He's absolutely right. Getting them out of the attic is always a little emotional for me. On the one hand, I've always loved Christmas. But on the other hand, there are some things that it hurts to remember.

Together, we go outside and harvest lots of pine-tree greenery and fir cones, throwing them into a large crate that was in the shed. Then Jed cuts down sprigs of holly with gleaming scarlet berries and I place them carefully on top of the other foliage. Jed hefts the crate into the house.

I set to work adorning the staircase banister, winding it with pine garlands, fir cones and holly, then I weave in some strings of tiny white fairy lights. Jed works at securing the Christmas tree in its pot, then we decorate it together, although I notice that Jed lets me take the lead. I'm relieved to be so busy. Once I'm in the swing of it, my earlier awkwardness seems to disappear and I find I can talk to Jed easily. Friendly but businesslike.

All this activity takes a good few hours, and by the time we've started feeling hunger pangs, it's after three and the winter light outside is already starting to fade.

We have the official 'switch-on' and I gasp at how gorgeous the room looks now, with the Christmas tree twinkling away, reflected in the window by the gathering gloom beyond, and the garlands over the mantelpiece, just waiting for the log fire to be lit. The staircase too looks magical, with its lush green foliage, holly berries and winking white lights.

'Brilliant.' Jed nods approvingly and grins at me. 'You've earned your money already.'

He brings out a variety of cheeses, cracker biscuits and red grapes, and we sit back down at the breakfast bar for a very late lunch with a glass of cider each.

Clemmy and Ryan still haven't returned from Easingwold.

'So, how long have you been a private caterer?' asks Jed, buttering a cracker. He's moved the stool round the other side, so we're facing each other to chat.

'Oh, not long,' I tell him airily. 'What's in that dish? It looks lovely.'

'Chutney.' He passes it across and I'm hoping that will be the end of that subject. Perhaps he'll imagine the glow in my cheeks is from our hard work.

'Great, thanks. Yes, I really hope I can make a go of the business because cooking and baking really are my passions. I work in a restaurant and do this on the side. But I really want to do it full-time.'

Jed nods slowly, studying me. 'I'm sure you will. A passion for your subject is half the battle when it comes to being successful. I bet, erm, *Harrison* is it?'

I nod.

'I bet he's really proud of you for having the guts to switch career like this. It takes courage to give up a regular job to strike out into the unknown.'

'Yes, I suppose he is proud of me. He was all for me giving up my job at the restaurant.'

'Great, well, that's a definite vote of confidence in you and the business, then, isn't it?'

I nod. 'I guess so.' It's not quite that straightforward, of course. Harrison would prefer me to make *him* my career by becoming a stay-at-home housewife. But I'd feel a bit disloyal, somehow, explaining that to Jed.

He raises his glass. 'Well, here's to the huge success of *Diner Might*! And to a load of delicious food and drink to put the merry into Christmas. Which reminds me, we need to get down to brass tacks.'

'Sorry?'

'Money.' He smiles. 'I'm assuming *Diner Might* isn't a charity?'

Colour surges into my cheeks. I've been so caught up in the novelty of having a real catering job, it's completely slipped my mind to bring up the subject of payment. He must think I'm *so* unprofessional! And what the hell should I be charging anyway? Mrs Morelli was a flat fee for one dinner party, but this will be totally different. I'll be cooking every day for almost a whole fortnight, if my mental arithmetic serves me correctly! I'll have to talk it over with Erin and somehow come up with a figure. And I'll also need to find out which days Erin can help me, and agree on a rate of pay for the work she does. I'll feel much more confident if she's with me in the kitchen here, especially for the first few days.

Taking a deep breath, I paste on a smile and say, in what I hope is a businesslike manner, 'Actually, I was planning on getting a quote together for you this evening and emailing it through to you so you'd have it first thing tomorrow morning?'

He nods as if this would be perfectly acceptable and I breathe a little easier.

'What I usually do with clients is draw up a selection of menus and send them through for their approval.' My fingers are crossed under the breakfast bar. Talk about having to improvise on the spot! 'Would you like me to buy all the food and then bill you for it?'

'Sounds about right to me,' says Jed.

So far so good!

'And I'd be cooking dinner every evening – including Christmas Day itself – and providing a home-baked cake for tea every afternoon?'

'Yes, please.' He smiles at me. 'You'll certainly be making my Christmas a lot merrier, Poppy!' His green eyes are full of warmth and a funny little shiver of pleasure runs through me. Those eyes of his are *so* mesmerising. Then, with a stab of foolishness, I suddenly realise what he means. I'll be taking the weight off his shoulders by doing the cooking, so he doesn't have to. That's why his Christmas will be merrier. My heart swoops a little in disappointment, which is ridiculous. I'm obviously just feeling over-emotional after everything that's happened. Starting with having to wave Harrison off at the airport…

I pick up my glass to cover my embarrassment. 'Well, here's to a Merry Christmas!' I only hope I can cook up a storm and give Jed Turner value for money.

There's a sound from the hall. 'Hello-o! We're back! Oh my God, the staircase is *amazing*!'

Jed and I go out into the hall, just as Clemmy bursts into the living room, stops short in front of the Christmas tree and clasps her hands to her chest. 'Oh my days! How utterly gorgeous.' She turns as we join her in the doorway. 'You clever thing, Poppy. Did you do this?'

I look modestly from her to Jed. 'With a little bit of help ... well, a lot, actually.'

'Poppy did most of it,' Jed says, smiling at me in a way that makes my tummy flip with pleasure.

Clemmy glances towards the door as voices float in from the hallway. A look of uncertainty flashes across her pretty, flushed face but she quickly replaces it with a big smile. 'You've obviously been really busy the two of you!'

Jed frowns and indicates the voices. 'Who?'

'Oh, Ryan's brought Jessica back,' says Clemmy. 'He thought you wouldn't mind if she joined us for Christmas.' She beams at Jed and then at me but I catch that same hint of vulnerability in her eyes as they dart once more towards the door.

Ryan walks down the hallway with a statuesque blonde woman. She's wearing a stunning white winter coat and high-heeled tan ankle boots that match the expensive, buttery leather bag over her shoulder. 'Hi, there,' he says, keeping his hand firmly round her waist. 'Sorry we're late. We – er – got a bit held up.' A flirty look passes between them.

I can hardly bear to look at Clemmy. Her cheekbones must be aching with the effort of keeping that smile fixed in place.

Jed ushers Ryan and Jessica into the living room.

Jessica glances around her with a look of vague surprise. 'It's smaller than I imagined, but at least it's warm.' She rubs her hands together delicately. 'It's bloody parky out there.' She wriggles away from Ryan and slips off her coat. Then she turns and looks at me. I start to smile and hold out my hand, only to have her drop the coat into my arms the next second. I only just manage to catch it before it hits the floor.

Her disrobing has rendered me temporarily speechless – but it's not just the fact that she could so obviously sniff out the hired help at twenty paces that's taken the wind out of my sails.

Ryan's guest has the most enormous surgically enhanced chest I've ever seen in my life in the actual flesh. And there's a *lot* of flesh, believe me, encased in a plunging cream-lace bra – just visible above her top – that really must be wired with the aid of cutting-edge-precision engineering. Her waist is jaw-droppingly miniscule by comparison and her shiny dark-pink lips appear to have been outlined in caramel with a road marker.

There's a sort of hushed silence in the room. Then Jed moves towards her. 'Hi Jessica. Great to meet you.' He encloses her hand in both of his as she bats her eyelash extensions at him. 'I'm Jed and this is Poppy, who'll be cooking all sorts of delicious food for us over the festive period,' he says, glancing at me. 'I'll take the coat, Poppy,' he murmurs, and I hand it to him with a grateful smile. He drapes it over the back of a sofa then rubs his hands together. 'Right. Drink, everyone? Jessica, what would you like?'

'Champagne, please,' says Jessica smoothly. 'If you have any.'

Jed disappears into the garage and returns with a bottle. Clemmy helps him with the glasses in the kitchen as I glance around, thinking it's probably time I took my leave.

When they bring in the champagne and Jed offers me a glass, I glance at my watch. It's four-thirty. 'Thank you but I think I'd better be going.' I look at the glowing Christmas tree and almost wish I could stay. But I've got so much to do.

The job starts properly tomorrow, when I bake my first cake for their afternoon tea, and cook the first of my three-course dinners, so I need to do shopping and get organised. And before that, I need to head to the hotel and try to persuade Mimi to let Maxine do some of my shifts over the festive period. I feel sick at the thought. I'm not sure what I'll do if she refuses.

'You've done a great job,' says Jed warmly, and for a second, I feel his hand on my waist. It's so unexpected, it feels like an electric shock.

I swallow, feeling a blush rise in my cheeks. 'Thank you. Right. Bye, everyone. Enjoy your evening.' Avoiding Jed's eye, my smile lands on Clemmy and she gives me a little wave and an enthusiastic nod. I wish I could stay and chat to her. I really can't imagine she's relishing an evening in the company of Ryan drooling over his busty model girlfriend.

Jed goes with me to the door. 'Till tomorrow then?'

'Yes. I'll be here around twelve, if that's okay?' I say, aiming for my most professional tone.

'That works for me.' He smiles and I walk quickly to my car, delving in my bag for the keys. But next second, they slip through my fingers and manage to land not just on the ground but underneath the car, out of sight. So then, of course, I have to bend down and peer under to retrieve them, all the while aware that Jed is standing there, patiently waiting for me to leave so he can get back to his guests.

Red-faced, I dangle them at him with a silly grin, then dive with relief into the driver's seat, start the engine and make my exit. Luckily, Jed's already closing the door as I grate the gears spectacularly. Not that he can have failed to hear it. There are probably people trekking in the Himalayas who paused for a second to wonder what the noise was.

*

On the way to The Pretty Flamingo, I think about Jed and Clemmy.

He was so keen to invite Clemmy for Christmas, yet it's as plain as the nose on Clemmy's face that she's mad about Ryan. But Jed doesn't seem too bothered. Then again, some blokes can be astonishingly bad at reading the emotional signs. Maybe he hasn't even twigged that Clemmy's in love with his brother?

That doesn't really ring true, though. Jed seems warm and sensitive to other people's feelings – like when he pointedly took Jessica's coat from me after she treated me like a hat-check girl. The memory of him doing that gives me a warm feeling inside.

Perhaps Jed sees what's going on with Clemmy but is hoping to change her mind? I don't blame him for liking her. She's so friendly and fun and sweet – a bit like a bouncy Labrador pup that you can't help but love. No airs or graces whatsoever. Clemmy is just a very genuine person. The opposite of that awful Jessica.

But perhaps I shouldn't judge Jessica. I've only just met her – and it could be that her arrogant manner is hiding her nervousness at meeting Ryan's family and friends for the first time. There's certainly going to be an interesting mix of guests at the Log Fire Cabin. Jed's Uncle Bob, a widower, is arriving tomorrow morning, and his new girlfriend, Gloria, is apparently travelling down from Newcastle with her two teenage children. That makes eight people to cook for tomorrow night, presuming that Jessica is staying.

Nervous excitement fizzes like a New-Year firework in my chest at the thought of preparing the food for tomorrow night. I've already got the menu all worked out in my head.

It's only as I'm pulling into the hotel car park that I remember it's Mimi's day off. But having psyched myself up to sort out my shifts, I decide to ask Mrs Nutter instead. Hopefully, she'll remember all the times I've stood in during staff shortages and will be fine about repaying the favour. I've already made sure Maxine is okay about doing some of my shifts. In fact, she's delighted because she's saving up to go to New York in the spring, so the more work the merrier.

'No way.' Mrs Nutter crosses her arms and my heart sinks. I can tell from the defensive glint in her eyes that she will not budge on this. 'You know full well there's no swapping shifts during the Christmas season, Poppy.'

'But it would just be for a few nights, and Maxine is happy to fill in for me. And I'll work extra shifts at other times to make up for it?'

The answer is still no.

A little burst of frustration rises up. I've helped the Nutters out on so many occasions, but apparently that means nothing to Mrs Nutter. She's clearly not prepared to even talk about it. There's a faint smile on her face. I think she's actually enjoying my dismay.

How can I cook for Jed Turner if I've got to be here in the evenings? It's impossible.

I drive away and head for Erin's place. I need to talk it over with her and as it's her day off today, I'm hoping she might be at home. I park up outside her block of flats and I'm briefly checking my phone for messages when the main door to the building opens and two people emerge. One of them is Mark. As he descends the few steps into the car-parking area, he turns to talk to a girl following close behind. Small and slim with smooth, strawberry-blonde hair swinging past her shoulders, she's wearing a cute, cream trouser suit and red heels, with a camel coat slung over her shoulders. She laughs at something he said and her whole face lights up. I watch them as they stand and chat beside a little red car that must belong to her. She keeps pulling the coat closer around her against the December wind. Their conversation seems very animated and from their body language and the way they keep beaming at each other, it's more funny banter than an ordinary chat.

Then Mark glances at his watch and says something

to her, at which point they both stop smiling and glance anxiously towards the road.

Quickly, she gets in her car, waves and drives away, and Mark lingers by the entrance to watch her leave. Then he heads straight towards me, walking rapidly, hands in his pockets.

Panicking, I instinctively slide lower in my seat and turn my head so he won't see me. Then I wait until he's walking away from me along the High Street before I sit back up in the seat again. Erin musn't be in. Feeling low because I really wanted to chat to her, I start up the engine and drive home.

It's only as I'm letting myself into the house that I pause to wonder why I slunk down in the seat like that. I suppose seeing Mark emerging from that matching agency the other day must still be preying on my mind. But there won't be anything fishy going on. I'm quite certain of that. Mark's mad about Erin. He wouldn't do anything to mess that up.

I'm fiercely protective of my best friend after her terrible relationship history, and honestly, there aren't many men who pass my 'good-enough-for-Erin' gauge, but Mark definitely does.

No doubt Miss Cute Strawberry Blonde will turn out to be a colleague from the estate agent's where he works. At least, I sincerely hope so.

Chapter 14

Wednesday 21st December

<u>Afternoon tea</u>
Cherry and coconut cake

<u>Dinner menu</u>
Figs, melon and parma ham
***

Tender beef casserole,
buttery mash, glazed baby carrots and garden peas
***

Amalfi lemon tart with whipped cream

This morning, I'm up with the lark, unable to eat breakfast because I'm so nervous about the day ahead. There's a fizzing sensation in my stomach – and already my heart is pumping faster – but everything is prepared for my first day of cooking for Jed Turner, so hopefully things will turn out fine.

As I dash out of the house, a text pings through from Harrison.

Flamenco dance class tonight. Black pants far too tight but Mother insists. Wish you were here xx

As I draw up outside Erin's, I'm still chortling at the thought of Harrison in full flamenco gear, with flouncy-sleeved blouse and trousers cutting off his circulation. His mum, Betty, is a forceful woman. What she wants, she generally gets. And poor Harrison will have to go along with it.

Then I remember I'm due in for a shift at the restaurant tonight and my heart drops like a stone. I'm going to have to phone in sick. It's going to be so blatantly obvious I'm swinging the lead after Mrs Nutter turned me down yesterday. But what else can I do? At least I know Maxine is standing by to fill in for me, so my absence definitely won't be leaving them short-staffed.

Erin comes down the steps, looking slightly preoc-cupied.

I'd assumed she'd be full of the joys because her Christmas break officially begins today. But she doesn't even get excited when I suggest we splash out at the delicatessen for the parma ham. (She's normally like a kid in a sweetie shop among all those exotic quiches, jewel-bean salads and German sausages.)

She perks up a bit as we drive along the bumpy road towards the Log Fire Cabin and she catches her first glimpse of the lake. It's another crystal-clear, blue-skied morning and the reflection of the cottage and pine trees in the water is perfect.

'It's such a gorgeous setting,' Erin murmurs. 'Mark and I used to come here for picnics when we first got together.'

I turn in surprise. 'Did you?'

'Yeah, it was really romantic. He'd buy stuff from the deli and bring a cool box with a bottle of chilled fizz. On summer days, we'd spend hours and hours just lying on a rug on the grass, being daft. We never seemed to run out of things to talk about.'

'Sounds heavenly.' I glance at her profile.

She sighs. 'Oh for the early days, when he was always trying to impress me.'

'Perhaps you could revive the picnic days? You can borrow my cool box.'

Even this doesn't raise a smile – and she loves that cool box! It's an electric one that you can plug in to the car to keep your bits and pieces nice and fresh. Harrison bought it for our first picnic together. He gets a bit jumpy about ham going off in the sun and random insects landing on his food.

'You know, Mark is so much more romantic than Harrison,' I say, to cheer her up. 'He buys you flowers for no reason, for heaven's sake. And he sits through entire episodes of *Hollyoaks* because you love it and he wants to be with you. What bloke does that?'

'That's true. I'm just being stupid.' She straightens up in her seat and points across the lake. 'Ooh, wouldn't it be lovely to buy that little cottage and do it up? It's so unbelievably cute.'

'It used to be a B&B.'

'Really? Gosh, I don't remember that.'

'It was many moons ago,' I say, recalling the creaky wooden stairs leading up to the sunny bedroom with its window seat and views over the lake. I loved that window seat. I'd sit with my feet up, curled sideways among the floral-sprigged cushions, gazing at the expanse of sky and the pine trees on the opposite side of the lake. That was long before the Log Fire Cabin was built. 'They did a brilliant breakfast fry-up.'

I'm dimly aware that Erin is asking me something about the B&B, but I'm lost in the past, remembering how Mum refused to eat anything that morning. She just hugged a coffee with an expression on her face that suggested the milk was sour. I, however, was in my element, demolishing bacon, eggs and sausages as we chatted away. Alessandro brought Italy alive for me and I remember being entranced by his halting English accent. I hung on his every word as he transported me to the pretty town of Sorrento in the heat of the summer, and drove me along the stunning Amalfi coast to Capri in an open-topped car. I could almost feel the warm wind in my hair and breathe in the scent of the lemon groves.

I still can't forgive Mum for not telling me the truth about Alessandro until it was too late and he'd gone back to Italy. But, looking back, I sometimes wonder if she was on edge the entire time he was with us because she could see I really liked him and she knew it could only end badly for me.

'Are you okay?' Erin is peering at me. 'You were miles away.'

'Sorry. I – er – I'm just trying to get everything sorted in my head for today.'

'Exciting, isn't it?'

'Or terrifying.' I force a smile, pushing Alessandro out of my mind. 'I can't decide which.'

I was up till three this morning, devising mouth-watering menus for the next twelve days, so I should be feeling exhausted but I'm not at all. Excitement is whipping up the adrenaline in my system, making me feel anything but tired. I feel like the battery bunny – I could probably keep going for days.

I'd emailed the menus and my quote through to Jed in the early hours and, by breakfast time, he'd emailed back to approve them. A wave of relief coursed through me. I'd been worrying I was charging too much but

Erin told me quite fiercely that I wasn't to undersell myself. I was a brilliant cook, she said, and I was charging a very reasonable rate for what she knew would be almost two weeks of first class cuisine.

The only picky eater, Jed noted in his email, was Ruby, Gloria's teenage daughter. But he'd bought in a supply of her favourite chicken goujons and vanilla ice cream, so we were covered for all eventualities.

When Erin and I arrive at the house, I use the key Jed has given me so we can come and go as we need to, and I introduce an amazed Erin to the splendours of the Log Fire Cabin. The place is eerily silent. I assume they've all gone out.

'Close your mouth.' I grin at her. 'Or you'll catch flies.'

'Oh my God, it's *gorgeous*,' she breathes, staring up at the Christmas tree. 'Hang on, are they your baubles?'

'Some of them. Yes.' I pause to admire the tree myself, remembering how Jed had to decorate the topmost branches himself because I couldn't quite reach.

We place our cartons and boxes on the breakfast bar in the kitchen and go back out to the car to collect the rest. When we return, Jessica is floating down the stairs in a silky Japanese-print robe and bare feet.

'Good morning, Jessica.' I smile. 'This is my assistant, Erin.'

'Hi there. Pleased to meet you,' sings Erin. 'What a beautiful dressing gown.'

'Thank you. It's a kimono.' Her glance is frosty as she sweeps past us. I guess it's not *de rigeur* for the hired help to initiate a conversation with a client.

We follow her into the kitchen and find Ryan making tea, wearing a skimpy cotton robe in dusky pink that shows off his fine hairy legs to perfection.

'For God's sake, Ryan!' hisses Jessica. 'I just bought that. It's bloody YSL! You'd better not spill anything on it!'

He ignores her and turns to us. 'Sorry about the lack of clothes, ladies. I thought we were alone.'

'Oh, don't mind us!' I say breezily, setting down the box I'm carrying. 'This is Erin, by the way.'

'Ryan.' He moves forward to shake her hand.

'Pleased to meet you.' Erin gives him a cheerful once-over. 'Can I just say you look ravishing in pink. But did you know your belt is coming loose?'

I could truly murder her. But thankfully, Ryan seems amused. It's the first time I've seen him smile properly, with his eyes, and he's really quite handsome. He should definitely smile more often.

'Any good at tying knots?' he asks Erin with a suggestively raised eyebrow.

Jessica hustles him out, clearly not enjoying the banter one bit, and her irritation explodes when she thinks she's out of earshot. 'And by the way, I can just about bear to *share a bathroom* with that *fat girl*, and use towels that have the texture of rush matting. But I *draw the line at wearing wellies*!'

'Prada heels aren't the best for a tramp through sheep shit,' points out Ryan.

'Well, then, I'll just stay indoors and *you* can go for a walk.'

'Clemmy's not fat, by the way. She's voluptuous.' Ryan's voice grows fainter as they climb the stairs.

Jessica barks a laugh. 'Yes, and her copy of *Hello* magazine is all about Einstein's theory of relativity. What's it doing in the bathroom anyway? Does she read it on the *toilet?*'

Their bedroom door slams shut.

I look at Erin and we both snort with amusement.

'No prizes for guessing Jessica would rather be anywhere but here for Christmas,' I murmur, rolling my eyes at Erin as I assemble the vegetables for her to prepare for the beef casserole.

'I know. Poor Ryan. Why on earth has he saddled himself with her?'

I grin at her. 'Apart from the obvious?'

'Well, there is that, I suppose. She has got an amazing figure.' She starts slicing an onion, screwing her eyes up slightly so that the spray doesn't make her cry. Then she looks up at me. 'This is it, then. The start of a whole new career. Your first real proper catering job!'

'Mrs Morelli was real, wasn't she?' I laugh. 'Not a figment of my imagination.'

'Yes, but we *knew* her so it doesn't really count,' says Erin firmly.

I smile at her enthusiasm. I only wish I shared her confidence that everything will work out fine. I might have been up half the night thinking about every last detail, but you can't plan for all eventualities. What if I have an unexpected cake disaster? What if the beef is tough? What if the lemon tart is too sharp/sweet for their taste?

I suddenly remember something and start hunting around in one of the boxes we've brought in. 'Ta-dah!' I pull out the gorgeous Christmas apron Erin bought me and put it on. Erin claps excitedly so I do a little curtsy.

'Thanks again for this.' I grin at her. 'I'm ready for anything now.'

'Are you making the cake first?'

'Yes. I'm going to dazzle them with the lusciousness of my baking!' I start delving in the boxes, setting out flour, butter, caster sugar, eggs, dessicated coconut and maraschino cherries. Then I start looking through the cupboards, memorising things. At home, I could probably bake a cake blindfolded because I know where everything is. But when you start cooking in an unfamiliar kitchen, it can be a little frustrating. Everything takes twice as long while you track down that vital piece of equipment – a whisk or a lemon-squeezer or a certain size of cake tin – that always seems to be in the very last place you look.

Erin has her iPod on softly, chopping in time to The Killers. We work away in silence for a while and, before too long, the kitchen is filled with the mouth-watering aroma of cherry-and-coconut cake baking in the oven.

The beef for the casserole is slow-cooking in a rich gravy of onions, red wine and stock with crushed garlic and a handful of fresh thyme. The beauty of the slow-cooker method is that it's guaranteed to make the meat so tender, it will practically melt in your mouth. And it also gives Erin and I time to nip out for a quick sandwich.

But first, I take a deep breath, pick up my phone and call The Pretty Flamingo, hoping against hope that Mrs Nutter doesn't pick up. Luckily, it's Daisy, the lovely receptionist, and I breathe a sigh of relief. She's so sympathetic about my imaginary flu, I feel a real fraud, then she tells me quite sternly that I mustn't even *think* of returning to work until I'm completely better. Erin's grinning broadly at me the whole time, which is a bit off-putting, to say the least. But I feel so relieved when I come off the phone, I actually laugh out loud.

'Good for you.' Erin, who's clearing up, waves a tea towel at me. 'You never take sick days. So don't feel guilty.'

'I'll try not to.' Grateful for her support, I go to check the cake, which is out of its loaf tin and cooling on the rack. I turn it over, hoping the cherries haven't all sunk to the bottom. But it seems fine. I'll slice and serve it with Earl Grey tea at four p.m. I check the slow-cooker, stirring the pot carefully, and Erin joins me, breathing in the lovely, rich herby aroma over my shoulder.

'Another triumph,' she says.

I make a face at her. 'Wish I had your confidence.'

She shrugs. 'You should. You're brilliant. You were *miles* ahead of me on that cookery course we went on.'

'Only because you were pining for Mark and texting him every spare minute.'

She laughs. 'I'd only just met him then.'

'Right, come on, let's go and grab something to eat.' I glance around the kitchen to make sure everything is in order and scoop up my keys before Erin has a chance to get despondent about Mark again.

I'm manoeuvring the car out of the parking area when a horn sounds loudly, making me pull on the break. A big blue people carrier skids to a halt on the road, just ten feet away. When I peer over, wondering whether to reverse back and let them in, a woman in the passenger seat with bright orangey-red hair waves cheerily then leans over and gives the horn an extra jolly toot.

'Who on earth's that?' breathes Erin, as we smile and wave back. She says it in a 'gottle o' geer' way, without moving her lips.

I frown and reverse back into a space. 'I think it must be Jed and Ryan's Uncle Bob and his girlfriend, Gloria.'

They park next to us, and two teenagers – a boy and a girl – emerge from the back seat.

I copy Erin's ventriloquist act. 'That'll be Gloria's kids – nineteen-year-old Tom and sixteen-year-old Ruby.'

'Oh dear. Ruby looks pretty cross. Maybe they've had a row.'

'She does look quite fierce,' I murmur. 'Her hair's pretty edgy, too. What would you call that shade?'

'Er ... brown and purple with grey highlights?'

I unclip my seat belt and get out of the car to say hello.

Ruby's door opens and her voice drifts out. 'It's total *shit,* Mum. When are you going to get on to the phone company and give them a bollocking? It shouldn't just break like that. I barely *touched* the bloody thing.'

Tom, getting out on his side, snorts loudly. 'You dropped it off the first-floor balcony onto concrete.'

Ruby reddens. 'Well, it still shouldn't have broken. I'm bloody sick of mobile phones.'

Gloria fixes her with a glare. 'Is that right? Well, in that case, you won't mind waiting till after the holidays for a new one. And *stop swearing.*'

'Get real, mother.' Ruby looks sulky. '*Bloody* is hardly swearing.'

'Ruby!' Gloria gets out and straightens her leopard-print top and lacy black skirt with a flourish, as if the action will herald a fresh start. She smiles a little desperately across at Bob, who's emerging from his side. 'Kids, eh? Who'd 'ave 'em? Of course, what our Ruby needs is a good feed. She's always grumpy when she's hungry, aren't you, love?' She tries to pat Ruby's cheek but her daughter whisks out of reach.

'I do not need "a good feed". I just need a new phone. How am I supposed to do *anything* without a phone?'

Tom, who's been calmly loading himself up with bags from the boot, suddenly hisses, 'Ruby, will you bloody shut *up* about your stupid phone. We've heard nothing else since we left Newcastle. There were people hurling themselves off the train just to escape your whinging.' He takes the bag his mum is holding and heads for the front door.

'Ooh, snap your beads, Tom,' calls Ruby. Then in a loud stage-whisper, just to wind up her brother, she says, 'He's fed up because he likes this girl, Charlotte, but he's too scared to ask her out.'

Tom turns and murders his sister with a look. 'I'm not scared. I just don't want a relationship right now.'

Ruby rolls her eyes. 'Yeah, right. And I'm Lady Gaga's costume designer.'

Gloria glances at Bob and laughs nervously. 'Proper comedian. That's our Ruby. Can I help, Bob?'

Uncle Bob has his head buried in the boot. From what Jed told me yesterday, the first time he'll have set eyes on Gloria's children would have been less than an hour ago, when he picked the family up from the station. I wonder if he's regretting it already?

He straightens up, smiles at Gloria and lays a soothing hand on her back. 'No, no, you go in, my dear. Make yourselves comfortable.'

He suddenly notices Erin and I, waiting by the car. His face lights up and he bounds across. 'You must be our delightful Christmas caterers? I'm Bob.'

We shake hands and I explain that we're just off for lunch but we'll be back to serve afternoon tea at four o'clock.

'Would you like some tea just now?' I ask, unsure if it's my place to offer.

His smile makes him look quite youthful. Jed said he was sixty-seven but he could pass for ten years younger than that. Bob's very tall, like Jed. But unlike Jed – who's broad and muscular – Bob has the slender frame of a marathon runner.

He shakes his head. 'Don't worry. I'll get refreshments on the go. But thank you. Off you go and have your lunch and we'll look forward to some fine dining tonight!'

'Excellent.' *No pressure there, then!*

'Can I ask what's on the menu?' He twinkles.

I reel off the three courses and he nods approvingly. 'Sounds delicious. Doesn't it, Ruby?' He smiles at her and she nods, trying to look enthusiastic but clearly not caring two hoots.

'I don't know about anyone else but I could eat a scabby horse!' says Gloria. 'What about you, Bob?'

Bob blinks at her. 'Well, I'm not sure Poppy mentioned 'scabby horse', my dear, but we could always order it in for you. Do you like it medium or rare?' He regards her solemnly for a moment and Gloria looks perplexed. Then, as a wicked smile transforms his face, she gets the joke and slaps him on the arm.

'Ee, Bob. What are you like!' She turns to Erin and me. 'Sense of humour dry as a witch's tit!'

Grinning, Erin and I clamber back into the car.

'I'm already thinking about that Amalfi lemon tart!' calls Bob.

'Uncle Bob's a sweetie,' says Erin.

'He is. I hope that cantankerous Ruby doesn't spoil their Christmas by moaning about her phone all the time.'

Right on cue, Ruby glances around her in distaste and says in her broad Geordie accent, 'Where's all the shops, then? The nearest phone store is probably about five hundred miles away from this skanky pit—'

Gloria grabs her arm and whispers urgently into her ear before turning back to Bob and fixing on a bright smile.

'Poor Gloria,' says Erin. 'Her first Christmas with her new man and she's got an obnoxious teenager ruining her chance of romance.'

'I've a feeling it's going to be an interesting Christmas, one way or another,' I murmur with a grin.

Chapter 15

It's ten minutes to eight. The diners are all sipping drinks in the living room while Erin and I quietly tend to the last little touches before the starter is served.

I'm feeling surprisingly calm and in control.

Then the door opens and Jed appears. And at once, my heart starts beating so fast, I think it might explode out of my chest and make a run for it.

So much for feeling calm!

Jed catches my eye and grins. 'We're just about ready for you. I'll get everyone seated and you can start serving in a couple of minutes?' He peers closer at the starters. 'They look amazing.'

A wave of heat washes over me and I smile shyly at him. 'We're all set. Would you like us to serve the wine?'

'No, no. We'll do that.' He rubs his hands together. 'Right. Looking forward to this.'

'I'm going to make this for Mark,' says Erin, standing

back from arranging slices of fresh fig on eight white plates.

I check the casserole once more for seasoning, letting the mingled flavours of tender beef, red wine, stock and herbs settle on my tongue for a second. Then I go and peer over Erin's shoulder, smiling at the gorgeous splash of colour from the damson-coloured figs against the juicy pink ham and fans of ripe honeydew melon.

'That's where I fall down. The presentation,' says Erin. 'I'm used to just slapping the food down in the middle of the plate, like Mum used to when there were six of us ravenous kids round the table.'

'Well, you're definitely learning.' I smile at her. 'Those plates look absolutely perfect. Oh God, I hope it's okay,' I murmur as we pick up two plates each.

Erin grins. 'Stop fussing. And *breathe*!' She pulls open the door.

We each take a gulp of air, and head out to the waiting guests seated around the long oak dining table.

'Ooh, it's just like being in a proper restaurant, isn't it, Ruby?' enthuses Gloria as I lay her plate down. She beams up at me, grabs her napkin and starts shaking it out. Her glass of white wine goes flying, all over the place setting next to her, which happens to be Jessica's.

Everyone freezes for a second.

Then Gloria is up on her feet, almost knocking the plate out of my hand and apologising profusely to

Jessica, trying to dab at a small wet patch on her top, dangerously near her plunging cleavage.

'It's all right,' Jessica snaps, stony-faced. 'Really, Gloria, leave it.' She waves her away and dips the corner of her own napkin in her water glass, rubbing delicately at the mark.

'Okay?' murmurs Ryan, who's sitting opposite her.

Jessica, flicking away at the tiny mark on her baby-pink chiffon blouse, doesn't even reply.

'Ee, you can't take me anywhere, can you, kids?' gasps a flushed-faced Gloria, wafting her napkin in an attempt to cool herself down. 'I'm like a bull in a china shop! And these bloody hot flushes!'

Bob, who's sitting opposite, leans forward and covers her hand with his. 'Never mind. It was an accident.' He turns. 'There's a very good dry cleaners in the village, Jessica. I will personally deliver your dress to them tomorrow.'

'It's fine.' Jessica thaws slightly under Bob's warm smile, and doesn't even point out that it's a top, not a dress.

Erin and I retire to the kitchen to start plating up the main course – tender beef casserole with a tureen of creamy mash and serving dishes filled with sweet garden peas and buttered carrots sprinkled with parsley.

Later, when Erin goes in to clear the main course, to my enormous relief, all the plates come back empty.

'They must have liked it!' I feel like doing a Highland fling around the kitchen.

'Of course they did!' Erin grins. 'Stop worrying.'

I smile at her, wondering if I'd have the courage to do any of this if I didn't have my best friend backing me up.

By the time we get to the dessert course, I'm feeling even more nervous. Bob made a point of saying he was really looking forward to my Amalfi Lemon Tart – so it has to be perfect! We take out the plates and Clemmy's eyes gleam as Erin sets down hers. 'Ooh, lovely, my favourite.'

There are lots of murmurs of approval round the table, then Jed, who's sitting next to Clemmy, nudges her and says, 'It was knickerbocker glories with extra squirty cream once upon a time.'

'That was in France when I was only sixteen.' Clemmy sneaks a look over at Ryan, who smiles. 'My tastes have got a bit more sophisticated since then. Although my pudding of choice does tend to change fairly frequently.' She leans in to Jed, looking up at him mischievously. 'There was the "treacle sponge in a tin" phase. Then the "family-size raspberry trifle" period, followed by the "chocolate ice cream with absolutely everything" era.'

Everyone laughs. Even Jessica.

Clemmy and Jed are smiling warmly at each other,

and I feel a strange sort of wistful pang at the obvious affection that exists between them. Clemmy is half-nestled up to Jed in a playful way. They're old friends, of course, from when their families used to holiday together. But still, I find myself wondering if maybe, now that Jessica is occupying Ryan, Clemmy is starting to feel more for Jed.

'I like a woman who enjoys her food,' Ryan says suddenly, and Clemmy darts a look at him, blushes and glances down with a pleased smile. Jessica purses her lips, having just made a point of waving away dessert.

As Erin and I leave the room, Jed is looping his arm around Clemmy's shoulders, pretending to drag her away from the dessert, and she's giggling like a smitten schoolgirl.

The scene lingers in my mind as we clear up, making me feel strangely unsettled. Harrison and I never seem to joke around like that. Or if we do, it's always because I've initiated it. Of course, the reason I'm feeling a bit morose is probably because Harrison has been away for several days now, and I'm starting to really miss him.

'Tired?' Erin gives me a quizzical look.

'A bit. It's been a long day.'

'But very successful.' She grins and holds up a plate containing the last remaining slice of cherry-and-coconut cake. It seemed to go down very well earlier in the day.

We finish it up between us, glancing guiltily at the door as Clemmy walks in.

'Caught you!' she smiles. 'But I won't tell.' She looks around. 'Tonic water?'

I point to the fridge. 'Side of the door.'

'Thank you. By the way, that was a truly gorgeous meal. And isn't Jed lovely?' She selects a bottle and turns. 'I mean, I've always known what a great guy he is, but he'll make someone a gorgeous hubby one day. Don't you think?'

Erin nods. 'Looks, personality and intelligence all in one package. I like him a lot.'

Feeling suddenly bafflingly tongue-tied, I nod awkwardly at Clemmy and turn away, picking up a tea towel to dry some dishes. The door opens and Jed himself is standing there. He's removed his jacket and loosened his tie. 'That was a triumph, Poppy. Thank you.'

Our eyes lock and a funny little shiver skitters right through my entire body. 'You're very welcome,' I tell him with a prim little smile.

'Right, Clemmy. Come on, we're playing charades.' He casually steers her towards the door.

'Everyone?' she asks.

'Well, no. Jessica's making an important business call in her room and she's demanded Ryan keep her company.'

Clemmy's face falls slightly.

Jed, noticing, murmurs, 'Sorry, Clem. Was it a stupid idea inviting you for Christmas?'

She paints on a smile. 'No, of course not. I'm really glad you did. I'm having a lovely time!'

He frowns. 'It would be lovelier if Ryan hadn't suddenly decided to bring—' He shrugs.

She gives her head a little shake. 'Doesn't matter. Right, Gloria needs her tonic water!' She hurries out.

'Clemmy's so lovely,' says Erin.

Jed nods. 'She is. I've been trying to cheer her up.' He grins sheepishly. 'I hope it wasn't too obvious. It's just my brother's choices can be a little – erm – puzzling sometimes. I really thought he and Clemmy might ...' He trails off and looks at his glass. 'Sorry, this is the whisky talking.'

The cogs in my brain are whirring into action. Without pausing to think, I blurt out, 'Oh, I see! So you invited Clemmy for *Ryan*, not you!'

He looks at me for a moment, an odd expression on his face. Then he grins. 'Yes. And that's the very last time I take on the role of Cupid.'

When he's gone, I smile at Erin, a funny little burst of happiness spreading through me. 'Hasn't today been amazing?' I busy myself packing stuff into boxes to take home, humming – for some odd reason – *All I Want for Christmas is You*.

Erin grimaces at the flat notes then gives me an arch look. '*You* seem perkier suddenly.'

'Do I? I suppose I'm just relieved it went so well today, that's all.'

She nods with a knowing little smile that I choose to ignore.

She seems to have got it into her head that I like Jed, which couldn't be further from the truth. I mean, I *do* like him. Just not in the way she's hinting at.

Admittedly, decorating the house with him yesterday was really good fun. I giggled so much, I swear my laughter lines were deeper than usual when I looked in the mirror last night. But I'm almost engaged to Harrison, and I can't have Erin getting the wrong idea. Perhaps it's time to tell her about Harrison's proposal. The trouble is, I'd then have to explain about the cooling-off period and I have a feeling she'd think that was hilarious.

'I think we deserve a glass of fizz back at yours,' Erin says. 'You know, to help you relax and dream up more amazing menus.' She sticks her tongue in her cheek.

'Ha! Any excuse.'

Before we leave, I pop my head round the living-room door, where the game of charades is in full swing. The lovebirds have rejoined the group and are cosying up in the same armchair, Jessica perched on the arm, draping herself across Ryan. Gloria is out front, rotating her hips suggestively, as Ruby cringes behind a cushion. Poor Tom looks as if he'd like the sofa to completely swallow him up.

Jed catches my eye and grins.

'We're going,' I mouth. 'See you tomorrow.'

'*Sex Tape!*' shouts Ryan.

Gloria shakes her head and rotates her hips more frantically, as if that will make her clue easier to solve.

Jed gets up and sees us off from the living-room door. 'You're a big hit with Bob, by the way.'

'We are?' I smile with delight.

He nods. 'I told him you specialise in Italian cuisine, and he's wondering if we could have an evening devoted to all things Italian, maybe on Christmas Eve?'

'Oh. Yes, no problem!'

'Good.' He leans on the doorframe and gives me a lazy smile. 'Great cake today, by the way. What are you baking tomorrow?'

'Lemon drizzle?'

'Definitely my favourite. I'll be hoping for seconds.'

The way he says it, with a hint of mischief in his eyes, brings a flush to my cheeks. I cover my confusion with a laugh. 'Well, what the client wants, the client gets.'

He grins and ducks back into the living room.

Erin raises one suggestive eyebrow. '*What the client wants, the client gets?*'

'What?' I laugh nervously. 'It's true, isn't it? The customer is king, as they say.' She just smiles serenely, which for some reason irritates me even more than if she'd made some clever-clogs remark. When we go outside, we find Clemmy leaning against the wall, staring up at the star-studded night sky, all bundled up in her lovely jade green coat and scarf. 'You're going, then?' she asks, straightening up and stamping her feet in the snow.

'We are.' I give her arm a swift rub. 'It's freezing out here. You should be inside.'

She attempts a smile but it doesn't quite come off. 'I'd rather be out here,' she says in a tight little voice. 'I can't stand seeing him with Jessica. I know it's stupid but I've been in love with Ry ever since I was a kid.'

I exchange a sad look with Erin. 'You're so much nicer than Jessica,' I tell her honestly. 'It's not fair.'

Erin snorts in agreement. 'Men! Why is it they *never* know when they're well off?'

I dig around in the box I'm carrying, bring out a paper napkin and hand it to Clemmy. She blows her nose furiously. 'Ry kissed me on that family holiday in France and after that, I thought we were meant to be together. The way you do when you're sixteen and incredibly naive.' She smiles. 'I should have fallen for Jed on that campsite instead.'

'But you didn't,' I say softly.

She shakes her head sadly. 'I mean, I do love Jed. But just as a friend. You can't help who you fall in love with, can you?'

'Ain't that the truth,' mutters Erin.

'Mind you, falling for Jed would be even less likely to end in happy ever after.'

My heart gives a funny little thud. 'Oh? Why?'

She shrugs. 'His long-term girlfriend, Katerina, broke off their relationship to go and be a lawyer in Australia. It hit him hard, the lovely man, because he was all set to marry her.'

'Oh, God. Poor Jed,' breathes Erin, as I stand there, mute with shock.

'That was two years ago and Ryan says he was starting to get over her.' Clemmy dabs at her eyes and gives a loud sniff. 'But then, would you believe it, she phoned Jed up out of the blue yesterday, talking about the "good old days" and hinting she wants to get back with him.'

'But she's in Australia,' points out Erin.

Clemmy shakes her head. 'No, she's not. Her contract out there was for two years. She flew back yesterday. Just in time for Christmas.'

Chapter 16

Thursday 22nd December

<u>*Afternoon tea*</u>
Lemon drizzle cake

<u>*Dinner menu*</u>
Warming butternut squash soup with
toasted lemon and garlic ciabatta
***

Mildly spiced lamb tagine and
fragrant couscous
***

Sweet plum tarts and whipped cream

When I wake this morning, wintry sunlight is already filtering through the bedroom window, telling me I've slept late. I don't think I moved all night.

I fell into bed, exhausted, after the enjoyable but hectic activity of the day before – not to mention the small matter of several glasses of celebratory champagne with Erin after we'd finished. I didn't have the energy to clear away the glasses after she left, or even to close the bedroom curtains.

I lie there for a while in the cosy warmth, enjoying the sensation of having the whole bed to myself and thinking about the previous day. As we were chatting to Clemmy just outside the front door, Bob – coming out to his car to collect a book – made a point of congratulating me on the Amalfi Lemon Tart. 'Not too tart, not too sweet. In fact, absolute perfection!' was his happy verdict.

The memory gives me a warm feeling inside. But at the same time, it makes me nervous. It's a lot to live up to. Resolutely, I push back the covers, spring out of bed and head for the bathroom. Then I quickly double back, grab my notebook and write:

Nine days until I'm engaged! The lovely thing about being married, I imagine, is being able to count on your husband for support. Harrison loves and encourages my cooking. And once he sees how excited I am about this new business venture, I'm certain he'll be really supportive of me.

As I lather up the shampoo, I wonder briefly if I should phone Harrison, but then I decide to leave it until I get back tonight and I've got more time to chat. Deep down, I'm a little afraid he might trivialise my modest success and – without meaning to – take away some of the excitement I'm feeling.

Two hours later, I'm back at the Log Fire Cabin, loaded down with boxes containing the food for the day. Everyone appears to be out, so I let myself in and head straight for the kitchen. Unpacking the fresh meat, the various cartons and the colourful array of fruit and vegetables, my stomach fizzes with a mix of excitement and apprehension at the prospect of baking Jed's favourite, lemon drizzle cake, and later on, serving up another three-course dinner.

Our arrangement was that Erin would be here the first day, then once I'd found my feet in the kitchen, she'd come along for a few hours every evening to help serve dinner. The silence in the kitchen seems odd after yesterday, so I flick on the radio and listen to the DJ getting excited about Christmas and playing all the old festive favourites.

Suddenly, the door opens and in flies Ruby. She glances frantically around her then dives nimbly under the breakfast bar. Peering out, she shushes me with a finger over her lips and whispers, 'I'm *not* going for a walk with Mum and that old man, and she can't bloody make me!'

'Bob?' I ask, surprised. 'He's not terribly old. And he seems really nice to me.'

'Sssh!'

A second later, Tom arrives. He hovers awkwardly by the door, flushing as he meets my eye. 'Is my sister hiding in here?'

I shrug and hold up my hands with a grin, as if to say, *Leave me out of this*!

He peers under the breakfast bar, where she's sitting cross-legged and grumpy. 'Ruby, you're such a plank.' He sighs. 'For God's sake, come on. They're waiting for you.'

Silence.

'You did agree to go for a walk round the lake with them,' he reminds her.

'Yes, but I only said it to get Mum off my back. Does she really expect me to be all pally-wally with her new *boyfriend*? Because if so, she can bloody whistle, as far as I'm concerned. He's old enough to be our *granddad*!'

'No, he's not.' Tom leans his elbows wearily on the breakfast bar and runs his hands through his mop of curly dark hair. 'Bob's only about fifteen years older than Mum. I think he's all right. You should give him a chance.'

'Why should I? He's not Dad and he never will be.'

He sighs. 'You should be thinking about Mum. It's nearly two years since Dad died. Don't you think she deserves to be happy?'

'No, I bloody don't.' Ruby's voice wavers. She sounds on the verge of tears. 'Mum's priority should be *us* now that Dad's gone. Not that ancient relic!'

'Ruby! Where are you, love?' At the sound of Gloria's approaching footsteps, Ruby shuffles out from under the counter and dives for the patio doors. A desperate fiddle with the key and she's out, slamming the door behind her and running across the grass.

I grin at Tom, hoping to cheer him up. Slouched over the breakfast bar, he's a sprawl of long limbs and untidy bed hair – and he looks as if he has the cares of the entire world on his shoulders. 'There's some hot chocolate that's almost reached its sell-by date here,' I say casually. 'I don't suppose you could use it up?'

He looks up without much enthusiasm.

I carry on beating the eggs into the butter and sugar. 'It'll just go to waste if you don't use it.'

He shrugs, as if he's too fed up to argue.

'Sit yourself down and I'll get the milk on.'

'Okay. Thanks.' He pulls out a stool and perches on it, dwarfing it with his gangly six-foot teenage frame. Then he stares resignedly out of the window.

I bustle about getting the hot chocolate ready. 'There you go. Enjoy!' I place the mug in front of him. 'Sisters, eh? It looks like Ruby would rather be anywhere else but here.'

'Anywhere there's a phone shop,' he murmurs. 'I take it you've heard that her whole life is in ruins?'

'I got that impression, yes.'

'She's so loud. And she's stressing everyone out,' he complains.

'Well, you've come to the right place,' I tell him, and he looks at me quizzically.

'The kitchen's a great place for chilling.' I stir in the lemon zest and flour, tip the mixture into a tin and smooth it over with a spatula. Then I pop the cake into the oven. 'In fact, I always think the kitchen is the most relaxing room in the house.'

'Even though you're working?'

I smile. 'Ah, yes, but I love cooking and baking, so it doesn't really seem like work to me.'

He nods and takes a sip of his chocolate. 'Nice.'

'So what's *your* passion?'

'Sorry?' He flushes slightly at the word 'passion'.

'The thing you love doing?'

He shrugs. 'I'm into cars. I want to be an engineer and get into car design. I'm supposed to be going to university next year.'

'Oh, that's brilliant.' I frown at his gloomy expression. 'Isn't it?'

'It could be.'

I suddenly remember Ruby baiting him about a girl he likes.

'You don't want to leave Newcastle. Is that it?'

He looks at me, startled, but says nothing.

I smile. 'When I first went away to college, I had to

leave all my friends behind and I found that really tough. In fact, I nearly chickened out altogether. The worst thing of all was having to leave this boy I really liked.'

'Yeah? So, what happened?'

'With the boy?'

He nods.

'It worked out fine. My college was only a couple of hours away by train, so he came to visit me and we ended up getting together.'

'Cool.'

I nod. 'Yes. It was.' I don't need to mention the fact that the boy in question went on to shag my flatmate after a drunken night out, at which point it all went completely pear-shaped.

'Is there a girl?' I ask casually, turning away and looking in the cupboard.

He sighs. 'Yes.'

'Have you asked her out?'

'No.'

'Why not?'

He shrugs.

'Are you friends with her?'

'Yes.'

I busy myself washing the mixing bowl and wooden spoon. 'Cool. What's she called?'

'Charlotte.'

'Lovely name.' I pause. 'But you're afraid if you ask her out, you might lose her as a friend?'

He heaves a sigh. 'What if she laughs? I couldn't stand that.'

I turn, looking at him thoughtfully as I dry the mixing bowl with a tea towel dotted with red-nosed Rudolphs. 'If she laughs, she wouldn't be much of a friend, would she?'

'I suppose not.'

'Do you think she likes you?'

He nods. 'She told a friend she does, and the friend told me.'

'Well, then, I think you just have to be brave, Tom. And ask her out.'

He groans and buries his head in his arms. My heart goes out to him. I so remember that teenage agony of being in love for the first time, but feeling painfully shy.

The door opens and Clemmy bursts in. She frowns at me, at first not noticing Tom slouched over the breakfast bar. 'I wanted to apologise to you about last night, Poppy. Honestly, I was feeling *so* ridiculously sorry for myself, standing out there staring at the stars like a love-sick teenager. But no more! I've decided. It's high time I moved on from Ryan and –' She catches sight of Tom. 'Oh. Hi, Tom!'

He raises his head, gives Clemmy an awkward half-smile and turns red.

'What's up? Are you all right, love?' she asks him.

'We're discussing relationships,' I tell her, to spare Tom the embarrassment of talking about his feelings.

She rolls her eyes. 'Ah. Say no more. They're the bane of my life.'

'I was saying you have to be brave, if you really like someone, and risk rejection. Because you never know, they might just say yes.'

Clemmy opens her eyes wide at Tom. 'Don't tell me a handsome lad like you is too scared to ask a girl out? Crikey, I would have thought you'd be absolutely spoilt for choice.'

Tom flushes even redder.

'Honestly, Tom, ask her out!' she urges him. 'And if she says no – and I have to say she'd be a first-class *prat* to turn down a lovely boy like you – well, then you can move on to someone else! At your age, the world is your oyster. You should just go for it.' She sniffs and looks at the oven. 'Ooh, lovely smell.'

'Lemon drizzle cake.' I glance at Tom, cringing on his behalf. Clemmy's lovely and her advice is well intentioned, but Tom, bless him, looks rigid with embarrassment at her lecture on romance.

There's a brief silence. Then Tom swivels round on his stool to face Clemmy. 'So, you think I should? Ask Charlotte out, I mean?'

'Absolutely! No question! And she's a fool if she says

no. Correct?' She turns to me and I nod firmly.

'So then if she *does* say "thanks, but no thanks", it doesn't really matter because the last thing you want, Tom, is to be going out with a fool!'

I laugh at her weird logic.

Tom grins. 'I suppose not.'

'Ooh, is that hot chocolate?' Clemmy's eyes light up. 'Do you mind?'

Tom shakes his head, watching as she takes a gulp from the other side of the mug.

I smile to myself. *Way to go, Clemmy! You've certainly given him something to think about!*

'Where's Ruby, Tom? Your mum was looking for her.' Clemmy licks hot chocolate from her lips and goes back for more, as I peer at my cake in the oven. Almost done.

Tom nods in the direction of outside. 'She's been desperate to explore that ruined cottage on the other side of the lake. Keeps going on and on about it, but Mum said on no account should she risk it because the place is falling down.'

I laugh. 'So that's probably where she'll be?'

He nods. 'My sister gets bored easily. She likes adventures. A slow walk around the lake with Mum and Bob would totally bore her to death.'

'Well, good for her,' says Clemmy. '*I* won't spoil Ruby's adventure if *you* won't.' She grins at me. 'I used to climb out of my bedroom window and slide down the wall clutching the drainpipe and that never did *me* any harm. Well, except for the time I split my head open, of course.' She laughs gaily at the memory.

'You put me to shame.' I smile. 'I'm rubbish at being brave.'

'But you're a fabulous cook so it doesn't matter! Is there a hoover that works round here, do you know? The pine needles are piling up through there, but the one in the utility room doesn't seem to be picking up.'

'I'll have a look at it,' Tom offers, getting off his stool. 'I'm good with machines.'

'Wow! Good-looking *and* handy. Devastating combo! How will Charlotte resist?'

She follows Tom out, turning back to tip me a wink.

*

With the scent of lemon drizzle cake filling the room, I start preparing the vegetables for tonight, all the time thinking about poor Clemmy's unrequited love for Ryan. What does he see in Jessica? Apart from the impressive boob job? Then I think about Ruby and the tremor in her voice when she spoke about the dad she's lost. She must miss him terribly. No wonder she's fed up that her mum appears to have found someone to replace him. It doesn't matter how nice Bob might be, that still must hurt.

When you lose someone close like that, whatever the circumstances, it's so hard. I know all about that. It must be worse for Ruby, though. She had her dad in her life for fourteen years and now he's gone forever. Whereas I only spent four days with mine. He's probably still alive but he could be anywhere in Italy. Anywhere at all. And impossible to track down ... not that I'd ever want to find him. He showed he didn't care. Why would I want someone like that in my life?

Suddenly, there's a hard ball of sadness in my throat.

The door opens and Jessica walks in. She stares at my shiny eyes and I blink rapidly. 'It's the onions.'

She gives the briefest of nods. 'I'd like a coffee with milk. In fact, make that two. And make sure the milk is hot. I can't stand lukewarm drinks.'

My eyes must have widened in surprise because she adds, 'That is what you're here for, isn't it?'

I smile at her as I cross to the oven to take out the cake. 'Well, not really, no. But I can certainly make you some coffee.'

Her look is glacial. 'Good. Bring it up to my room, will you? I'm not in the mood to be sociable.' Gloria's raucous laughter drifts through the open kitchen door and Jessica grits her teeth.

'No problem. But I have something to attend to first.' I untie my apron and pull on my coat, telling her cheerfully, 'Coffee with milk coming up, just as soon as I get back.'

I disappear before she has a chance to pin me down to a time.

Bloody cheek of it! She must think I'm some sort of maid. I didn't mind at all making hot chocolate for Tom, but Jessica's attitude leaves a whole lot to be desired. Ryan's far too good for her.

As I walk through to the hall, Jed comes out of the living room. 'Okay, Poppy? Are you off for your lunch?'

'Actually, I'm going in search of Ruby. Gloria was anxious to find her and I think I know where she might be.'

He looks at me quizzically.

'At the broken-down cottage,' I explain.

'Ah, yes. She did mention it.' He grins. 'More than once. Do you want some company?'

'Um … yes.' I smile up at him, thinking what an unusual green his eyes are. Emerald with little flecks of amber. 'That would be great.'

Chapter 17

Ve head outside and set off, skirting the lake along a well-trodden path set back from the water, along the tree line. It takes us a good half hour, walking fairly briskly. Jessica will no doubt be furiously awaiting her caffeine fix but I really don't care.

As we approach the cottage, my stomach is churning like a cement mixer. I want to see inside it. But at the same time, I'm torn in two. On the one hand, I'm experiencing a self-preserving urge to run as fast as I can away from the place. But on the other, I desperately want to go in and see if it's the way I remember it.

Jed tries the door and finds it open. He must sense my hesitation because he turns to me and says, 'You don't have to go in. I'll find Ruby. If she's here.'

I paste on a smile. 'No, no. It's fine. I'll come with you.'

He pushes open the door, and instantly my knees turn to water at the sight before me.

Wooden stairs lead up to the first floor, still covered in the same wine-coloured-cord carpet I remember, and there's a closed door on either side of me. If I remember rightly, the one on my right leads to a little breakfast room with four small tables and prettily mismatched chairs. The white tablecloths bore an embroidered pattern of tiny blue forget-me-nots and the tantalising aroma of frying bacon drifted through the hatch from the kitchen. The door on my left opened into a little lounge where guests sat to read the daily newspapers. Both rooms commanded lovely views over the lake.

Jed calls for Ruby, then pushes open the doors on the ground floor to look inside, before heading up the stairs. He pauses halfway up and looks back at me. 'Stay there if you like. I'll see if she's up here.'

I take a deep breath. 'I'll come up.' As I pass them, I glance into the rooms, but they're empty. All the furniture I remembered has gone.

We find Ruby in one of the front bedrooms, the one with the window seat. I catch my breath as I walk in. This is the room I slept in with Mum. Alessandro had the room across the landing.

'Ah, there you are, Ruby. Your mum was wondering where you'd got to,' says Jed matter-of-factly. He glances around. 'Nice place to escape to. Although if I were you, I wouldn't lean against that window. All the frames in this house look rotten.'

'Oh, okay,' says Ruby. 'I like this window seat, though. I wish I had one in my room at home.'

Jed grins at her. 'Have you explored the other rooms?' He nods at the landing. 'This place dates back to the nineteenth century, although it was obviously modernised when it became a B&B. It's in a great spot.' He moves near the window and peers out. 'Be a shame if no one stepped in to rescue it.'

I frown. 'Is it safe to walk around?'

Heading for the door, he grins back at me. 'If you hear me shout, you'll know I've landed in the room below.' He disappears off to explore and we hear the floorboards creaking ominously on the landing.

'It would be funny if he *did* fall through a hole in the floor,' says Ruby, looking anything but amused by the idea.

'Are you okay, Ruby?' I ask. 'Why didn't you want to go on the walk with your mum and Bob?'

'I don't know.' She looks down at her hands then starts gnawing at one of her nails. 'I just keep thinking Dad should be here. He'd have sorted out my phone by now and we'd be doing fun things.'

'Like what?'

'I don't know. Just not this shit.' She shrugs petulantly. 'No one talks about Dad any more. Especially Mum. It's all "Bob does this" and "Bob does that" and "Bob has the bloody sun shining out of his—' She stops and flicks me a sheepish glance.

'Bob does seem really nice,' I say carefully, going over

and perching on the other end of the window seat. 'Maybe you should give him a chance. If he makes your mum happy.'

She's on the verge of tears and my heart goes out to her.

'I know what it's like,' I say softly. 'Not to have your dad in your life. It hurts.'

She looks up, surprised. 'Is your dad dead?'

I shake my head. 'No. But I don't see him. It's complicated.'

She nods, thinking about this. Then she groans. 'Plus I haven't got a phone. It would be *so much better* here if I could talk to my friends. Mum took me to the phone shop and I wanted a blue one as a replacement but they didn't have any in stock, so they had to order one for me. Which means I won't get it till after Christmas.' She sighs. 'They had grey phones in stock. I should have just taken one of those. But Mum says it's too late and I'll just have to wait and be patient.'

I smile in sympathy. Gloria's got a point, though. Kids tend to need everything *right now* but I suppose they have to learn that they can't always have their heart's desire immediately. 'What's your favourite cake?'

'Chocolate brownies.'

'Good choice. How do you fancy baking chocolate brownies for everyone tomorrow? I could get the ingredients for you.'

'Me? Make cake for everyone? Are you nuts?'

'You could come shopping with me tomorrow morning for the ingredients if you like.' I remember Jed saying Ruby loves her fast food. 'We might even pass a McDonald's on our way back.'

'Really? God, that would be nice. No offence but I'm not really into different-coloured food.'

I grin. 'You mean vegetables?'

'Hey, they've got a wine cellar!' Jed calls from downstairs. 'With wine!'

Ruby raises her eyebrows at me in amusement and gets up, clearly bored with staring out at the view. As she goes downstairs, I linger where I am for a moment, staring over the lake towards the Log Fire Cabin on the opposite shore. Last time I sat on this window seat, all those years ago, there were trees on the far bank, but no buildings at all.

*

I hear Jed calling my name and my heart does an odd little flip. I get up from the window seat and walk slowly down the stairs. They're both in the musty cellar. I can hear the clank of bottles and Jed's voice exclaiming over the vintage.

'Right, I'll see you two back at the house,' says Ruby, climbing the steep, grimy staircase and joining me at the top. She marches off outside, then Jed appears, shaking his head in amazement over the wine, abandoned by the owners when they left.

He closes the cellar door and we collide in the small space. His hands touch my waist briefly and when I trip slightly on a warped floorboard as we make our way out of the cottage, he steadies me from behind.

'Oops.' I laugh in confusion at the feel of his hands pressed against my sides, and turn to make a joke of it. He's still holding me and there's barely an inch separating us. His thick winter jacket is open and I'm transfixed by the pale grey sweatshirt he's wearing underneath, which subtly moulds to the contours of his broad, muscular chest. I have an urge to smooth my hand over the material to explore its softness and feel the contrasting hardness of Jed's body beneath. The musky scent of him makes my head spin.

My gaze travels shyly upwards and my heart leaps in my chest as his eyes lock onto mine. For a second, an intensity flares in their burnished-gold depths that makes the breath catch in my throat. His smile fades and so does mine.

The space between us vanishes as I lean in to him and feel his body hard against me. My head swims and my lips part. I'm melting against him...

Then, through a dazed rush of feeling, I'm suddenly aware of Jed's hands gripping my upper arms, as he gently but firmly moves me away from him.

He lets go of me and fixes his eyes ahead, out of the open door. 'These rickety floorboards need replacing,' he mutters, his voice sounding strained. Then he strides out of the cottage and stands, hands in pockets, scuffing the grass and staring out over the lake.

'They do,' I agree, pulling the door behind me, wondering why my legs feel so shaky.

We walk at a brisk pace back to the house, Jed slightly ahead of me, whereas on the way to the cottage, we walked side by side. My legs still aren't working properly and I'm struggling to keep up with his long strides. I'm almost glad when the path narrows, requiring us to walk in single file.

My head is still spinning. But I tell myself it was nothing and that I probably imagined the jolt of attraction between us. It probably happened because I'm missing Harrison so much and temporarily deprived of cuddles.

And Jed? I watch him covering the ground at speed, clearly wanting to put as much distance between us as possible. Eyes closed briefly, I relive the shameful part where I leaned in close, and the gallant way he gently dissuaded me from snogging his face off.

I feel *so embarrassed*...

Chapter 18

Back at the cabin, Jed tends to the log fire, marching straight out to the wood store and slamming the back door, while I scuttle to the safety of the cake-scented kitchen.

My heart is still beating frantically, probably because of the speed with which we made our way back along the lake. I stand in a daze and look at the cake I baked earlier, trying to focus on the plan for this evening, but failing completely. My brain has turned to mush.

What is wrong with me?

I feel suddenly overwhelmed with emotion. Am I missing Harrison so much that I fling myself at the first reasonably attractive man I find myself alone with? It's not like me at all. But I suppose Christmas is an emotional time for everyone – it's the season, more than any other, when we draw closer to family and friends, and think about loved ones who are missing from our lives. Being here at the lake at Christmas-time is sure to make me feel a little wobbly, thinking about the past. It has nothing to do with Jed Turner. Nothing at all.

I walk to the patio doors and stare out at the lake.

It looks as pretty as a Christmas card, with the glitter of frost on the trees. What must it be like to have a normal, hectic but happy, family Christmas? The sort that most people take for granted?

A pang of loneliness hits. It's like a real, physical ache deep inside.

I should have gone to Spain with Harrison.

But next minute, I realise that would have been impossible. I need to be near Mum over the festive season. She always says she'd cope perfectly well on her own, and maybe she could – but *I* certainly couldn't. She's all the family I've got, and I couldn't bear the thought of not being with her. Especially on Christmas Day.

Often, I feel like *I'm* the mum in the relationship. It's as if I'm caring for my grown-up teenager, who's flown the nest but isn't quite mature enough to cope alone and is likely to forget bin day and eat beans straight out of the can for dinner. Going round to check up on her every day certainly takes some planning, but I wouldn't have it any other way. In between my catering duties at the Log Fire Cabin, I'm going to make sure we have the best Christmas we can, just her and me.

The thing with Jed earlier, which has sent me into a tailspin, was just a symptom of my confused feelings about everything. Ever since meeting Harrison, my life has trundled along a well-worn track, and now, all of a sudden, things are starting to change and, naturally, it's a little unsettling.

Feeling in need of fresh air, I open the patio door a fraction and take some cautious deep breaths, telling myself not to be so silly about earlier. It was a fleeting moment with Jed, soon to be forgotten. And later on this evening, I'll be able to talk to Harrison and everything will feel perfectly normal again.

The air is so icy cold out there, tears spring to my eyes. A few snowflakes drift down from a sky that's promising more. Quickly, I retreat inside, shutting the door and locking it.

*

With Mum on my mind, I decide to call in at hers and take some sandwiches for lunch. I ring the bell then let myself in, to save her the complicated manoeuvre to the front door.

'I've got a catering job over Christmas,' I call, as I wade through a sea of debris and boxes to reach Mum, who's standing in the living room waiting for me. It's always an effort to get anywhere in this place, like when you're in a traffic snarl-up and it takes the longest time to travel a few yards. 'But don't worry, we'll still be able to spend most of Christmas Day together.'

She smiles. 'Good for you, love. I've always thought

you should use those marvellous cooking skills of yours. Where's the job?'

'Oh, it's a holiday chalet place – about ten miles out of Easingwold.' I hold up a cuddly hippo. 'Any reason you're keeping this?' I ask, lightly. 'Harrison and I aren't planning on giving you grandchildren any day soon, you know.'

She gives me her slightly stiff smile. The one she gives me any time I dare to question an item in her mountain of junk. 'You never know. So where exactly is this chalet?'

I shrug. 'Hard to explain. It's right in the middle of nowhere. You'd never find it unless you already knew where it was.'

She nods.

'Sandwich?' I make it through to the living room and we sit down on the two-seater sofa. I chat about the job and what it entails, adding that I'm hoping Uncle Bob might give me my big break and hire me to cook for him occasionally.

'He's requested an Italian-style dinner on Christmas Eve, so I'll have to pull out all the stops to make it really special.'

'Well, you've certainly had plenty of practise over the years,' she says. 'Cooking Italian food, that is.'

I nod. 'I guess it runs in the family. I must have got the taste for pasta from my dad. My *real* dad.' I glance at her but her expression remains neutral.

The words hang in the air between us. It would be the perfect opportunity for her to start a dialogue. But, as usual, she chooses silence instead. Looking away, she reaches for a gingham-patterned cushion that's lying on the floor. She sets it on her lap and smoothes her hand over the fabric, and for the millionth time, I wonder why she finds it so hard to talk to me about him.

We eat our sandwiches and chat about something safe instead – our arrangements for Christmas Day. I'll be collecting her in the morning and bringing her over to mine to open gifts. Then I'll leave after our lunch, around four, to head over to the cabin to cook dinner.

'I'm looking forward to it,' Mum says, rubbing her hands together, and for once looking genuinely happy.

I smile at her. 'Me too, Mum. We'll have a good day, I promise.'

She comes to the door to wave me off, back to the cabin.

'It's come round so quickly, Christmas.' She gives a little sigh. 'Remember when your dad used to bring in a real tree two weeks before the big day? I just adored the scent of it.'

My heart turns over at the wistful look on her face. She's obviously forgotten that the fallen needles would end up annoying Martin so much that there'd inevitably be a huge row even before Christmas Day arrived. She must miss him still, even after everything that happened

– all the arguments and the bitterness and the silences. It's amazing how the mind can erase the stuff you'd rather not remember. And I suppose she did love him once.

'I could get a real tree if you like,' I offer. 'We could have it at mine for Christmas Day.'

She shakes her head. 'Don't worry, love. You sound as if you have enough to do. You'd better get back.' We hug and I find there are tears in my eyes. 'Has this cabin place you're working at got a real tree?'

'Yeah. It has, actually. They've got quite a bit of land and there's a little copse of fir trees by the lake. It came from there.'

Mum narrows her eyes. 'The lake?'

My heart misses a beat.

'Yes. The – um – cabin sits on a small stretch of water. It's hardly a lake at all, really,' I add, trying to backtrack.

'The Cottage on the Lake B&B?' She studies me intently, and I know there's little point denying it. She's very sharp, my mum. There's not a great deal that gets by her – not even now, when her head seems so full of trivialities.

I nod. 'Near there, yes.'

We stare at each other, thinking of that long-ago time when we stayed there one night. Out of nowhere, a big lump appears in my throat. I know I shouldn't say what's on my mind but I'm powerless to stop it. I've suppressed the question for so long that when it falls out of my mouth, the strangled tone doesn't even sound like me.

'Why did he never come back, Mum?'

The expression on her face is anguished and when she opens her mouth, I really think she's going to tell me at last. But instead she gives her head a little shake and turns away.

*

Later, I collect Erin to help me out serving dinner.

She's in a cheerful mood today, chatting away about the film she and Mark saw the night before.

'Not in the same class as *Pretty Woman*. Obvs,' she says, beaming at the mention of her all-time favourite movie. 'But good nonetheless.'

'You actually *are* Julia Roberts, aren't you? Or should I say *Vivian*.'

'Oh, yes.' She grins. 'Big mistake. *Huge*,' she adds, holding up imaginary bags and quoting her favourite line from the famous Rodeo Drive shopping scene.

'How *is* Mark?' I ask.

'He's mighty fine, thank you.' Erin swings back her hair. 'Actually, I'm lucky he was actually talking to me last night. I was such a bloody idiot.'

'Really? How?'

She sighs. 'Well, I found a lipstick in the bathroom

by the basin. A frosted pale pink, which I would never use. And honestly, I swear my heart actually stopped.'

An image of a girl with stunning pale-red hair sweeps into my mind. I glance anxiously at Erin, but she's smiling away, looking perfectly relaxed.

'So was it yours after all?' I ask her, my heart drumming faster.

'Well, I definitely didn't recognise it and I went a bit silent on Mark.' She grimaces. 'Bless him, he looked *horrified*. Like he couldn't believe I would suspect him of entertaining another woman in our flat.'

I frown at her, wanting desperately for there to be a plausible reason. 'So the lipstick belonged to?'

'Me! It was Mark who suddenly remembered that I'd been clearing out my make-up junk in the bathroom the other day. You know how you collect all sorts of free samples that aren't your colour at all but you hold onto them anyway? So that pale-pink lipstick must have been one I was going to throw away.' She grins. 'I'd accumulated such a huge pile of useless stuff, it's not surprising I didn't remember that one lipstick.'

I try to smile at her but my face won't oblige. Should I tell her about the strawberry-blonde haired girl I saw him with that time, coming out of their flat together?

She frowns. 'Is something wrong?'

I shake my head. 'No, not at all.'

My head is in a spin. *Shall I mention her? Or shall I*

keep quiet? Chances are it was totally innocent anyway.

What would I want Erin to do if the shoe were on the other foot?

That's my answer. Because I'd definitely want to know.

I force a light, nonchalant tone. 'It's just that I did see Mark the other afternoon coming out of your flat with a girl. Perhaps one of his colleagues at the estate agent's?'

Erin frowns. 'Oh? What did she look like?'

I shrug, as if I barely remember, it was so unimportant. 'Er ... small, I think, with long, strawberry-blonde hair? Ring a bell?'

I can feel Erin staring at me as she thinks, and my face starts to burn. *Oh God, I wish I could take it back!*

There's the longest silence ever. Then Erin snaps her fingers. 'I know! That'll be Sophie, Mark's old friend from university. They've known each other for yonks. She lives in London now. Long red hair?'

I nod happily, relief flowing through me. 'Quite pale red. But definitely red.'

'Oh.' Erin looks pensive. 'It used to be a really vivid red but maybe she's dyeing it a lighter shade these days. She's lovely, Sophie. She must be back from London on holiday, visiting her parents. So perhaps it's her lipstick. Mark must have forgotten she was at the flat.'

Thank you, thank you, thank you! (I'm not sure who I'm actually thanking, but I'm so relieved there's a perfectly innocent explanation.)

After all Erin has been through with men, I truly don't know how she'd cope if Mark were to break her heart, too.

*

Back at the cabin, as the time for dinner approaches, the atmosphere in the kitchen is fairly calm with just a hint of suppressed panic on my part. The sweet-pastry plum tarts, just out of the oven, are browner on top than I would have liked. But we combat the singed look by shaking caster sugar on top of them.

It's a good sign when the starter plates come back empty. And when we take the main course out, everyone 'oohs' and 'aahs' – all except Jessica, who peers at the lamb tagine as if she suspects some kind of foul play.

Once the desserts are served, with a generous dollop of whipped cream on each individual plum tart, Erin and I collapse back against the worktops for a moment, taking a well-earned breather.

Seconds later, a commotion breaks out on the other side of the door.

Two female voices, one raised in anger, one rather more placating in tone, carry through to us in the kitchen.

'Trouble?' whispers Erin.

I strain to hear. 'Sounds like Jessica's upset about something.'

Sure enough, next moment her rage carries through to us. 'Right, that's fucking it! I'm leaving. Someone call me a taxi to collect me in *precisely* thirty minutes.'

Heels skitter up the wooden stairs and a bedroom door slams. Erin dashes to open the kitchen door a crack to listen.

'Erin!'

'What?'

'It's none of our business.'

But curiosity gets the better of me. Shaking my head, I join Erin and we hover by the door, but the remaining diners appear to have been stunned into silence.

'She bloody hated that dessert,' Erin whispers, grinning.

'Well, I've never known *anyone* reject my plum tarts.'

'Arf arf.'

'Oh, God. Maybe I should be brewing a soothing tea for everyone. What shall we do?'

'Hide in here is my preferred option. Until Jessica's taxi removes her from the scene.'

'Poor Ryan. Do you think he'll go with her?'

'Probably.' Erin considers this for a second. 'Poor Clemmy.'

'We need to clear away.'

'That's just an excuse to go out there.'

I make a face at her. 'You know me too well.'

We bustle out with a businesslike air, looking as if we haven't heard a single syllable of Jessica's explosion.

Gloria, slumped at the head of the table, is mopping her red face with her napkin, looking bewildered and hotter than ever. 'I only asked her where she got her boobs done. It was a compliment, really.'

Ryan grins. 'She likes people to think they're all natural.'

I can't help thinking he looks remarkably calm for someone whose girlfriend has just stormed upstairs and is packing to leave.

'Well, *I* didn't know that,' wails Gloria.

'Perhaps you should think before you speak,' Bob snaps. He sighs and runs a hand through his hair. 'Look, I'm going to bed. See you all in the morning.'

Ruby snorts. 'Jessica's boobs are about as real as my hair colour.'

'Ruby!' chides Gloria, staring with alarm at Bob's departing back. 'Oh God, shall I go up and talk to her?'

'I'd leave her, if I were you.' Ryan pours himself another glass of wine and swallows half of it in one go. 'Once Jess makes up her mind, there's no shifting her.'

'But I could at least say I'm sorry,' offers poor Gloria.

'Nice thought, but it won't make any difference.' Ryan slugs down the rest of his wine and reaches for the bottle. 'She turned down Christmas on a yacht in the

Med to come here so she's understandably pissed that it hasn't worked out.'

'But I feel so guilty.' Gloria slumps lower in her chair.

Ryan shakes his head. 'You shouldn't. Jess was just looking for an excuse to escape.'

'It's not *your* fault she didn't enjoy herself,' points out Ruby, siding with her mum for once. 'If you walk around with a face like a slapped arse all the time, like Jessica does, you can hardly expect to be happy!'

'Ruby!' Gloria looks horrified. 'Oh bugger, me and my big mouth. And now you're taking after me, Ruby.'

'No, I am *not*!' Staring at her mum in disgust, she scrapes back her chair and marches out, leaving Gloria on the verge of tears.

Erin and I clear the table as quietly as possible, studiously avoiding eye contact.

After a while, Clemmy speaks up. She's been sitting in worried silence but now she looks at Ryan and murmurs, 'You should go up to her.'

Ryan looks at her questioningly, as if he hasn't a clue who she means.

'Jessica,' says Clemmy. 'You should go and talk to her. Explain that Gloria didn't mean to upset her.'

Ryan looks away with an indifferent shrug. 'If she wants to leave, let her. I'm not bothered.'

But something about the rigid set of his mouth tells me that he *is* bothered. A great deal.

Jed, having gone to build up the fire while all this kicked off, looks up and gives me a weary smile as I pass him, in Erin's wake. In return, I give my head a little helpless shake at the abrupt way the evening has ended.

It's the first time that Jed has actually looked at me since our close encounter in the hallway of the lakeside cottage, and a little burst of joy runs through me. I can't believe the relief I feel at knowing things are okay between us again.

I push backwards through the door into the kitchen, feeling lighter in spirit, as if a weight has rolled off my shoulders. If I'm to be working here until after New Year, there can't be any awkwardness between Jed and me. He's my client. I need to keep our relationship pleasant but firmly businesslike.

And so it will be, from now on...

Chapter 19

Friday 23rd December

<u>Afternoon tea</u>
Ruby's chocolate brownies

<u>Dinner menu</u>
Smoked salmon and king prawns
with dill and lime mayonnaise
and Scottish oatcakes
***

Vodka lemon chicken
with creamy mashed potatoes, broccoli florets and mini
glazed carrots
***

Squidgy chocolate and pear pudding

Harrison, bless him, seems to have entered a whole new level of flamenco-dance hell.

I tried to call him several times last night but his

phone must have been out of charge. Then a text came through first thing:

Sorry missed calls. Paella evening got bit out of hand. Very loud. Mother has entered us into flamenco dance competition xx

Poor Harrison. He'll be *hating* it! But I'm so proud of how thoughtful and kind he's being with his mother. It can't be easy for her, the first Christmas without her husband. I can't wait to see him on New Year's Eve!

Later, at the cabin, I've got Ruby in the kitchen with me, teaching her how to make chocolate brownies. Actually, she's surprisingly clued up already, reeling off the difference between plain and self-raising flour, and creaming the butter and brown sugar together like a pro.

'I like your purple hair,' I say truthfully. 'It's really striking.'

'It's not purple,' she corrects me, looking pleased nonetheless. 'It's called chocolate-mauve.'

'Well, it suits you.' I nudge her, nodding at the brownie mix in her bowl. 'You've done this before.'

'Dad liked baking and I used to help him.' She smiles at the memory. 'He used to work at the office on Saturday mornings then come home and make flap-jacks. He said it helped him to relax, and when he smelled the biscuits baking in the oven, he knew his weekend had begun.'

'Perhaps we could make flapjacks some other time?' I murmur. 'In your dad's honour.'

'Maybe.' She focuses on beating the cake mix, her expression neutral, but I notice the slight flush in her cheeks.

Ryan wanders in around eleven and asks if there are any biscuits. I rummage around and find half a packet of digestives and he eats them standing by the patio doors, staring out. He looks so deep in thought, he's probably only vaguely aware of Wizzard blasting out 'I Wish It Could Be Christmas Every Day'.

He seems to have spent the whole morning prowling around restlessly, like a caged panther. He came into the kitchen earlier with a newspaper and sat at the breakfast bar after asking if minded. I smiled and said of course I didn't, and I made him some coffee, wondering if he was in here in order to eascape from everyone. He looked preoccupied and definitely wasn't reading his newspaper. Instead, he spent a lot of time just staring out over the lake, only leaving when Jed came in and asked for his help with something.

'Thanks,' he says now, screwing up the empty biscuit packet and tossing it in the bin.

'No problem.' I smile, and he slopes out.

'Do you think he's had The Letter?' murmurs Ruby,

carefully tipping out cocoa powder into the weighing scales.

I smile at her as little puffs of the delicate chocolate powder rise up and scatter on the bench. 'What letter?'

She looks solemn. 'You know, the letter from Santa informing him that as he's been a bad boy this year, he won't be getting presents.'

I start to laugh.

'What?' Ruby stares at me. 'Why are you laughing?' She clutches my arm. 'Oh no, please don't tell me Santa isn't real!'

She looks so totally devastated, my heart misses a beat. Oh God, does that mean I've ruined Christmas for her? But she's *sixteen*. Surely by now she...

Ruby's peals of laughter reveal I've been taken for a complete mug.

'Crikey, Ruby, perhaps you should be an actress when you grow up,' I tell her, laughing. 'That was a very believable performance.'

'I've acted in the school musical.'

'Yes? What part did you play?'

'The singing nun. I got into the *habit* of running round the hilltops.' She grins at me. 'Boom boom.'

'You were Maria von Trapp?'

'That's the fella.'

'Wow, I'm impressed.'

'It got me out of having to join the school choir. How

boring would *that* have been?' She snorts. 'We used to try climbing up the scenery backdrop when Mrs Chance, the music teacher, was off flirting in a corner with the drama master.'

I smile at her, thinking how I'd like to have been that cool at her age. Instead, I did exactly what I was told and shied away from putting myself out there. 'Perhaps you should study performance art.'

Ruby shakes her chocolate-mauve head firmly. 'I love extreme sports. I want to do something outdoors for a job. Be a rock-climbing teacher or something. Dad took me whitewater rafting once and it was the most awesome thing I've ever done.'

I nod. 'Sounds exciting.'

'Or I could be a cook.' She looks at me thoughtfully. 'Do you think I'd be any good?'

'Maybe. Let's see how the brownies turn out first, shall we?' I nudge her teasingly.

'I wish there was stuff to do round here. You know, exciting things. But Mum won't even let me dive into the lake. She says my extremes would freeze.'

'Your extremities.' Laughing, I tell her about the traditional New Year's Day lake swim and her eyes light up. 'Where do I get a wet suit?'

'I'm sure they'll be able to rustle up one for you from somewhere,' I assure her. Personally, I'll be giving that swim a very wide berth...

Soon, the heavenly aroma of warm, melting chocolate is filling the house, and Ryan wanders in to investigate just as the brownies are emerging from the oven. 'Very nice. When can we eat them?' He grins at Ruby when she slaps his hand and says he has to wait until they've cooled down.

'Poppy and I were just talking about extreme sports,' says Ruby. 'Have *you* done anything exciting like that, Ryan?'

He perches on the edge of a stool. 'It's not exactly extreme, but I'm learning to fly a plane. I'm hoping I'll have my licence some time next year.'

'Yeah?' Ruby's eyes light up. 'I'd *love* to be able to fly a plane. Is it difficult?'

Ryan laughs. 'It is when you're not great with heights.'

Ruby's eyes widen. 'You're scared of heights but you still go up there?'

He shrugs. 'My dad's a pilot.' A shadow passes over his face. 'I guess I got the bug from him.'

I glance at him, puzzled. I'm sure Jed mentioned that his mum was spending Christmas in Australia with their sister this year and that his dad had died several years ago. Perhaps they're half-brothers and Ryan's dad is still alive?

Gloria pops her head round the door and summons Ruby for a game of Monopoly then bustles off to find Tom.

'The excitement is mind-numbing,' Ruby says with such a deadpan expression that I can't help laughing.

'Go and trounce them all,' I tell her. 'And stay out of jail!'

She trails out of the kitchen and Ryan grins. 'She's a good kid when you get to know her. At first, I wanted to murder her, what with all that mobile-phone stuff.'

I murmur my agreement then cautiously ask him if he's feeling okay.

He looks surprised. 'Me? I'm fine.'

'You're probably missing Jessica, though.'

He makes a variety of faces, considering this, but ends up saying nothing, just shrugging.

'Is your dad coming for Christmas?' I smile. 'The pilot?'

'Never see him.' His reply is brusque.

'Oh, why not?' The instant the question is out, I wish I could take it back. Judging by the look on Ryan's face, it's obviously a painful subject.

He sighs. 'I wasn't even supposed to know he's my dad. Mum only told me about him when I was eighteen. I'd grown up thinking Jed's dad was my dad, too. But then I found out.'

I raise my eyebrows but don't press him for details, although I'm curious to know more.

Ryan shrugs. 'The fact is, Mum had a brief affair while Dad – well, I *thought* he was my biological dad – was working in Dubai, and she ended up having me.'

'Do you see him?' I ask. 'Your real dad?'

'Not really. He's a great guy but he's got a family of his own now and they live in France. He's a pilot for British Airways. He says I can go over and stay with them any time I want, but ...' He shrugs.

'So, why don't you?' I can tell from his expression it's eating away at him.

'I don't know. It would be awkward for everyone, especially his other kids,' he says. 'I don't really belong.'

'But you do! You're his *son*! Honestly, Ryan, if I were in your position and I'd been invited over to France by my real dad, I'd be there like a shot. Wild horses couldn't keep me from booking that flight!'

Hot tears surge up. Embarrassed, I turn away and start cutting up the brownie slab to serve later for afternoon tea.

There's a tense silence. Then Ryan says, 'Well, maybe I'll phone him.'

'You should.' My voice sounds clogged with tears.

'Do your mum and dad live locally?'

I blink furiously, paste on a smile and turn. 'Mum does. But Dad – isn't in my life anymore.'

'Oh.' There's a tense silence. Then he says, 'The food's been brilliant, by the way. Jed says your partner is in Spain visiting his mum.'

'Harrison. Yes, he is. And he's being forced to take up flamenco dancing.'

'Yeah?' Ryan laughs. 'Poor bloke. I bet he thinks it's great, you switching career like this.'

I grin. 'Well, actually, I think he'd rather I was a stay-at-home housewife. Not that he'd stand in my way, if this is what I wanted to do.'

'And is it? What you want to do?'

'Definitely. One hundred per cent.'

'Then I'm sure Harrison will support you and be proud of your achievement.'

I nod and smile, wishing it were that easy. It's impossible to dispel the sneaky feeling that Harrison probably wishes I *wasn't* so keen on a career change. I'm starting to think he'd rather I was there in the background, the little woman supporting him in *his* career advancement. It's only since he's been away that this has suddenly become clear to me. It's as if distance has given me perspective.

'You're lucky your life is so sorted.' Ryan groans. 'I don't think I'll ever settle down and have a family.' He smiles sheepishly at having confided something so intimate. I'm surprised, too. But then, I've always considered a cosy kitchen the perfect place to relax, mull things over, off-load...

'Are you in love with Jessica?' I ask carefully.

He looks surprised. 'Er ... no. We get on okay and she can be good fun sometimes. But I definitely couldn't see us growing old together.' He plays with the handle on his cup. 'No, I'll just be the eternal bachelor. The indulgent uncle to Jed's five kids. Far less complicated.'

'Maybe you go out with the wrong women?' I suggest, turning to count the brownies cooling on the rack to hide my reaction at the thought of Jed with five kids. 'I mean, I might be wrong, but Jessica doesn't really seem ready to settle down any time soon. Perhaps you choose girlfriends who haven't the power to hurt you.'

He sighs heavily. 'Oh, that's deep. Far too deep for a simple guy like me.'

'What about Clemmy?' I ask, after a pause. 'She's lovely.'

'Clemmy?' He frowns, shifting around on his stool. 'Clemmy's nice. But I've known her since she was a spotty kid with braces, and our families are so close, we're practically related.' He shrugs. 'I can't start dating my sister, can I? I'd get arrested.'

I laugh. 'Yes, but she's not *really* your sister. And she's not spotty now.'

'No braces, either,' he muses.

'I think she likes you. A lot.'

'Yeah? More fool her!' He slumps lower over the bench and stares moodily out of the window.

'Here. Have a brownie,' I say, to put a smile on his face.

'Thanks.' He wolfs down the largest one on the plate I'm holding out. 'Mm. Nice one, Ruby. Listen, sorry for interrupting your work and for being such a gloomy arse. All this "relaxation" is a shock to the system. I think I need to get back to work.'

'You work far too hard, according to your brother.'

Ryan gives me a broad smile. 'Got to fill the time, otherwise you end up thinking too much. And that's dangerous.' He doesn't smile often – not properly – but he's actually really handsome without that slightly sulky set to his mouth. 'Thanks for the counselling,' he says, spinning off his stool. 'I do actually feel better.'

'Come back for coffee and a packet of digestives any time!'

He winks. 'I may well do that, Dr Poppy.'

I quickly place the rest of the brownies in a tupperware box for their tea later, then grab my coat and bag and head out. I'm meeting Erin in Easingwold to mop up the rest of our Christmas shopping.

As I head out the front door, Clemmy and Tom burst in, chatting and laughing. Tom seems quite transformed from when he first arrived. Gone is the awkward teenage air. He and Clemmy seem to be getting on like a house on fire.

Clemmy beams at me. 'There's nothing like going for a country walk in winter!' she says, shrugging off her coat and struggling to unzip and remove her boots. Tom offers a hand to steady her. 'Thank you, Tom. And thanks for your company.' She beams at him. 'Just remember what I told you! Play it cool.'

Ryan comes out of the living room. 'Hey, everyone. I was just about to saunter around the lake. Fancy it, Clem?'

Clemmy looks surprised. 'Oh. Thanks, Ry, but Tom and I have just hiked for miles and we're knackered. And I've been fantasising about a mug of hot chocolate for the past half hour.' Her face is flushed from the chilled air outside. She heads off to the kitchen. 'Want one, Tom?'

'Yeah, great,' says Tom with enthusiasm.

He follows her, leaving Ryan standing there, looking slightly bemused.

'Maybe tomorrow, Ry?' calls Clemmy.

'Fine.' Ryan shrugs. 'I guess it's just me, then.'

*

It's later than usual – nearly seven – when Erin and I get back to the cabin to serve dinner. Driving through a busy Easingwold, splashes of vibrant Christmas colour sparkling at every turn, the festive-season traffic was extremely slow-moving. Even getting out of the car park seemed to take forever.

Not that Erin seemed too bothered by the hold-ups. She was still on cloud nine because Mark had bought her a huge and very expensive-looking bunch of flowers the day before. They were waiting for her on the kitchen table, apparently, when I dropped her off at their flat late last night, and there was a note from Mark saying he was sorry he'd been neglecting her lately and that he knew he was so lucky to have her. And once things at work were less hectic, he'd make it up to her, he promised.

'It's just a shame he has to work tomorrow,' she says as we get out of the car. 'But at least it means I can help you without feeling *I'm* neglecting *him*.'

I frown as I lock up. 'But it's Saturday tomorrow. And it's Christmas Eve. Will Mark's office be open?'

She shakes her head. 'No, but Mark always says that's the best time to work – when there's no one there and the phones aren't ringing. He wants to clear all his paperwork before Christmas.'

I glance at her uneasily. Of course it's lovely that he bought Erin flowers. Although, thinking about it, a bouquet and a box of chocolates from Mark seemed to be practically a weekly occurrence until fairly recently. Perhaps he really is snowed under at work. And of course the 'honeymoon period' in a relationship never lasts forever...

All the same, I decide I'll call by Mark's office in the morning. Just to wish him happy Christmas because I probably won't see him again until after the Big Day. I'm taking Mum out shopping so I'll fit them

242

both in before I arrive at the cabin to prepare the special Italian dinner Bob has requested for Christmas Eve.

My heart beats faster at the thought. I spent a long time last night, going over the menu and checking I have everything I need to cook a dinner that will impress Bob so much, he'll absolutely *have* to use my services in the future! A tingle of excitement runs through me. I can't afford to waste this golden opportunity. Tomorrow night's dinner has to be absolutely perfect in every detail.

I keep thinking how amazing it is that one wrong number led to this – the perfect opportunity to win an important client and forge the career in catering I've longed for. If Jed hadn't mis-dialled when he was trying to reach Clemmy, none of this would have happened.

As soon as we enter the cabin, it's clear that a happy Christmas atmosphere is sorely missing. Loud music is coming from upstairs and, at that moment, Gloria – wearing a skin-tight red dress over her ample curves, and matching jewelled ballet pumps – hurries into the hallway and yells, 'I've told you to turn that down, madam!'

When the volume remains unchanged, Gloria looks at us in despair. 'She's just doing this to rock the boat. She's trying to split Bob and me up, and the awful thing is, I think she's succeeding.' Tears wobble in her eyes then splash down her cheeks, taking half her mascara with them.

She looks so forlorn and vulnerable, I want to grab her and give her a hug. But next second, she draws herself up to her full height of five foot nothing and roars, 'Right, young lady!' She charges up the stairs, meaning business, her generous, scarlet-clad rear end shifting swiftly from side to side.

The living-room door is open. Clemmy is curled up reading a magazine, and Ryan, Jed and Tom are watching some sport on TV. Bob is nowhere to be seen.

Erin and I grimace at each other and hurry into the kitchen.

Bob must have been in his room because he appears when dinner is served and makes a valiant effort to talk to a sulky Ruby, asking her what music she likes – as if he hasn't spent half the afternoon having his eardrums burst by Justin Bieber.

Gloria chats away nervously in the face of Ruby's monosyllabic replies, but the atmosphere around the table is subdued, to say the least. Ryan looks sunk in gloom again, and even Jed looks preoccupied. Only Clemmy and Tom seem to be in the Christmas mood, vying with each other to remember the most pointless gift they've ever received.

'Bloody hell,' says Erin, back in the kitchen. 'Talk about a typical family Christmas! I felt like slapping

Ruby for being so rude to Bob. But then I suppose she's missing her dad.' She pauses then says sadly, 'I keep thinking back to last Christmas. It was so lovely.'

'Your very first with Mark,' I murmur. 'I remember. He gave you those gorgeous diamond earrings hidden in a toiletries gift box.'

'Ah, well.' She sighs wistfully. 'This year is going to be *even better*!'

We smile at each other and I really hope for her sake that it is.

It's a relief when dinner is over and we can get cleared up. It's been a sombre evening and I'm only hoping there's more of a Christmassy atmosphere around the table when we serve up the special Italian meal tomorrow night.

In the car, the temperature gauge is at two degrees below zero, and I realise I've left my gloves in the kitchen. Leaving the engine idling, I blast the heater for Erin. 'Back in a sec.'

I hurry into the kitchen but my gloves aren't there, so, hearing no sound from the living room and thinking everyone must have escaped to their rooms, I pop my head around the door. To my surprise, Jed is there, sitting forward on an armchair angled towards the log fire, elbows resting on his thighs, staring into the depths of the dying embers. He looks up, startled from his reverie.

'Sorry to disturb you. I've lost my gloves. But I'll look for them tomorrow.'

I start backing out, but he says, 'No, come in. We'll find them.'

Chapter 20

It doesn't take long. They're on top of the piano. I must have left them there when I arrived back this afternoon.

I stroke the glossy lid of the piano. 'Gorgeous instrument. Shame no one plays it.'

'Ryan plays.' Jed lifts the lid and tinkles a few keys with his long fingers.

'He does? I haven't heard him.'

'He got up to Grade Seven as a kid. His piano teacher had high hopes for him, and so did Bob's wife, our Auntie May, who lectured at a college for the performing arts.' Jed shrugs. 'He doesn't play any more.'

'But what a shame. Why not?'

Jed pauses, his jaw tightening. 'He gave up playing after he heard about his real dad. He gave up a lot of things then.' He glances at me. 'Ry told me you had a chat about it. I think you made a difference. He was talking last night about getting back in touch.'

'Oh, that would be brilliant!' My face falls. 'If his dad would welcome Ryan, that is.'

Jed frowns. 'Yeah, it's a risk. I suppose Ryan's afraid of rejection and I can't really blame him. Especially since the guy has a family in France.' He sighs. 'I wish Ry would sort his head out, though. It's like he pours every last scrap of energy into his work. He never seems to stop. He hates London and he's permanently knackered. And he's had a string of relationships – if you could call them that – with vacuous blondes that he seems to choose precisely because he's not likely to fall in love with them.'

Our eyes collide and hold when he says this and the air is suddenly charged. My heart jumps into my throat.

'Yes, I –' My voice emerges as a squeak. I clear my throat, blushing furiously for some reason, and I'm the first to look away. 'I wondered that myself. He told me he picks the wrong women. It's so sad.'

The fire spits loudly and Jed moves away from the piano. 'He and Clemmy had a thing at one time, when they were just teenagers,' he says, mesmerised by the embers again.

'They'd be great together.'

'I don't know. Clemmy might be kind and generous, and very pretty, but she hasn't got blonde hair and legs up to her armpits. When I invited Clemmy, I did hope something might happen between them. But ...' He turns and shrugs helplessly.

248

I go over and stand beside him and we both stare into the fire's glowing depths. Jed glances sideways and catches my eye, and a happy, tingly feeling trickles through me as we stand there in silence, only inches separating us. The fire is such a wonderful focal point, even now, when the embers are only partially glowing. The scent of the ferns and the holly berries, and the winking white lights along the mantelpiece, add up to the perfect Christmas scene. All I need now is the man I love.

Tears prick my eyes. What is it about Christmas that makes people so emotional?

'Did you know you have flour in your hair?' Jed says softly. 'Here, let me ...'

I turn towards him and his fingers brush my face instead. His hand freezes there and the pert comment on my lips fades away, forgotten. His eyes are locked onto mine, burning with intensity and echoing my own uncertainty right back to me. His hand slides down my cheek and rests near my mouth and, instinctively, I turn my head ever so slightly, closing my eyes and placing my lips against the rough skin of his palm. For a moment, my head whirls with a mix of wonder and panic at the sensations coursing through me.

Then I feel Jed's hands around my waist, pulling me in to him and crushing his mouth down on mine.

Back in the car, minutes later, my head is spinning crazily.

Did Jed break away first? Or was it me? I need to believe it was me, because I'm going to have a hard enough time living with the guilt as it is, without having to face the fact that I didn't want Jed to stop kissing me!

But the problem is, I don't really know. It all happened so quickly. I just keep recalling Jed's ragged breathing and intense expression as we locked eyes a second after we broke apart. It should never have happened. We both knew that. I could see it in Jed's shocked expression. It was as if he couldn't believe he'd allowed himself to be drawn in again and was already regretting it...

The thought of Harrison over in Spain, blissfully unaware of everything going on here, is enough to make me want to bury my hot face in my hands and weep. But I can't because Erin is sitting beside me, lolling sleepily against the headrest in the greenhouse-warmth of the fan heater. So I reverse out of the car park area and bump the car onto the snowy, potholed road. In the dark, the icy surface seems even more treacherous but eventually we make it back to the smooth main road, which has been gritted for tonight's sub-zero temperatures. I'm driving as if in a dream, which makes me glad there are so few cars on the road. Questions keep circling round and round in my head.

I kissed Jed! How could I do that to Harrison? I'm supposed to be meeting him on New Year's Eve for a grand reunion.

How the hell am I going to face him?

*

Later, back home, I'm too restless to even think about sleep.

I need to speak to Harrison. I just need to hear his voice because, seriously, I am perilously close to going online and looking at flights to Spain. Leaving in the next few hours! But again his phone is obviously either switched off or out of charge.

I try to watch some late-night TV but I can't concentrate. I just keep thinking about how devastated Harrison would be if he knew I'd kissed Jed. The fact that he doesn't even know that Jed is my client makes the guilt even worse. So many layers of deceit! Perhaps I should phone Jed tomorrow and say I can't work for him any more. But what would that achieve? I'd still be guilty of kissing him. And I'd have wasted a huge opportunity to get my business off the ground.

After much soul-searching, I finally decide that the best thing to do is to look upon the kiss as just a blip.

Part of me wants to throw off the terrible guilt by coming clean with Harrison. But while that might make *me* feel better, getting it off my chest, I know Harrison would be really hurt. I need, however, to make damn sure I never get into any situations where I'm alone with Jed. Not that anything like that would happen again. I'm fairly certain about that. It was just a weird moment, never to be repeated.

It's well after midnight before I head for bed, but sleep is still elusive. I lie there, images from the day flying around my mind, unable to switch the endless film show off.

For some reason, I keep coming back to the conversation I had with Ryan in the kitchen, when he told me about his real dad being a pilot. Ryan's sadness is painfully clear. And the very fact that he, too, is training to be a pilot is just so poignant. If he can't have his dad in his life, he wants to emulate him and experience the things that really mean something to the man.

My eyes well with tears. I hope Ryan has the courage to get in touch with his real dad and give himself the chance of forming a loving father-son relationship.

And then it hits me.

The tears are for Ryan. But they're also for me...

I lie there, staring into the darkness. My real dad is out there somewhere. And my feelings towards him are so mixed up. I've tried so hard to forget him. It's obvious he doesn't want me in his life because he's made no attempt to stay in touch with me. I came to the conclusion a long time ago that I must have disappointed him. Clearly, I wasn't the sort of daughter he'd hoped for, so he'd allowed the fragile connection between us to fade away into nothing. I've spent years telling myself I don't care. If he doesn't want me in his life, that's his loss, not mine. But now I'm realising, with startling clarity, that far from deleting Alessandro from my life, I've actually done the very opposite. I'm fascinated by the country of his birth and drawn like a magnet to the culture and the food of Italy. Florence and Venice have long been at the very top of my 'must visit' list. And, of course, I want to be a cook, specialising in Italian food. Just like Alessandro is a chef in Italy!

So almost without realising it, I've spent years doing exactly the same as Ryan – keeping the connection with my dad alive, without being fully aware that's what I'm doing. Has this flair for cooking really been passed down to me? Or is it just that, like Ryan wanting to be a pilot, I've always longed to have my real dad in my life whichever way I can?

My heart beating faster, I scramble out of bed and grab my childhood box of secrets from the back of the wardrobe. Settling myself back against the pillows, I open the box and pluck out the maroon exercise book containing the diary I wrote that long ago Christmas when I was twelve and life seemed so full of joyful possibilities. Flicking through the pages, one section in particular jumps out at me:

We swam in the lake today and it was freezing but so much fun. Mum refused to put on the wet suit. She just stood there on the shore, watching sternly with her arms folded, presumably worried he might be about to drown me! She said Al was an old friend from university, so I don't know why she would think that! I don't know why she didn't just stay in the B&B lounge. She could have watched us from the window. It's sad because she hasn't joined in with anything at all, however much we've begged her. I really don't know why. Martin would have swum today if he'd been here, but he's had to work in London all of Xmas.

This has been the coolest Xmas of my life and I never want it to end!

There's a painful lump in my throat. It's an innocent childhood account of one perfect Christmas. But what makes me emotional is knowing that as she wrote it, that child – the much younger me – had no notion of the heartache that was to follow.

I place the diary back in the box, reflecting that there's one major difference between Ryan and me. His biological dad told him he was welcome to visit him in France. But Alessandro never really cared.

Chapter 21

Saturday 24 December

<u>Afternoon tea</u>
Italian chocolate panettone

<u>Dinner menu</u>
Caprese salad
(mozzarella, tomatoes and basil)
***

Italian meatballs in a rich, herby tomato sauce, served
with spaghetti
***

Panna cotta with berry sauce

As soon as I wake up, the memory of kissing Jed last night by the log fire flies into my head.

Groaning, I bury my face in the pillow. 'Guilty' just doesn't cover it. I really don't know what came over me but I desperately need to talk to Harrison. Although we've sent each other texts, I haven't spoken to him properly since he got to Spain. I need to hear his voice. Being here alone is clearly getting to me.

But it's Saturday. Christmas Eve. And I have a special dinner to prepare for tonight. Plus, I'm running really late because I didn't get to sleep last night until after three. I take a quick shower, put on a little make-up and flee the house with the groceries for the day in a cardboard box. I still have to pick up meat and cheese but I can do that at lunchtime. It's only when I'm in the car that I look at my phone and realise Harrison sent me a text last night. I quickly read it, feeling terrible that I've only just noticed it.

Watched marathon of British soaps last night, dubbed in Spanish with subtitles. Mother wants a party. I want to come home. Wish you were here xx

The last four words bring a lump to my throat. I wish I were there, too. Things would be a whole lot simpler if we'd gone to Spain together. Poor Harrison hates parties and drinking and soaps! Bless him, he sounds like he's having an awful time, doing all this stuff to please his mother. Whereas I'm having this big adventure, cooking for all these lovely people – *and kissing Jed*.

Oh, God!

A flush of shame creeps over my entire body.
Quickly, I text him back:

*Lots to tell you. I'm cooking for a party of seven over
Christmas! Dying to tell you all about it. Could you
call me tonight? Love you xxx*

*

The atmosphere in the Log Fire Cabin as I make my
special Italian chocolate panettone is very far from
festive. I'm trying to remain upbeat, but lack of sleep
and an emotional hangover the size of Australia is
undermining my good intentions. Regret with a capital
'R' is adding to my brain fog, colouring my day a dull
sort of grey. I shouldn't have succumbed to reading the
diary last night because doing so has released all sorts
of repressed emotions that are still flying around inside,
making me feel slightly nauseous. And I should *definitely*
not have kissed Jed!

The house guests seem equally morose and unsettled.

Ruby is in a huff because Gloria has gone out for a
walk with Bob, taking her phone with her. (She's been
letting Ruby use it from time to time.) So Ruby is
roaming around at a loose end, which means she keeps
coming into the kitchen to bend my ear about how
rotten her life is. My suggestion that we make the flap-

jack her dad used to bake is met with a dejected sigh, so I abandon the idea.

When I arrived, I glimpsed Ryan in the living room, flicking through a men's magazine, back hunched against Clemmy and Tom who were over by the window, heads together, being all chummy as usual. I'm starting to think Clemmy might be trying to make Ryan jealous, showering the lovely Tom with lots of attention. Still, at least she seems to be cheering Tom up, bringing him out of his shell and helping to banish his shyness. If nothing else, it's good practice for him getting up the courage to talk to the girl he fancies.

Bob has just gone off on a lone hike, taking his binoculars in a rucksack and a packed lunch I made up for him, consisting of ham-salad rolls and left-over chocolate brownies. I have an awful feeling it's just an excuse to escape the house, and who could blame him?

The one person who I desperately wish *was* out of the building is currently occupying the sofa in the living room, long legs stretched out and tripping everyone up, reading the newspapers and drinking sugarless coffee, which I happen to know he detests.

He was there, making coffee, when I arrived twenty minutes earlier, and my heart missed a beat at the sight of his tumbled mane of chestnut hair and solid physique in washed-out jeans and sweatshirt. I could tell by his sheepish expression that he'd been hoping to get it made before I arrived. We muttered a good morning with an awkward flick of the eyes and stepped around each other carefully as if there was an unexploded bomb buried under the kitchen floor. Then Jed left abruptly with his mug of coffee, forgetting to stir in the two teaspoons of sugar I know he likes. So he's out there, drinking revolting coffee, because he feels too embarrassed to face me after last night's clinch.

It's all so depressing.

Added to which, I feel a weird sort of responsibility for making Christmas at the Log Fire Cabin a success for everyone. I know it's silly because, of course, I'm simply the hired chef, and the fact that things aren't going brilliantly is absolutely nothing to do with my food. But for Bob to be inspired to hire me to cook for him once this festive job is over, I kind of feel it's important he has a good time.

Right on cue, Ruby yells, 'No, Mum. I'm *not* going to play "Jingle Bells" on the piano.' Footsteps thump along the hallway and disappear upstairs.

I grimace to myself. Poor Bob probably wishes he'd never invited Gloria and the obstreperous Ruby to this ill-fated festive gathering. Especially since he could have been sunning himself in blissful peace and solitude at his villa in Barbados instead.

Thankfully, the panettone cheers everyone up. The buttery aroma from the oven starts drifting through the house, working its magic, and Ryan appears in the kitchen saying the general consensus is that it should be eaten immediately, so that it's still warm and oozing chocolate, which I agree is a mighty fine idea. I'm just disappointed Bob isn't here to enjoy it.

It's amazing, the soothing effect delicious food can have. Even Ruby smiles at the huge tray I carry through, although she turns up her nose at coffee and asks – very politely – if I could please make her a hot chocolate instead. I manage to serve a slice of panettone to Jed without once looking him in the eye, and he mutters a gruff compliment, I suspect also without glancing my way. It's all so unbearably awkward between us now. However hard I try, I can't stop my mind looping back to that kiss, and thinking how devastated Harrison would be if he knew what I'd done.

I escape the cabin after that, glad to feel the fresh air of freedom against my cheeks. I've said I'll take Mum shopping this lunchtime, and I'd also planned to pop into Mark's place of work to wish him 'Merry Christmas' as a cover for spying on him. But I've got all sorts of disjointed thoughts tumbling around in my tired brain – Jed avoiding me, guilt over Harrison, Alessandro, the diary – and all I really want to do now is drive home, crawl into bed and pull the covers over my head.

Life is too confusing and I crave oblivion.

When I arrive at Mum's, she seems even more brittle

than usual, so I have to tread carefully. She gets a little freaked out having to leave her house and come to me for Christmas, although once she's settled in, she's usually fine.

The trouble is, ever since reading the diary last night, I've been plagued with questions about Alessandro. Usually, I try not to think about him. But the diary has opened the floodgates, and suddenly, I need to know more. Driving into Easingwold, I finally break the silence. 'What's he like? My real dad, I mean?'

There's a stunned pause. Then Mum gives a little sigh. 'I don't know, Poppy.'

'What do you mean? Of course you know,' I say gently.

When she turns to look at me, her eyes are shiny. 'I haven't seen Al for nearly twenty years.' She swallows hard. 'How would I know what he's like now?'

'But what was he like back then? When you met him in Italy for the first time? I bet it was really romantic.' My heart is racing, knowing I'm straying into forbidden territory. There's an electric silence and I realise I'm holding my breath.

'Don't do this, Poppy,' she whispers at last, dashing a tear from her eye. She turns angrily away from me and stares out of the passenger window.

'But why?' I fight to keep my tone calm and reasonable. 'I just want to know a little bit about my real dad.

That's not too much to ask, is it? Why did he wait twelve years before coming to see me? If I had a baby, I could *never* stay away that long. Even out of simple curiosity, you'd think he'd have wanted to see what his own child was like. Are you sure we never met before that Christmas visit?'

'No, of course you didn't.' Her voice sounds strangled and strange. 'Just let it be, Poppy.'

I drive in silence for a while, recalling my first meeting with Alessandro when I felt sure I recognised him from somewhere. Mum swears I couldn't possibly have met him before. But then, there's such a lot she prefers to bury her head in the sand over, rather than have to face up to reality.

'Mum, don't you think you should talk to someone about your feelings? A professional who can help?' I venture after a while. 'You've had no life really since you and Martin went your separate ways. Every time I bump into old friends, they ask how you are and if they can see you. Wouldn't you like that? Instead of being stuck at home on your own all the time?'

She sniffs, but says nothing. I take that as an encouraging sign and wade on. 'There's a really lovely counsellor that Erin knows who'd be perfect for—'

'Poppy, I do *not* need psychiatric help!' There's a note of real panic in her voice.

I swallow hard and turn into the packed car park.

'No one's saying you do, Mum. I just think it would be good for you to talk to someone who's trained to help people—'

'I don't *need* that sort of help,' she snaps. 'Look, there's a space over there.'

Sighing, I manoeuvre the car into the tight gap. Mum pulls a hanky out of her handbag and dabs her nose. 'I hope the charity shops aren't too busy,' she says with forced jollity.

I grit my teeth. The conversation is over before it even got started.

After we've done her shopping, I take Mum and her bags back to the car and leave her reading a magazine while I pop into the nearby delicatessen to pick up meat and cheese for tonight's dinner, then head over to see Mark. My fingers are firmly crossed that he'll be there at his office, doing exactly what he told Erin – working at clearing his paperwork backlog. Then I can breathe a sigh of relief and stop fretting about my best friend's romantic life.

As I'm waiting to cross the road, I spot Mark coming out of the office building and relief floods through me. He was telling the truth. I'm about to turn round and go back to the car, when the lights change and the green man flashes – and some instinct or other makes me cross the road and follow him. His trail leads me along side streets to a rather seedy part of town and the entrance to a salvage yard, of all things. At that point, I'm tempted to turn around. He must be buying something for the flat. But instead of going straight into the yard, he hangs around the entrance, looking back along the road as if he's waiting for someone. I lurk in a nearby bus shelter, watching, and then I spot the girl I saw him with last time, with the strawberry-blonde hair. She looks at her watch as if she's late, then she hurries up to Mark at the gate and, laughing, they walk into the yard together.

What on earth's going on?

Luckily, the bus shelter has a seat because they're in the yard a good twenty minutes before they finally emerge. They both check their watches and head across the road to a café that's horribly near my bus stop.

I walk by and glance furtively in the window. They're standing at the counter, heads together, chatting and laughing, and pointing at cakes beneath the glass. I'm desperate to challenge Mark and find out who she is, but I'd need to get him on his own to do that and it doesn't look as if the two of them will be parting company any time soon. They look far too cosy.

I frown. Something tells me Mark definitely won't have told told Erin about this meeting...

*

Finally I drop Mum off, but I don't really want to leave her alone. Ever since I mentioned Alessandro, she's been very subdued and I can tell she's stewing over our conversation. I wish I'd never said anything.

But I can't stay. I need to get back to prepare the special Christmas Eve dinner. I draw up outside her bungalow and, on an impulse, reach over to hug her. She looks surprised. We're not usually that demonstrative. She grasps me tightly for a moment and I breathe in the perfume she's worn for years, feeling suddenly quite teary. Then she gets out without a word.

Back at the lake, I park up and let myself in, just as Ruby storms down the stairs with a determined look on her face. 'Hi,' she says, and bolts straight past me, out of the cabin. I just have time to register this, when I become aware of raised voices coming from the living room. Ryan seems to be involved in some kind of shouting match with Tom. Clemmy appears at the living-room door, her pretty face flushed, and yells, 'It's a game of Monopoly, for heaven's sake! You're acting like kids, the pair of you. And you, Ryan, should know better, since you're the actual grown-up. Or at least, you're *supposed* to be!'

She sees me, gives an agitated shake of her head, and opens her mouth to explain what's happening, just as Gloria appears on the stairs.

'Have you seen Ruby?' She looks anxious.

'Er, she went that way.' I point at the open front door.

At that moment, the noise of a car being revved angrily splits the air.

'What the—' Gloria bustles down the stairs, flapping the front of her blouse to ward off another hot flush. 'I didn't think she'd actually—'

She hares out of the front door, shouting, 'Ruby! Get back here! Ruby!'

Clemmy and I glance at each other in alarm and rush out after her, just in time to see Bob's car lurch backwards up the slight slope from the car park area – driven by a scared-looking, but very determined, Ruby.

Chapter 22

'Oh my God. Stop her!' yells Clemmy, and we all charge towards the car. Ruby has managed to get the vehicle up onto the track but, thankfully, she's turned the steering wheel the wrong way and is moving jerkily in the direction of the circular route around the lake, rather than heading towards the main road.

I manage to draw level with the driver's door and run alongside, banging on the window. Ruby looks at me, wide-eyed, then swings the steering wheel away from me, at which point the car leaves the track and starts bouncing down the frosted grassy bank towards the lake.

We all stare helplessly after her.

'Bugger me,' murmurs Gloria, apparently paralysed with shock. 'She's going in the lake.'

'Oh my God, she's heading for that wooden post!' yells Clemmy. 'Brake, Ruby, brake!'

'Ruby! Middle pedal!' I shriek.

There's a horrible grating sound as Ruby executes an emergency stop by ignoring the clutch and simply slamming her foot hard on the brake. The car slews to a stop – but not before the front-left side slams into the post.

We all hare down the bank and Gloria gets there first, shouting to make sure the handbrake is on tightly and helping a shaking Ruby out of the car.

'Oh my God. Bob's going to kill me, isn't he?' she wails. 'I'm so, so sorry, Mum. I just got so fed up not being able to talk to my friends and I thought I was going to literally explode if I didn't actually *do* something.' She breaks away from Gloria, who's stroking her hair to calm her down. 'I thought driving would be easy but it's really not. Look at the dent in the car. God, I'm so stupid!'

'At least you're in one piece,' murmurs Gloria, who appears to be taking it all surprisingly well, considering Bob's damaged bumper is sure to drive an even bigger wedge between him and Ruby. 'It'll be all right, love.'

Ruby looks distraught. 'No, it won't,' she squeaks. 'I'm such a major pain in the arse, aren't I? I'm surprised you haven't had me fostered out by now.' She buries her face in her mum's shoulder and sobs genuine tears.

Clemmy and I exchange a sideways glance. Now that we've established that Ruby is unscathed, we start to edge indoors, suddenly noticing how cold it is outside.

'Come on, let's get inside,' says Clemmy. 'It's freezing out here.'

We all start walking back to the house, Ruby full of anguish and apologies. 'I'm so sorry, Mum. I just kept thinking how if Dad were here, we'd have gone off on an adventure, and then I got all sad because Dad always said he was going to teach me to drive. But he's not here, so how am I going to learn now?'

'There there, love,' comforts Gloria. 'I'll teach you.'

Ruby looks at her, horrified. 'I'm not that desperate, Mum.'

Back in the kitchen, I get on with tonight's food, aware of the comings and goings beyond the door as the small matter of Bob's damaged car is sorted out by Jed and Ryan. Every now and then, I hear a wail from Ruby, proclaiming how sorry she is. She must be dreading Bob's return.

I need to get on with the meatballs for the main course so they can firm up in the fridge before I cook them. But when I look in the groceries box, the meat isn't in there. So where...? Ah yes, the white plastic bag that also contained the cheese...

My insides go cold.

I can't believe it. I've left the bag somewhere. Frantically, my mind tracks back to when I was standing at the bus stop over the road from the café, watching Mark and his mystery woman go into the café.

I must have left the bag on the bus stop seat!

My head spins with horror. What am I going to do? This is supposed to be a special dinner for Bob and there's no meat. I've ruined everything. They'll have to order a takeaway.

Calm down!

Taking a few deep shaky breaths, I tell myself everything will be okay. My change of plan worked really well at Mrs Morelli's dinner party, so I can do it again. It will have to be a vegetarian main course tonight. Risotto? Maybe. I check in the fridge. There's some Portabello mushrooms, courgettes, red peppers, carrots, garlic and corn on the cob. And some pancetta. My brain whirs into action and in the end I decide to roast the vegetables and use them to make vegetable ravioli, then fry the pancetta so it crumbles with a delicious saltiness over the pasta. And I'll make a light, lemony sauce to go with the dish.

By the time Erin arrives as planned at seven to help with serving up, I'm feeling well in control. She admires the neat ravioli, pasta parcels filled with fragrant vegetables and just the right hint of garlic, and declares that the lemon sauce is to die for.

'It's bloody hot in here, though,' she gasps, shedding her coat.

I touch a radiator only to find it's burning hot, so I turn it to a low setting. With the last of the ravioli simmering in a pan on the hob, I run my wrists under the cold tap to cool myself down. We made it! And even Ruby will probably tuck in heartily because she absolutely adores pasta.

Erin fans herself with a discarded lettuce leaf, and holds back her hair from her neck. 'I need to put it up but I've lost my hair tie.'

'Food hygiene rules.' I waggle my eyebrows at her. 'I have to do it right if I'm to run a successful business.'

'Ooh, listen to you!'

I grin back at her. Actually, I surprised myself. Saying it out loud like that, with such confidence, is a far cry from the timid me of only a few weeks ago. Sadly, it's just wishful thinking, though. There's no way I can give up my waitressing to do this full-time, however much I might want to. It just wouldn't be practical financially.

The food goes out and when Erin brings the plates back, to my relief, they're mostly empty.

'Did they like it?' I'm always anxious for feedback.

'They did.'

'Are you sure?' I stare at her suspiciously. She's avoiding my eye and looks very flushed.

'Yes.' Her tone is defensive.

'Erin? What's going on?'

She turns miserably. 'Bob found what he thought was a worm in his pasta.'

'A worm?' I shriek, staring at her, appalled. 'Don't be ridiculous!'

'Except it wasn't a worm.'

Erin holds out Bob's plate and I peer closer. Carefully pushed to the side is a brownish circular object, coated in pasta sauce.

My mouth opens in horror. 'Your hair tie?'

She winces. 'I knew I'd lost it. But how the hell it got in the ravioli ...'

'Oh, Erin!' I don't know whether to laugh or cry. The person I was keen to impress the most *has* to be the one to find the stray bloody bobble in his food! 'What did he say? Was he disgusted?'

'Well, probably. Wouldn't you be if you found someone else's hairy—'

'Yes, yes. For God's sake stop rubbing it in.'

'Actually, he thought it was funny. And he'd pretty much finished by the time he found it. He asked if there was a prize for the person who found the worm in their pasta.'

I breathe a sigh of relief. Thank God for Bob's sense of humour! Although I really ought to go and apologise for—

My mobile starts to ring, making me jump.

'News is getting around,' grins Erin. 'That's another order for your hair-tie pasta speciality.'

I'm still laughing when I pick up.

'*Poppy?*' The voice on the other end is more of a shriek.

'Mum?' I stare in alarm at Erin. 'What's wrong?'

She starts to speak but the noise of a police siren in the background drowns out her words. 'Mum! What's going on?' I yell.

Erin puts down the plate she's drying and comes over, looking worried. My heart is in my mouth.

And then I hear Mum, loud and clear.

'Can you come, Poppy? Now! I'm trapped in the living room. And it's on fire. Can you be quick?' There's a muffled sound, like a stack of boxes tumbling to the floor.

Mum screams.

And the phone goes dead.

*

I dash from the lodge, with Erin shouting to the others what's happened.

Jed, Clemmy and Gloria gather at the front door, watching anxiously as I reverse onto the track then drive like the wind over the dips and bumps, back to the main road. The car is practically airborne at one stage, we're speeding along so fast. Erin insists on coming with me, which I'm really glad about. My heart is in my mouth, wondering what I'm going to find when

I get to Mum's. It was always my worst nightmare, that Mum's hoarding would lead her into danger, and now...

As we drive into her cul-de-sac, the first thing I spot is an ambulance, and my heart goes into overdrive. Two fire engines are parked up front and the door is wide open, light pouring out of the house. The piles of boxes and crates that were stacked in the hallway have been tossed into the small front garden and for some reason this panics me more than anything. Mum will be furious at her stuff being treated so casually!

There's no sign of smoke or fire damage from here, but the air is thick with an acrid smell of burning that starts Erin coughing and grows far worse when we get out of the car and dash over to the ambulance. Firemen are visible through the front door, moving about between the living room and the hallway, but I can't see any flames or smoke. Maybe they've put out the blaze already.

To my enormous relief, as we rush for the front door, we see Mum sitting wrapped in a blanket in the back of the ambulance, wearing her Shaun the Sheep slippers and sipping something from a plastic cup. She looks completely forlorn, staring down at her feet as the paramedic – a small, dark-haired woman of about thirty – bends over her. Mum looks up and spots Erin and me. A look of pure relief spreads over her face and my heart twists with love.

274

'Oh, Mum.' I sit beside her and take her free hand, rubbing it to help warm her up. 'Are you okay?'

'She's doing fine,' murmurs the paramedic, crouching down beside her. 'Aren't you, Donna?'

'Yes,' says Mum in a small voice. 'Thanks to you lot.'

Gently, I ask how it happened.

Mum looks sheepish. 'Stupidly, I decided to have a brandy and a cigarette. Not that I really smoke,' she adds, for the benefit of the paramedic. 'I just keep a packet for stressful situations.'

I squeeze her hand, my heart sinking. It's my fault she needed an emergency cigarette. I shouldn't have brought up the subject of Alessandro in the car earlier. She's probably been stewing over it ever since.

Mum gives a shuddery sigh. 'The brandy made me sleepy and I must have nodded off with my cigarette alight because next thing, I was waking up to the smell of burning and a tower of cardboard boxes on fire only inches away from the sofa. They tumbled down when I was speaking to you on the phone and I just managed to move out of the way, otherwise God knows ...' She trails off, silent tears streaking down her face. 'I'm so sorry, Poppy. I'm about as much use to anyone as a chocolate fireguard these days.'

'Hey, come on.' The paramedic takes Mum's cup from her shaking hand and I pull her into a hug, rubbing her back and shushing her. 'It's all right. Don't worry.

The main thing is you're absolutely fine.'

She hiccups. 'I didn't think I'd make it to the front door. But luckily I had my phone with me and the emergency team were here in minutes.'

'They're brilliant, aren't they?'

I smile up at the paramedic, who remarks jovially, 'Aw, shucks! Tell that to my husband when I've woken him up for the umpteenth time frying bacon when I get back after a shift! My name's Alice, by the way.'

I smile at her. 'Thank you *so* much, Alice.' Then I turn to Mum. 'You really had me worried. But you're okay – and it doesn't look as if there's too much damage in there.' I crane my neck to see, hoping I'm not being overly optimistic.

'You won't be able to get back in until it's declared safe,' Alice says, looking over at Mum's house. 'We'll need to have you checked over at the hospital, Donna, and then perhaps you can stay at your daughter's?' She looks enquiringly at me.

'Yup. Sorry, Mum.' I keep my tone relentlessly jolly. 'But you're going to have to put up with me and my spare room tonight.'

*

Much later, when we arrive back from the hospital, I put fresh linen on the bed in the spare room and turn on the heating in there to take the chill off the place. Then I pack Mum off to have a shower, before getting her into bed with a mug of cocoa, some digestive biscuits and a hot-water bottle for good measure. I can tell she's fretting about her house and belongings, although only once does she ask me when she'll be able to go home. I tell her I'll phone the police first thing next day to find out, but that for now, she must just rest up and allow me to spoil her.

Smiling, I brush a smudge of soot from her cheek that she's missed in the shower, thinking how lucky we are that she emerged from the fire completely unscathed. Every time my mind wanders to what could have happened, my blood runs cold.

Clemmy phones, anxious to find out how Mum is and I reassure her that she seems absolutely fine, no harm done, just shaken up. It's lovely to know that everyone at the Log Fire Cabin is thinking of me. I've only known them a few days, but it hits me that I've grown fond of every single one of them. Especially Clemmy. And Jed.

Once I'm sure Mum's nodded off, I retreat to my room and phone Harrison's mobile. I can't believe he hasn't responded to the text I sent him this morning telling him about my new catering job. If he'd sent news like that to me, I'd have phoned him straight back.

His phone goes straight to answerphone. Again. I

throw my phone down, feeling suddenly lonely and tearful. Then I reason that maybe he didn't even get my message. International connections can be a bit dodgy sometimes. So I phone again, and when the automated voice finishes speaking, I say, 'Hi, love, hope everything's fine over there in Spain. Could you ring me when you get this message? Mum had a fire at her place. She's fine, so don't worry, but it would be great to chat. Miss you!'

Of course, there's one thing I definitely *can't* mention, and that's my intimate encounter with Jed Turner. The dreadful guilt has been gnawing away at me all day. I close my eyes in despair. I'll make it up to Harrison somehow. I promise I will.

I drift off to sleep with my mobile under my pillow, just in case he calls.

Chapter 23

Christmas Day dawns.

I wake at seven-thirty a.m. to a text from Harrison that's just arrived:

> *Merry Christmas, Puss! Feeling sick. Drank too much sangria at Mother's party. Boring night. Average age of guests about seventy-three. Hope your mum is okay and that she's realised hoarding is a bad thing*
> *xx*

I stare at the message, reading it over again.

Why did he send a stupid bloody text instead of phoning me? Couldn't he hear in my voice that I really needed to talk to him? If *he'd* phoned *me* to tell me about a fire, it wouldn't matter how hungover or sick I was feeling, I would call him straight back. And it's a little insensitive, rubbing it in about Mum's hoarding. We all know it's a bad thing, but surely there's a time and a place to point it out?

I'm feeling a little crushed, but I haven't got time to dwell on it. I need to see how Mum is doing after last night's ordeal, so I shrug on my fleecy robe and slippers, and peer into the spare room. Mum is lying on her back, snoring gently, the remains of the cocoa I took her last night congealing in the mug on the bedside table.

I make tea and go back to my room, standing at the window and staring out at the houses opposite. A feeling of loneliness washes over me. There's not a single soul about. Everyone is cosy indoors, unwrapping presents or perhaps still in bed, anticipating a day of fun and excitement. My head is still full of the horror of last night: panicking when I got Mum's call, hearing the fear in her voice; racing over there, my heart in my mouth, desperately afraid of what I would find; the revolting, acrid scent of burning belongings and melting plastic that greeted us. The smell is still in my nostrils. I can even taste it in my tea.

I have a horrible sick feeling inside, knowing how close I came to losing Mum. It's what I've dreaded for so long. A fire – started by one of her occasional ciga-rettes – blocking off the only exit with Mum trapped inside. It chills me to the bone, thinking what could have happened to her. As it is, she's had a shock but, thankfully, she seems unharmed.

My mind wanders to the Log Fire Cabin. Will Ruby

be up early this morning, demanding to open presents, or has she reached the age where she prefers a lie-in? I need to get organised fairly soon if I'm to cook Christmas dinner for them this evening. The turkey I bought is fairly large and will need a good few hours in the oven.

Soon after nine, a policewoman phones and gently broaches the subject of Mum's hoarding. I do what I can to reassure her that I will be helping Mum to gut the house of the clutter. I sound confident and certain – which is not at all how I'm feeling. More than ever now, I know that I need to persuade Mum to accept help for her hoarding. But that's easier said than done. It has to be her decision to see a trained professional. No one can force her. Not even me. Is she even aware of how close she came to total disaster last night?

I take in a cup of tea when I hear her stirring and she gazes at me mournfully, looking as if she's aged a hundred years overnight. 'I'm so sorry, Poppy.'

My heart swells with love and relief that she's okay. I take her hand in mine, smiling through my tears. 'You're okay, Mum, and that's all that matters.'

'I'm not going to smoke ever again. I promise.' Her chin wobbles. 'I'm such a burden to you, love, and I really don't mean to be.'

'Don't be silly. Of course you're not!' I pull her into a hug and she clings tightly to me, making little strangled gasping noises as she tries to hold back sobs. I laugh softly. 'You're a bit of a pain at times, obviously, but I'm used to that and I wouldn't have it any other way. You're my mum and I'll always be here for you. You know that.'

Eventually, she calms down and drinks her tea.

The doorbell rings around ten.

'I bet that's Erin.' I spring off the bed, putting on a cheerful front for Mum's sake. 'She probably wants to make sure you're all right.'

But when I pull the door open, it's Jed.

My treacherous heart does a little leap at the sight of him standing there, his big shoulders filling the doorway, hands thrust deep in his jacket pockets. He looks exhausted.

'Hi, Poppy. Hope you don't mind me calling round but I wanted to make sure you were both okay. What with – um – Harrison not being here to support you.' He gives an awkward half-smile.

A painful lump rises in my throat at his kindness. I suppose I've been too busy up until now to afford the luxury of breaking down. But all of a sudden, to my horror, hot tears are pricking at my eyes.

'Hey, hey, you're okay. Come here.' Suddenly Jed's arms are around me, powerfully strong and comforting. 'Clemmy said your mum was fine when she phoned last night,' he murmurs into my hair. 'Is that true? You weren't just putting on a brave face?'

'No, no. She is. She's okay. Just very tired, that's all.' My face is crushed against his big chest, and in my weakened state, I feel like I'm drawing strength from the solid feel of him. I want to stay there, in his firm embrace, for a long, long time.

Eventually, he moves his hands to my shoulders and tenderly moves me away from him so he can look at me. 'You've had a tough time. Especially with Harrison away in Spain. Is he on his way back now?'

'Sorry?'

He shrugs. 'I thought he'd probably want to be here for you. But I suppose it's not easy to get a flight on Christmas Day.'

'Er, no. It's not,' I croak, avoiding his eye. 'But I'm fine. Honestly. And Harrison has to stay and look after his mother.'

'Right.' He lets go of me and stands back, and I feel cold and desperately alone without his protective arms around me.

Suddenly, it occurs to me that he probably wants to know about Christmas dinner tonight. How stupid of me not to have phoned the cabin to let them know! Not very professional at all.

'I'll be over about four to start cooking. If that's all right?' I tell him hastily.

He frowns. 'You'll do no such thing. You'll stay here

283

with your mum today and make sure she's okay. You don't have to worry about us.'

'Oh, but I can't!' I'm taken aback by his generosity. 'I don't mind coming over and cooking. Really I don't. Mum will be fine for a little while on her own.'

He shakes his head firmly. 'It's all in hand. I make a mean fried chicken and chips. The chicken portions are defrosting as we speak.'

'Chicken and chips? For Christmas dinner?' This brings a wary smile to my face.

He grins. 'Yeah, why the hell not? Nandos, eat your heart out.'

'Well, at least Ruby will be pleased.'

'Good point. It pays to keep the teenage contingency happy.'

'The thing is, I've got the turkey and the pudding and everything in the kitchen. Do you want to take it?'

He nods. 'Okay. It would be a shame to waste it.'

I lead him through to the kitchen and he hefts both large boxes of food out to the car.

'Why don't you and your mum come over and join us later?' He closes the boot and turns. 'I promise it will be edible.' A smile lingers on his mouth as he gazes at me, and I'm suddenly covered in blushes at his lovely offer.

'That sounds great, but—' I glance quickly back at the house. 'Mum – um – she doesn't like venturing far from home. I think she'd prefer that it was just her and me.' I shrug apologetically.

'Hello?'

We swing round. Mum is standing at the door in my dressing gown, smiling over.

'Mum! Get back inside. It's freezing out here.'

Jed strides over. 'You must be Poppy's mum. Hello. I'm the very fortunate man your daughter agreed to cook for over the festive period.' They shake hands. 'And I'm delighted to see with my own eyes that you're okay.'

'Thank you.' Mum smiles up at him in surprise. 'It's so kind of you to go out of your way for us. Isn't it, Poppy?'

I smile at Jed, a lovely warm feeling creeping over me, despite the sub-zero temperatures. 'It is.'

Unless my eyes deceive me, Mum is actually blushing slightly under Jed's warm gaze. I can be quite cynical about charming men. Martin was good at turning on the charm – usually when he wanted something. But in this case, I feel sure it's all perfectly genuine. Jed is just a lovely, caring man.

'No need to rush back,' he assures me as he leaves. 'We won't starve.' Then he smiles that lovely lazy smile again. 'But that's not to say it won't be brilliant to see you when you come back.'

From nowhere, a little arrow of desire shoots through me.

Jed slides into the driver's seat of his car and I stand there, rooted to the spot, watching him drive off. Then I think of Harrison, far away in another country, watching dubbed soaps, drinking sangria to stave off boredom, and flamenco dancing in uncomfortable pants to please his mum. I turn quickly and head back into the house.

It's probably a good thing Harrison is away, really. Having Mum here wouldn't be quite so easy if it wasn't just her and me. I'd like to keep her here as long as I can – and perhaps if she's away from her familiar environment, you never know, she might start opening up a bit about how she feels about everything. Then maybe I can persuade her to accept help.

'That Jed is nice,' she remarks when I go in. 'He reminds me of Al.'

'Does he?' I remember Alessandro as medium height and fairly slim, whereas Jed is powerfully built and very tall.

Mum stares away into the distance, a wistful look on her face. 'I meant his kindness.' She turns to me with a strange half-smile. It feels as if she's apologising for something. For refusing point-blank to discuss Alessandro yesterday, maybe?

We settle in for a fairly normal Christmas Day, cooking the turkey and trimmings together. Erin calls round in the afternoon for a jolly half-hour, keeping us amused with her tales of dried-out turkey and Mark drinking far too much champagne. Mum's spirits seem to be reviving as the day goes on, especially after she's indulged in a small sherry or three.

When Erin leaves, I go with her to the door and she drops the jolly front.

'Mark's crashed out in front of the TV, snoring his head off. So much for a romantic Christmas, just the two of us.'

I grin. 'Sounds like a pretty normal Christmas Day, really.' But she doesn't smile back.

'There's something not quite right.' Her eyes are sad.

'How?'

'I don't know, it's like there's something on his mind. I've tried to gently quiz him but he's not giving anything away.'

I shrug. 'Perhaps he's having problems at work and he doesn't want to bore you.'

Just as she's leaving, a gleaming white Mini Clubman pulls up smartly outside the house. Puzzled, I peer in and so does Erin. Who could be calling on us uninvited on Christmas Day? I don't recognise the car.

'Visitors?' murmurs Erin, as a woman gets out of the driver's seat. Dressed in a fake fur and heels, she slams the door, locks the car and walks determinedly up to our gate.

My heart sinks into my fluffy slippers. 'Oh, shit!' I

mutter to Erin. 'It's Mimi Blenkinsop. Come to check I'm really dying of the flu, no doubt.'

Erin frowns in sympathy. 'Do you want me to stay?'

'No, don't worry. I'll cope.' I smile to show I'm fine, although inside I'm a bag of nerves, and Erin walks away.

'So, fighting fit, I see?' Mimi launches in. 'I guess you'll be able to return to work tonight, then.'

'Er, no. I won't, I'm afraid. Mum's still recovering so I really can't leave her.'

Mimi's expression remains as hard as granite. Maybe she hasn't been told what happened. I try again. 'Mum had a fire at her house. I did phone this morning to explain and Maxine said she'd pass on the message? It was all such a shock when it happened, I've barely managed to get my head together. Mum could have died in the fire.'

Far from understanding, Mimi actually laughs. 'Yes. We did get your message. But domestic problems are nothing to do with the hotel. We have a business to run. And if I can't rely on my restaurant staff to show up when they're supposed to be on duty, then we have every right to sack you.'

I stare at her incredulously. I've done the right thing, phoning to explain my absence, but it's apparently not good enough.

'I've spoken to the Nutters about this,' she sweeps

on, her nostrils flaring angrily, 'and they're in full agreement. I'm to issue you with a written warning, Miss Ainsworth. And if you're not back at work within two days, then don't bother coming back at all.'

A fury is building up inside me.

I can tolerate Mimi Blenkinsop's nastiness because I don't know her and she certainly doesn't know me. But the Nutters have known me for fourteen years and I've worked my arse off for them. Yet she's saying they know about my family crisis but are completely unsympathetic! How many times have I gone the extra mile for them, for the sake of their stupid hotel? I really wish I'd never bothered!

'You may be a good worker, Miss Ainsworth, but you are not indispensible. Mr and Mrs Nutter are *furious* at you for letting them down like this!'

'I know I'm not indispensible,' I tell her coldly. 'No one is.'

'So, can I tell them you'll be back at work tonight?'

My whole body is trembling, but I swallow hard and say, 'No, you can't. I need to look after Mum. She's infinitely more important than my poxy job.'

That's silenced her!

'In fact, you can tell the Nutters they can stick their job, because quite frankly, I've had enough. I've given my all to that place and this is the thanks I get. Well, no more!' My heart is racing so fast, I think I might be about to keel over. As confrontations go, this is a corker. But I'm determined not to give in meekly the way I usually do.

I draw in a long breath. 'I'm resigning!'

She blinks several times, very quickly. 'Really?'

I smile cheerfully. 'Yes, really.'

Mimi eyes me nastily. 'You'll regret this when you're jobless.'

'Well, I won't be. As a matter of fact, I'm setting up my own catering company, specialising in Italian food. So you can bugger off, Mimi, because I have no intention of setting foot in that hotel ever again. And can I just say this feels incredibly liberating? God, I should have done it years ago!'

Mimi, red in the face with shocked indignation, stalks back down the path to her car.

'Oh, Mimi?'

She turns, probably expecting me to start grovelling and changing my mind about resigning.

'I do great dinner parties. Would you like a business card?'

*

When I get back inside, I'm trembling so much that Mum's really worried about me. She makes me sit down and put my head between my knees, then brings me a cup of hot, disgustingly sweet tea 'for shock' and stands there waiting while I drink it.

I tell her about Mimi and the Nutters, and she smiles admiringly. 'Well done, love. This catering business of yours is going to be brilliant. I always knew you could do marvellous things if you tried.' She winks. 'You *are* your mother's daughter, after all.'

We smile rather wistfully at each other, and I wonder if she's thinking what I'm thinking. *I'm also my father's daughter, and he's a chef. So maybe I was born to it!*

I phone Harrison again, but when I get through, I can barely hear him. It sounds like last night's party is still going on in the background.

'The Flamenco crowd,' Harrison groans. 'It's a nightmare, Poppy. They're all several sheets to the wind and practically dancing on the tables.'

I giggle. 'Can't hear any castanets! What are you drinking?'

'Lime and soda.'

'Oh, poor you.'

'I've also realised that Mother didn't much like my father.'

'*What?*'

'Yeah. This is basically a party to celebrate her new status as free and single. Can you believe it?'

'Wow.'

Actually, I really *can't* believe it. I met Harrison's

mother once and she was strait-laced and rather stern, with a fondness for twin sets and brogues. I can't imagine Mrs Ford kicking up her heels in wild abandon at a flamenco class and toasting the passing of *Mr* Ford. I suppose you just never know what's really going on in people's relationships.

'Oops, better go,' says Harrison. 'The turkey won't fit in the oven and Mother's trying to butcher it with a hacksaw.'

'Harrison?'

'Yes, Puss?'

'I resigned from the restaurant today and I've decided to go full steam ahead with the catering business.'

There's a brief silence. Then he says, 'Gosh. Well. That's a bit of a bombshell.'

'I know.'

'We'll have lots to talk about when I get back, then.'

'I can't wait. I've been really missing you.'

'You, too, Puss. You, too. Right, better go.'

He rings off, leaving me feeling decidedly out of sorts. Not being able to see his expression, I've absolutely no idea how he really feels about me resigning. I can't wait for him to come home so things can get back to normal.

For some reason, I think of Jed Turner's strong arms around me, when he was comforting me earlier, and my insides do a funny loop the loop. But I give my head a little shake. I'm just missing Harrison, that's all.

Once he's back, I'm never going to let him go to Spain alone again. I can't wait to let him know that, after our 'cooling-off period', my answer is the same as it was when he first asked me to marry him.

A big fat *yes*!

Chapter 24

I feel closer to Mum than I've felt in years.

However much she tried to mediate between Martin and me, we could never be as naturally affectionate with each other as we might have wanted to be. Martin resented our closeness so we tended to play it down when he was around.

This week, it's felt really easy to be around each other. I think the fire is making Mum think about her situation, and I'm even hoping she might be amenable to some clearing out, although I certainly won't be rushing her. It has to be her decision.

In the kitchen this morning over breakfast, she quite naturally starts talking about Alessandro. It's as if mentioning him yesterday made her realise that the world won't actually come crashing down on her head if she talks about him.

'I loved Al so much, you know, but I thought I was too young for commitment. I was in Naples for my gap year with my friend, Joan, serving coffees in a little side-street café, and it was just a holiday romance. Or so I thought.'

'You must have been really sad having to leave Italy – and him.'

She nods. 'It was really hard. But I was so single-minded then. I'd made up my mind to study medicine and I had my university place, so the only solution was to bring you up alone.' She sighs heavily. 'Little did I know that I'd never feel the same way about any man ever again in my life.'

I pause in buttering my toast. 'Not even Martin?'

'Not even Martin. I loved him at the start but, of course, he was on his best behaviour then. We all are at the beginning of relationships. He even seemed to take to you, and I was so delighted because that was always my goal: to find you a lovely dad.' Her smile is wistful. 'It was only later, I realised what a damaged man he was.'

'He didn't have the greatest of starts in life.' Martin's parents had died in a car crash when he was eight and he grew up in children's homes.

'I know. I thought I could change him. Mellow him,' she says. 'He did try. But in the end, he didn't try hard enough.' She reaches for my hand. 'It broke my heart, knowing he couldn't love you the way I wanted him to.'

'You could have left him when you realised it was never going to work.'

'Yes, but I had you to consider. I kept thinking that two parents were better than one. That's why I married him, really. I felt deeply guilty that I'd deprived you of a proper dad. I kept telling myself things would get better eventually, and the years just rolled by.'

I can't believe she's talking about it at last. It's as if being away from her crowded bungalow – essentially her prison, where she's been stuck for years – she can finally breathe new air and see her situation from a different angle.

There's one thing I really need to know, though.

'I wish ... I wish you'd kept in touch with Alessandro. Al. Why didn't you, Mum? You've just admitted he was the love of your life.' I stare at her sadly, wanting desperately to understand.

But that's clearly a question too far, and I can almost see her retreating into her shell.

'I think I'd like to go over to the house later,' she says, and my heart sinks. I really don't want her to go back there just yet..

'Actually, Erin and Mark have offered to go over there with me,' I tell her. 'Just to check out the extent of the damage. So maybe you could just take it easy today. Watch that old black-and-white Bette Davis movie you were talking about?'

Mum smiles. '*The Old Maid*. Yes. She lost the love of her life, too.'

A car draws up outside. It's Jed. Instantly, my heart starts beating faster.

I open the door to him, feeling oddly shy after blubbing all over him the day before. 'Hi! How was the turkey?'

'Very good, actually. Clem and Ryan took over the kitchen and wouldn't let anyone else in. They did a great job.'

'So Ryan isn't missing Jessica too much, then?'

'Doesn't look like it.' He smiles. 'Listen, do you need any help at your mum's house? That's why I'm here.'

'That's so good of you, thank you.' His offer takes me completely by surprise.

'No problem. Happy to help.'

I nod gratefully. 'I just need to make sure Mum knows how to work my TV system, then I'll get changed and be with you.'

'Don't worry about that. Go get changed and I'll show her.'

I smile knowingly at him. 'I'm sure she'll *love* that.'

Ten minutes later, we set off in his car to Mum's bungalow, a few minutes' drive away and instantly, my stomach starts grinding round like a washing machine. I'm dreading seeing the state of the place. I psych myself up to follow Jed through the front door, trying to breathe through my mouth because the smell of smoke is still so disgustingly strong. The boxes normally piled up near the front door have been forcibly shoved to the sides of the hallway or trampled underfoot by the firemen in their haste to get to the source of the fire in the living room. Even this small space will take ages to clear up.

But what is stressing me out even more is the fact that Jed has now seen the state the house is in. I know Mum will hate that. And I can't help feeling a little bit embarrassed myself.

Jed, to give him huge credit, doesn't do what most people do when they see it for the first time. Generally, jaws drop open and people's eyes grow large and as round as saucers as they mutter something like 'Jeez' under their breath.

'Mum's a bit of a hoarder.' I have to say something by way of explanation, even if it is stating the obvious.

Jed turns and grins. 'She's certainly got some stuff. I suppose we all have our crutches in life.'

I laugh. 'That's one way of putting it.'

We make our way along to the living room. On the way, I pick up a maroon coat that Mum sometimes wears. It's on a pile of other clothes, but when I hold it to my nose, it reeks of smoke. I throw it back on the heap.

'All her clothes are going to stink of smoke. *Everything* will.'

Jed turns. 'White vinegar and baking soda in the wash gets rid of the smell apparently.'

'Really?'

He chuckles. 'Yeah. I'm a mine of useless information like that.'

I smile at him, my eyes welling up. 'Thank you.'

'What for?'

'Just for being here.' I swallow hard and he nudges me gently.

'Hey, any time.'

We're standing in the living room where the fire originated, and I suddenly catch sight of Mum's sofa, where she always sat. It's completely destroyed, along with the standard lamp beside it. It really brings it home to me what a lucky escape she had.

'Mum should see this sofa for herself.' My voice catches. 'It might make her realise just how dangerous her hoarding has become.'

Jed nods, looking around him, assessing the damage. 'So I guess today you just want to rescue a few belongings you think your mum will need over at yours?'

I nod. 'I don't want to start clearing lots of stuff out without her here. She has to want to do it.' I glance up at him. 'It's so great to have your support, what with ...'

He nods slowly, guessing what I was going to say. *What with Harrison not being here.*

We're standing next to each other. I look up at him, and he's staring down at me with an intensity that makes the breath catch in my throat. Our eyes lock, and a shiver runs through me. The small space between us seems super-charged, and when he reaches over and puts his arm casually round me – meaning to give me some support and comfort, I suppose – my entire body responds. Little electric impulses shoot right through me, to parts of my body I'd almost forgotten existed.

Swept away on a tide of emotion, I curl into him, against his body, and he slips his other hand around my waist and holds me firmly against him. My gaze drops from the green depths of his eyes to his beautiful, firm mouth. And then we're kissing, and he's holding me against him even tighter, with a sort of urgent desperation, and I'm tangling my fingers in his hair then slipping my hands under his coat, running my fingers over the hard muscles of his chest as our bodies meld together and stars start exploding in my head.

Then suddenly, he pulls away, leaving us both gasping for breath. He catches my arms as I lurch forward, wondering what's happening.

'Sorry.' He steadies me, then pushes his hands through his hair, staring down at the ground. 'That was my fault.'

'No, it was mine,' I murmur, the quiver in my voice echoing the shaking in my body. I think of Harrison and a feeling of guilt and despair surges through me.

Jed was just being gentlemanly, claiming he made the first move.

It was all down to me.

*

When we leave Mum's house a while later, I've brought a bag of clothes, which I'm going to put through the washing machine to try and get rid of the acrid smell of smoke. Also in the boot is a box that's slightly charred but holds papers and documents that are unscathed by the fire.

As we drive the short distance back to mine, Jed's phone rings on his internal Bluetooth system and the name that comes up is 'Kat'. My heart squeezes painfully. Katerina. Jed's ex. The girl he wanted to marry...

As he talks, I stare out of the passenger window, doing my level best not to appear as though I'm listening in. When I glance at his profile, his expression is neutral. He's not exactly beaming from ear to ear at hearing from her. But who knows what's going on under the surface? They seem to be arranging to meet for a catch-up. Not that I was straining to hear above the radio that's still playing. Not at all...

I stare miserably at my hands, clasped together in my lap. Right now, I feel like a tiny boat on a boiling sea

– tossed high in the air one moment, then hurled down into the depths the next. Sitting so close to Jed but feeling as if there's a football-pitch-sized space between us is torture. I'm acutely aware of his gravelly voice, still talking to Kat, in my ear; strong hands on the steering wheel; long, muscled thighs splayed out, within tempting touching distance.

I give myself a little shake. This is no good at all. I can't possibly have feelings for Jed if I'm going to marry Harrison.

The thought swirls around in my head for a moment. Then a disturbing realisation starts to dawn – before hitting me with the full force of a tree crashing through the roof of a house.

Oh my God. I've got feelings for Jed!

But I can't have. What about Harrison? I'm going to marry Harrison!

I sit there, bolt upright, staring ahead in utter horror. I've fallen hook, line and sinker for the man sitting next to me. A man who happens to be in complete ignorance of the torrent of emotions that's tumbling through me right this minute—

'Are you okay?' When he speaks, it's such a shock, I practically jump into next week.

'Er, yes. Fine, thanks.' *Apart from the fact that my heart is attempting to break out of my chest.* 'It was really great of you to help me face the chaos over there.'

'No problem.' He smiles at me and I melt.

He honestly has no idea how dangerous those smiles are. The scorching effect on my body is enough to heat the water in three hot tubs simultaneously.

We agree that I'll be back cooking dinner for them the following night, and he says he has to be somewhere right now so he needs to dash off. So we transfer the clothes and the box of papers to the boot of my car (I don't fancy the smoky odour permeating the house) and I wave him off.

There's a heaviness in my chest. No prizes for guessing where he has to be in a hurry.

Kat.

Chapter 25

Tuesday 27 December

<u>*Afternoon tea*</u>
Date and walnut cake

<u>*Dinner menu*</u>
Italian meat and cheese antipasti
***

Classic spaghetti carbonara
***

Raspberry semifreddo

I wake, sweating, from a very odd dream.
   I'm sitting in a Jeep next to Indiana Jones and we're bouncing along this forest track desperately searching for some sacred temple or other. I'm panicking a bit because we need to get there before the bad guys catch up with us. But I'm feeling fairly safe with the fearless

Mr Jones at my side. I mean, who wouldn't? The man is rock solid. A legend.

But just as we enter the temple and are about to finally get our hands on the ancient and mysterious Pink Flamingo Diamond that is sure to save the human race from immediate extinction, I'm seized by an ape of a man with huge muscles, wearing nothing more than a loin cloth and a very sexy smile. Indiana Jones charges to my rescue and the two of them roll around on the ground, panting and getting filthy. Then Mimi Blenkinsop, in a black catsuit and mask, appears from nowhere, looking even more evil than usual, and threatens me with death by steak-and-kidney pie if I don't get to my shift at the restaurant on time. Those pies are deceptively solid, which is why I wake up sweating.

I lie there for a second, wondering who would have eventually triumphed. Indiana Jones? Or the ape man? I guess I'll never know.

Then as the dream fades, my memory of the day before – the devastating shock of realising I've fallen hard for Jed Turner – swoops into my mind, obliterating all other thoughts.

Groaning, I faceplant the pillow in despair, bumping my nose and making my eyes water. I don't often swear. But what the *fuck* am I supposed to do now? Harrison will be back in precisely four days' time and he'll be asking me to marry him again. He'll want to know if, after careful consideration during our cooling-off period, my answer is still 'yes'?

What will I say to him?

A moment later, I sit up straight and rub my nose.

I'll say 'yes', of course. Harrison and I were meant to be together. I've always had a sense of destiny about our meeting, and I'm not going to let what's probably just a silly crush on Jed Turner spoil my future with Harrison.

All the same, when someone raps on the bedroom door, panic flutters in my throat for a second. *What if it's Harrison himself, back home early and wanting an answer now?*

But of course it's not. It's Mum and she looks anxious.

'What's wrong?' I ask, sitting up.

'I've been thinking, love. I need to get all that stuff out of the bungalow. Now. I've hardly slept all night thinking about it. Do you think we could hire a skip and do it today?'

I stare at her, speechless. There are bright spots in her cheeks and her eyes are darting about as if she can't settle. She looks exhausted – as if she really has been up all night thinking about her house.

I hold out my hand and pat the side of my bed. 'Come and sit down and we can talk about it.'

She perches on the very edge of the bed. 'Probably

the best thing to do would be to get a skip and a handyman, don't you think? Then he can get rid of the lot in one go.' She frowns. 'Maybe *three* skips?'

I smile. 'Yes, I think it would take at least three. But Mum, while I think it's great that you want to tackle your house, I'm not sure just getting rid of the lot without sorting through it is the right thing to do.'

'Why not?' She looks alarmed. 'I thought you'd be pleased.'

'I am.' I smile encouragingly. 'It's great that you're thinking about it. I just think we need to tackle the *reason* for your hoard – er, collecting, otherwise the house will just fill up again. Do you see?'

She nods. 'I'm not having counselling, though.'

'Okay. Well, we could definitely start going through your things, room by room, and you could decide what you want to keep and what you want to donate to the charity shop? How about that?'

Her chin wobbles and she tries to hide it with a smile. 'I don't know what I'd do without you, love.'

We hug and she goes off to make some tea, and I lie there thinking about our conversation. That seems like progress to me. The shock of the fire seems to have flicked a switch in her brain, making her realise the dangerous way she's been living. I can't help thinking a professional trained in this sort of thing would do a much better job with her than me, though.

Still, I'm more hopeful than I've ever been that Mum will get through this and come out the other side, more like the strong, independent person she used to be.

I'm cooking at the cabin tonight so, after an early lunch, I pack a box with the food I need and take it out to the car. My heart is already doing energetic star jumps at the thought of seeing Jed again. Oh God, I'm going to have to avoid him if I can – which will be pretty hard since I'm supposed to be serving him dinner. I'll get Erin to do it instead. I just need to get through the next few days, giving him as wide a berth as possible, and then I'll never have to see Jed Turner ever again.

The bag of clothes and the box of papers is still in the boot from yesterday, so I take them inside and push the smoky, smelly clothes into the washing machine and set it off. I'm about to put the lid-less box into a cupboard to tackle some other time when my eye catches my name on an envelope inside it. Addressed to me, it's still sealed.

Puzzled, I glance at the postmark.

Napoli.

Heart beating fast, I stare at the handwriting. The only person I know who lives in Italy…

With trembling fingers, I quickly slit open the envelope and pull out the single sheet within.

My dearest Poppy,

How wonderful to meet you at last! I have never enjoyed a Christmas as much as the one I spent with you and your mother last week. What fun it was teaching you how to make the pasta and getting very cold swimming in the lake. And of course having the best snowball fight ever!

It was also lovely to be with Donna again, although I am not sure she felt quite the same! I know she thinks only of you in everything she does. You have a very brilliant, kind and beautiful mother, and you will grow up to be just like her.

I hope you are very well and happy, chica. We will meet again very soon, I am sure of this.

Love from

Alessandro

In shock and wonder, I glance at the envelope. The letter was sent just a few days into the New Year. January 1999. He must have written to me as soon as he got back to Italy after the Christmas we spent together.

But why did I never receive this letter? Why was it in this box?

Confused, I go in search of Mum. She's in the living room watching a game show.

'Mum, why was this letter from Alessandro at your place, unopened?' I hold it up, my heart drumming fast.

'Do you remember it arriving?'

She stares at it, as if shocked at the sound of Alessandro's name.

'Where was it?' she asks at last.

'In a box with other papers and official letters.'

'Oh.' Her eyes slide away, back to the TV screen.

I stare at her, my brain ticking over rapidly. 'Did you know it was there? Were you keeping it from me?' I'm barely able to believe what I'm asking her.

Mum swallows but continues staring at the TV screen, her lips pressed together.

'He says he'll see me soon, but he never came back. Is that because I didn't reply? Because you never actually let me read my letter?' My voice sounds hollow and strange to me, and the whole situation feels unreal, as if it's happening to someone else. 'All along I've thought that the reason he didn't return was that he simply didn't care about me. That's what I've come to believe.'

Mum turns. 'No. It wasn't like that at all,' she says firmly. 'I could tell that time he was here, he thought you were ... enchanting.'

'Enchanting?' I snap. 'That's a strange word to use. I don't think I've ever been described as enchanting!'

'That was his word,' she says softly. 'About you.'

I should feel happy. But instead, I feel cold all over. 'Why didn't you give me the letter, Mum?'

Her mouth is trembling. She sits forward in the

armchair and mumbles something, rubbing her temples distractedly.

'Sorry?'

She looks up at me, her eyes full of anguish. 'I thought it was for the best. I honestly did.'

'For the best?' I shake my head in disbelief. 'How could it be for *the best*?'

She swallows hard. 'I still had hopes back then that you, me and Martin could be a proper, loving family. And I had to make it work because I swore when you were born that I would give you a dad. That's why I married Martin. But I knew that if Alessandro became part of your life, Martin would be jealous and he'd make life even more difficult for us.' She shrugs. 'I didn't care about me. But I couldn't bear him being cold with you. That used to break my heart and I knew if Alessandro was around, it would get worse. So I thought if I kept his letters, he would eventually—'

'Hold on. *Letters?* There were others?'

She nods. 'He wrote to you every fortnight for six months. I—' Her voice sounds strangled, as if she can barely get the words out. 'I burned them. I must have missed that one.'

I'm so stunned, I can't speak for a moment. I take a long, slow breath to try and gather myself together. 'But he was my *dad*. He came to see me and it was one of the best times of my life. You knew that. I just don't

311

understand how you could deliberately keep us apart.'

She whispers something I can't quite catch. Then she clears her throat and repeats it a little louder: 'I thought I might lose you.'

'How would you lose me?'

She sighs. 'I knew you weren't happy at home, with Martin in our lives. I thought if you got to know Alessandro, you'd love him so much, you might decide you wanted to go and live with him instead. And I really couldn't have borne that.'

I stare at her incredulously. 'I'd never have left *you*!'

'But you might have,' she whispers, staring at me beseechingly, willing me to understand.

I shake my head. 'Of course I wouldn't.' My throat is so choked up, I can barely get the words out. 'I just wanted to have my real dad in my life. Was that really too much to ask?'

Close to breaking down completely, I blunder out of the room and flee upstairs.

Lying on my bed, I stare at the ceiling, trying to get used to the idea that my dad – my real dad – thought I was enchanting and wanted to spend time with me. He really wanted to be part of my life. How terrible for him, then, that his letters to me went unanswered. What must he have thought when I didn't reply? How can I ever forgive Mum for causing us both such grief? I know she was worried she'd lose me but it was still a terrible thing to do, burning those letters. Even she must know that.

Then a single, perfect thought breaks through the chaos in my head.

My dad loved that Christmas just as much as I did!

The tears that spring to my eyes are bitter sweet. If only I'd known that when I was twelve. What a difference it would have made to my life.

Mum tries to talk to me as I get ready to leave for the cabin, but I'm not in the mood for her attempts at an apology. There's nothing she can possibly say that will ever make it better.

Erin is horrified when I tell her. 'I can't imagine how you must feel, knowing you could have had your dad in your life all that time.'

'I don't even know where he is now. I Google him from time to time but there's never any trace of him.' I swing the car off the track at the Log Fire Cabin and park up. 'He lived and worked in Naples when I met him all those years ago. But he's probably moved from there now. He could be anywhere in Italy.' I switch off the engine and look across at Erin. 'When I was eighteen, I went looking for him on the island of Capri.'

Erin's eyes widen. 'What happened?'

I laugh softly. 'I didn't find him. Obviously. He'd mentioned that he wanted to live there one day and, like the daft, innocent teenager I was, I really believed that if I went to the island, I'd find him.'

Her smile is sad and full of empathy. 'Isn't there an address on that letter you have?'

I nod. 'There's a telephone number as well. I tried phoning it but the number was unobtainable. No wonder. He wrote that letter eighteen years ago!'

'You could try writing to the address. Whoever lives there now might know where he's moved to.'

I groan. 'Bit of a long shot, but I will try.'

'You should. And keep Googling him. And maybe try Twitter? And Facebook? You never know, one day ...'

She trails off and we look at each other gloomily. We both know the chances of finding him after all this time are very slim.

We sit in silence for a while, staring at the cabin. Then Erin heaves a sigh and says, 'It must be the day for shocks. I'm now fairly certain Mark is cheating on me.'

I swing round. 'Really? Why? What's happened?' Perhaps she's seen him with that red-haired girl?

She shrugs. 'This morning he said he was going in to work to tie up a few loose ends, which I thought was a bit strange because it's a bank holiday. I phoned the office but there was no reply, so I went down to the office in person but the whole building was dark and locked up. When I asked him about it, he told me some nonsense about not having been able to get in so he went for a walk and bumped into an old mate of his.' She rolls her eyes at me. 'They went for a drink, apparently.'

I frown, thinking about this. 'Maybe he did. Go for a drink?'

She shakes her head. 'He looked really awkward. I could tell he was lying.'

'Shit.'

'I know.'

'What are you going to do?'

She heaves a despairing sigh. 'What *can* I do? Accuse him of seeing someone else when I haven't actually got any proof?'

'But you can't carry on like this, just hoping against hope that you're wrong. You'll go round the bend.'

She frowns but says nothing.

And right then, I decide it's time I put my plan into action. I'm going to tackle Mark myself. I've been putting off doing it because, like Erin, I can't bear to imagine Mark has fallen for someone else. But I can't avoid it any longer. If he's cheating, he's cheating. And it will be terrible. But Erin needs to know.

I'm going to find out once and for all.

*

It's a relief to be cooking at the cabin tonight. It means I don't have to be around Mum.

I'm feeling surprisingly calm, all things considered. Until Clemmy comes in to ask about Mum and happens to mention that Jed is out tonight for a meal with Katerina, and won't be having dinner here.

I'm weirdly relieved yet achingly disappointed all at once, and I feel annoyed with myself that it should matter at all.

Just before we serve up, I manage to snatch some time to phone Harrison. He's just leaving for the flamenco-dance competition and he seems a bit distracted.

'Your dad?' he asks, when I tell him about the letter I found. 'You mean, Martin?'

'No. My real dad. You know, the one who came to see me when I was twelve.'

I told Harrison all about Alessandro when we first met, so I'm a little irritated that he seems quite vague on the subject.

'But didn't he forget all about you after he went back to Italy?' he points out. 'Do you really want someone like that in your life? I think not.' There's a crackling noise as he presumably covers the phone. '*Coming, Mother.*'

'But that's the point, Harrison. Harrison? Are you still there?'

'Yes, sorry. Mum's anxious to leave.'

And I'm anxious for him to share in this amazing news about my dad! 'The thing is, Harrison, he *didn't* turn his back on me. He wrote me lots of letters but Mum intercepted them so I never saw them. He wanted me in his life! Isn't that amazing? I always thought he didn't care. But he did! And I'm determined I'm going to find him.'

'Good. Great! Listen, I'm going to have to dash, Puss. We can talk about this another time, okay?'

My heart sinks. I've recently started to realise that 'talking about it another time' generally means we never do – unless I bring it up again. It's Harrison's code for *I'm bored with this. How can I wriggle out of the conversation without seeming rude?*

'Okay. Good luck tonight.'

'Thanks, Puss. Toodlepip!' he says cheerfully, totally missing the sharpness of my tone.

He sounds as if he can't wait to get off the phone. And he seems in a very upbeat mood. In fact, I'm beginning to wonder if Harrison protests too much – if all the talk about being a rubbish dancer and only doing it for his mother is actually a cover for the fact that he's developed a bit of a passion for it!

I'm still annoyed, though.

Surely good news about my dad is far more important than his stupid contest. It's not as if he's competing in

Strictly Come Dancing, for goodness' sake.

Later, at home, I lie in bed, our conversation going round and round in my head, wishing Harrison could be a little more interested in what's going on in my life. Because, so often, our life revolves around what *he's* doing. The talk is always about his promotion and never about what I'd like to do in my career. I'm always really supportive of his hobbies, even though drain covers quite frankly bore me to tears. But I've made an effort to be interested because they're his passion. Sometimes I feel that our relationship is rather one-sided.

I'd been keen to tell him all about the letter and Alessandro. I'd thought he'd be happy for me and might even help me work out a way I could start looking for my dad. But he didn't seem to realise what a big deal it was for me. He was off the phone in a jiffy.

If I'd told Jed about the letter, he'd want to know more. He'd ask me questions and want to talk about it. He'd be interested because it was affecting me.

Harrison was more interested in the dance contest.

But then, I suppose I've always known that the thing Harrison is actually most interested in is – Harrison. And I don't mean that in a nasty way. Not really. It's just he gets so wrapped up in the things that are happening in his life, he often forgets to be interested in mine.

I shuffle around in bed, trying to find a comfortable

position but failing. There are too many jarring thoughts tumbling around inside my head for me to relax. I'm still deeply angry with Mum and now Harrison has also let me down. And on top of everything else, I keep thinking about Jed and wondering if he's back at the cabin yet. What if he's staying at Katerina's tonight?

I punch the pillow and collapse back down with a sigh. Jed's relationship with his ex is actually none of my business and I'm annoyed at myself for stewing over it. It really doesn't matter to me *who* Jed is romantically involved with, because I'm going to marry Harrison.

Harrison is my rock; my safe harbour in a storm. Okay, he can be a bit self-obssessed at times, but we all have our little foibles. Harrison will always be there for me and, in an often harsh and uncertain world, that means everything.

Chapter 26

<u>Dinner menu</u>
Hors d'oeuvres
(with mulled wine and fruit punch)
***
Chilli con carne and jasmine rice
***
Chocolate bombe

Things are still uneasy between Mum and me.

She's given up trying to apologise and now seems to be in a major huff with me, which is a bit rich, really, considering that, technically, she's an arsonist and I could probably have her arrested for tampering with my post. We step around each other all morning, being coldly polite. The idea of her having to stay here until her own house is sorted and redecorated is a total nightmare.

Then, just before midday, Clemmy phones me in a panic. 'Ruby's gone missing and poor Gloria is absolutely demented with worry.'

'Oh, God, that's awful. And she hasn't got a phone. Where on earth would she go?'

'Well, Tom said she'd probably got the bus into Easingwold to look at phones. And when Jed said there *are* no buses from here, Tom mentioned the word 'hitching', which obviously sent Gloria into a state of hyper-frenzy.' She sighs. 'We wondered if Ruby had said anything to you about her plans?'

'I'm afraid not. When did she leave?'

'Some time this morning. We were all planning to go to Bob's opening ceremony but the plan has changed. We need to look for Ruby.'

Bob's latest architectural project, a stylish office building on the outskirts of Easingwold, was completed back in November, and I knew all about his plans to invite his associates and the local press to an opening ceremony.

'Can I come with you to search for her?' I ask, feeling Gloria's pain and hoping Ruby is all right. (Also, Mum just passed through the hall and gave me a sly 'daggers' look.)

'Great!' Clemmy sounds pleased. 'The more the merrier, Poppy. Pick you up in twenty minutes.'

The search party arrives in Jed's car. Calling to Mum

that I won't be too long, I hurry out to the car and peer surreptitiously inside to check who's in there. Gloria's sitting in the front, next to Jed, and Clemmy is in the back.

There's no sign of Katerina.

My relief is instant – perhaps I won't have to alter the quantities for tonight's dinner after all!

I slip into the back seat next to Clemmy and she beams at me. 'Great news. Bob's just phoned. Ruby's with him at the opening ceremony, sort of as his right hand woman. Well, *girl* ...'

Gloria turns round in her seat. 'She didn't bother to tell her mother, of course. Cheeky mare just waltzes off without a single thought of how I might think she'd been murdered or something even worse!'

'It's nice she's making an effort to get to know Bob, though,' says Clemmy cheerfully.

Gloria grunts. 'True. It's been full-scale bloody hostilities up until now. Although I can't for the life of me think what's softened her attitude towards Bob.'

It does seem a little odd. Ruby has been *so* anti-Bob, it's felt more than a little awkward at the cabin. Especially, I imagine, for poor Bob himself.

'At least we know where she is now,' remarks Jed who, up till now, has been silent, staring straight ahead, concentrating on the driving. He's so tall, his hair brushes the roof of the car. I stare miserably at his big, solid shoulders. He didn't even turn round to say hello when I got in the car. I can only assume he's regretting our passionate clinch the day before yesterday.

Gloria groans. 'I just hope she isn't planning to derail Bob's event.'

Jed turns. 'It's just a ribbon-cutting ceremony. There's not much Ruby could do to sabotage it.'

'You don't know my daughter,' mutters Gloria darkly.

Clemmy raises her eyebrows at me and I grin.

When we get to Easingwold, Jed finds the building and parks on the other side of the road. We all stare up at the stylishly modern structure with its impressive glass frontage.

'Very posh.' Gloria sounds proud of her man. 'Wait a minute!' She leans right across Jed to stare out of the window. 'What's going on? Are there *people* hanging off that building?'

'Oh my God, you're right,' says Clemmy.

We get out of the car and walk over the road towards the small crowd gathered near the entrance. Several representatives of the local press are there, training their cameras skywards.

I screw up my eyes. 'Looks like they're abseiling down the building.'

Two figures, looking like ants from this distance, are about level with the fifth floor and are moving slowly, bit by bit, down the side of the new office block.

'*Abseiling?*' shrieks Gloria. 'Oh my God. Is that Bob? And *Ruby?*'

She runs the last few yards, yelling, 'Ruby? Come down this minute! You might fall!'

'She'll be fine. Don't worry,' Jed reassures her. 'Bob wouldn't cut corners when it comes to safety. There'll be a professional crew in charge.'

Gloria's panic subsides a little. 'Now I know why she didn't tell me. She knew I'd say no if I thought she was doing something like this. But I can't believe *Bob* didn't let me know what was happening. The two of them must have been in cahoots!' She covers her mouth. 'Christ, she's coming down way too fast. *Slow down, Ruby!*'

Jed grins. 'I don't think she can hear you.'

'She's such a daredevil,' says Clemmy admiringly. 'You wouldn't catch *me* signing up for that.'

Gloria sighs. 'Bob's exactly the same. A thrill-seeker, I think you'd—' She stops. Then her mouth curves slowly up into a smile. 'The clever bugger! He'd have known Ruby couldn't say no to an extreme sport. I think he might just have played a blinder there.'

*

The gang at the Log Fire Cabin have decided to have a hot-tub party tonight.

When we get back from Easingwold, I call Erin to ask if she wants to come food shopping with me. I'm going to serve lots of little savoury nibbles to soak up the mulled wine and, specially for Ruby, a non-alcoholic hot spiced punch.

'Yeah, great,' she says, sounding totally lacklustre. 'A party at the cabin sounds way more exciting than anything happening in my flat.'

We end up buying quite a lot of booze for the drinks and I put Erin in charge of making the mulled wine and the punch to try and cheer her up.

'Do you think we've bought enough alcohol?' Erin asks, on the drive over to the cabin. 'These party drinks need to pack a punch.'

'Hey, *you* won't be drinking them, so don't even think about it! They're for the client and his dinner guests!'

She frowns. 'I know. I'm just saying. You want this party to be memorable, don't you?'

I laugh. 'It will hopefully be memorable because of the delicious food, not because they all have massive hangovers the next day. Anyway, if we run short, there's always the alcohol left over from the vodka lemon chicken we made the other night.'

'Oh, yes. You lost the lid, didn't you?'

I nod. 'Decanted it into another bottle. It's in one of the cupboards.'

'Righto, boss.' She grins. 'By the way, can you manage

a night at the cabin on your own? I don't mean tonight. It's the day after tomorrow. Mark and I are having a special meal.'

'Oh. What's the occasion?'

'No occasion,' she says gruffly. 'I think we both just feel we need to talk. Spend some quality time together …'

I wince inwardly. Sounds ominous. 'Your idea?'

'No. His, amazingly.' She frowns. 'Maybe he's feeling guilty for working late so often.'

I decide to broach the subject of their relationship with her later – to find out how Erin's feeling about everything – because talking things out can often work wonders. But as it happens, we barely have time to draw breath, we're so busy in the kitchen. We're making four different types of hors d'oeuvres to serve with Erin's mulled wine and punch, before everyone sits down for the big pot of chilli con carne I've made for the main course, and the chocolate bombe for dessert.

I cast a last eye over the two big platters of nibbles before we take them out. 'They look so tempting,' says Erin. 'Let's hope they eat loads to soak up the alcohol. When I went out there with more of the punch, they were all quite merry already, and it's not even eight o'clock yet. Gloria seems to be on the Baileys, drinking it by the half pint!'

'Bloody hell. Let's get these eats out. Then we can serve the chilli in half an hour.'

Everything seems to be going down well, and when Erin returns with the main-course plates, she has a special request from Gloria.

'She wants dessert in the hot tub.'

I eye the ultra-squidgy chocolate bombe and shake my head. 'I can't see it mixing with the steam, can you? It would be a disaster.'

The door opens and Jed comes in.

Our eyes meet and my heart does a giant lurch.

'Ignore Gloria.' He runs a hand through his hair and grins. 'She's halfway down a bottle of Baileys and has lost all sense. We'll have dessert at the table, I think. Then Gloria and Ruby can dive into the hot tub afterwards.'

'Ooh, lovely!' says Erin.

'You're welcome to use it yourselves, if you like,' offers Jed, smiling at Erin. He flicks his eyes across at me and I glance down at my feet. I presume I'm included in the invitation, even though he was pointedly talking to Erin. 'The hot tub's all ready. I've even put candles around it,' he adds, to no one in particular.

'Well, I'd have been up for it,' says Erin after he's gone. 'If I'd brought a swimming costume. The cooks definitely deserve some fun.'

'It wouldn't be very professional, though, would it?'

And I'm not sure I want to stick around, only to be ignored by Jed.

'Spoilsport!'

Erin takes in dessert then we start clearing up the kitchen, humming along to Christmas songs on the radio. When the door bursts open, my heart leaps, thinking it's Jed. But when I turn, it's only Clemmy. 'Oh God, that chocolate bombe was absolute heaven,' she says. 'You really are a genius, Poppy! Well, both of you!'

Erin grins. 'Thanks, Clemmy. But she's the genius. I'm the dogsbody.'

'You make a mean mulled wine, though. I don't suppose there's any more?' Clemmy's eyes are extra-sparkling and her cheeks are flushed. I think she might have drunk quite a lot of it herself.

'Erin?' I glance across.

Erin salutes. 'On it, boss.' She smiles at Clemmy. 'I'll make it a good 'un.'

'Brilliant! Oh, by the way, we're playing Truth or Dare and we need more people. Will you come and join in?'

She sees my hesitation. 'Please, Poppy. It'll be great fun.'

I think about the frosty atmosphere back at home. I've no real desire to get back until Mum's safely out of the way, in bed. So, I give in and smile my agreement.

Clemmy whoops and rushes out of the kitchen. 'I'll drag Gloria and Ruby out of the hot tub!'

In the living room, everyone is lying about on the sofas or the floor. Clemmy and Ryan shuffle along their sofa to make space for Erin, and I sit on the floor, leaning against the arm.

Jed, who's lounging directly opposite me in one of the armchairs, rubs his hands together. 'Right, who's going to start?'

Eventually, it's decided that Tom will go first. He opts for a dare.

'Ooh, I've got a brilliant one,' smirks Ruby. 'Tom, you have to phone Charlotte up and ask her out.'

Tom turns as white as the baby grand piano. 'No way.'

'You can do it, Tom,' says Jed, and Gloria nods. 'Go on, my son. I bet she says yes.'

Ryan grins. 'If she says no, you can always tell her it was just a dare in a game.'

Clemmy leans over and digs him playfully in the ribs. 'That's typical of you, Ry. Always cagey when it comes to being truthful about – *ooh!* – feelings.'

He throws a balled-up sweet-wrapper sideways and it bounces off her head.

'I don't have to do this, do I?' Tom looks appealingly at Clemmy.

She nods. 'Yes,' she tells him firmly. 'Yes, you do, Tom. Be brave.'

So he does, looking excruciatingly embarrassed, with everyone listening. He's red as a beetroot and, after he's asked the question, there's a long stretch where Charlotte talks and he listens. When he hangs up, everyone is on the edges of their seats – well, apart from Ryan, who's as laid-back as ever.

Tom swallows. 'She says she's busy tomorrow night.'

There's a chorus of groans and 'well, never mind, it's her loss,' and 'at least you tried'.

Poor Clemmy looks quite tearful, no doubt wishing she hadn't urged him to accept the dare. 'Never mind, Tom. You did it. And that's what counts.'

Erin is up next, and hers is a Truth.

'When was the last time a boy did the dirty on you?' blurts out Ruby, and everyone laughs.

'What?' Ruby demands, colouring up. 'It's a good question, isn't it?'

I glance anxiously at Erin. With such a dire romantic past, she's got so many 'boys' to choose from.

'It's a great question, Ruby,' Erin murmurs, attempting a smile. She looks around the room, pauses, then says softly, 'I thought I'd found the perfect man for me. We were so happy together. But now I think I'm losing him and it's killing me.'

There's a stunned silence, and it occurs to me that maybe Erin has been 'testing' the mulled wine rather too much while making it. Why else would she be revealing her most-personal feelings to people she doesn't know that well?

Ruby breaks the stunned silence. 'So you think he's about to dump you?'

Erin nods miserably.

'Well, *you* should chuck *him* before *he* chucks *you*,' says Ruby. 'You're much too nice to put up with any crap, Erin!'

'Language!' Gloria points an admonishing finger at her daughter. In her alcoholic haze, she's actually pointing at Jed, but we all get the drift.

Erin laughs sadly. 'Wish it was that easy.'

Ruby starts chanting, 'Dump him! Dump him! Dump him!' Then everyone's telling her to be quiet, although Erin seems to think it's quite funny.

Ryan, who's sitting next to Erin, puts his arm around her and whispers something to her. It must be a compliment, because Erin smiles bashfully at him. I see Clemmy's face fall as she watches them, and my heart goes out to her.

'Can we go back in the hot tub?' begs Ruby.

'No, it's Bob's turn.' Jed grins.

He opts for a dare, and Ruby shrieks, 'You've got to slide down the banister then sing 'Rudolph the Red-Nosed Reindeer' at the bottom.' She springs up and starts unwinding some of the foliage and fairy lights from one side of the stairs.

'Ry can play the piano!' shouts Clemmy. 'He can play while you sing, Bob!'

Everyone looks at Ryan, who folds his arms and says flatly, 'I don't think so.'

I feel sure the rather-reserved Bob will also flatly refuse but, to my surprise, he drains his whisky glass and gets to his feet. Walking rather unsteadily, to chants of 'Go, Bob!' from everyone, he gets to the top and slips one cheek onto the banister.

'Careful, Bob!' shouts Gloria.

She needn't have worried. Despite being very obviously pissed, Bob manages to slide to the bottom of the stairs in one piece, and even with a certain degree of elegance. He takes a bow then launches into a jolly rendition of 'Rudolph', and everyone else joins in when he starts forgetting the words.

Clemmy nudges me and giggles. 'I've never seen Bob so "relaxed". What's in that punch?'

'It's non-alcoholic. Basically, fruit, some spices and lots of fruit juice. We made it with Ruby in mind.'

She snorts. 'Well, Bob's been on it all night and it looks a bit less harmless than that!' She raises her glass of mulled wine. 'Cheers, Bob!'

He raises his glass in return and nearly over-balances. 'Nice stuff, this. Any more?'

'That's the second batch,' says Erin. 'I'm afraid there's no lemonade left. But there's plenty of mulled wine.'

Bob shakes his head. 'I don't drink.'

'Could have fooled me,' whispers Erin, grinning at

me. 'Ooh, it's your big moment, Poppy. You're up next!' She points at Clemmy.

'Right, Poppy. Truth or dare?'

My head feels a little woozy and at first I don't catch on. I've been on Erin's hot spiced punch, like Bob. But, also like Bob, I'm feeling as if I've drunk half a bottle of wine, at least. Has the punch been *spiked*?

Come to think of it, everyone seems pretty hammered. Even Ruby...

I'm about to ask Erin. But Clemmy's big smile looms in front of me. 'Truth or chair?' She explodes into giggles. 'Sorry, *dare*!'

'Um ... truth!'

Gloria and Ruby are arguing about mobile phones again. Clemmy clears her throat and shouts at them to pay attention. All eyes turn to me. Except Jed. He's gazing down at his glass, a pensive expression on his face. Maybe he's thinking about Katerina and wishing he were with her, instead of with us rowdy lot?

Thinking about that makes me think of Harrison and a wave of emotion rolls over me. So when Clemmy says, 'What's the most exciting thing that's ever happened to you?', I barely hesitate.

'My boyfriend has proposed and I'm going to marry him!'

There's a moment's stunned silence. Then a lot of whooping and congratulations. Erin looks at me incredulously. 'Is this true? Why didn't you tell me?'

Oh, God. Why did I let it slip out? I never meant to tell anyone till after New Year. No wonder Erin looks perplexed and a little hurt.

I'm so painfully aware of Jed sitting opposite, as soon as he gets up, my gaze swivels in his direction. 'I'm really pleased for you, Poppy,' he says, fixing me with those green eyes. Except they seem darker somehow and closed off to me.

'We need champagne to celebrate,' he says softly, and goes out to the kitchen.

I watch him leave, my stupid heart yearning to follow him. With that mane of chestnut hair, he's like a glorious jungle animal prowling around his territory ... *oh God, I really am pissed!* 'Erin, did you put anything else in that punch?'

She frowns. 'No, just some lemonade I found in the cupboard.'

Lemonade?

Oh God, no. When we lost the cap for the vodka, I had to find another bottle to pour it into. A lemonade bottle.

'Shit! Everyone, the hot spiced punch has vodka in it!'

Ruby raises her glass. 'Cheers, Poppy. It tastes brilliant!'

Gloria gets up and snatches the glass from her hand,

334

then downs it herself before Ruby can object. 'My turn! I choose dare!'

Her dare turns out to be dipping all ten toes in the lake for ten seconds.

'But it's freezing!' protests Bob. 'You can't, Gloria.'

She laughs. 'Eeh, don't worry, Bob. We're tough, us Geordie lasses.' She takes off her shoes and we all get up and follow her to the patio doors. She slithers over the snow-covered grass to the water's edge, turns round, flings her arms in the air and yells, 'Here goes!' Next second, she loses her balance, staggers back-wards and lands with a gigantic splash in the icy water.

'Oh my God. Mum!' Ruby tears down to the water in a panic and starts trying to heave Gloria out, but she's a dead weight. She's flailing around, gasping in the sub-zero temperatures. We're all on our feet but Bob gets there first. Acting amazingly quickly, consid-ering he's the worse for drink, he grabs a fleecy throw from the living room and runs after Ruby and, together, they finally manage to pull Gloria out of the water.

She seems unharmed, except for the fact that her teeth won't stop chattering, even when Bob wraps her up tightly in the throw.

Bob seems overwhelmed with relief. 'I was worried your heart might not stand the shock,' he says, walking her back to the cabin. 'Never do that again, Gloria. Promise?'

'Never.' She gives an extra-violent shiver as she steps back through the patio doors into the warmth.

'I love you, Gloria.'

'You do? Even after all the temper tantrums and the rows about mobile phones?' She looks sharply at Ruby, who has the grace to look ashamed.

'*Especially* after everything,' smiles Bob. 'Gloria, you have rocked my safe-but-boring world and it's taken a bit of getting used to. But now I never want to be without you.'

There's a chorus of 'aaahs'.

'Oh, Bob.' Gloria kisses him full on the lips. 'Let's keep on rocking into old age!'

'I think I might be there already.'

'No, you're not. You came down that banister with the speed and suppleness of a man half your age.'

'You flatter me, my love.'

As they head for the stairs, Gloria giggles. 'I'm sure we could find other ways of putting that suppleness to good use.'

'Oh, puh-lease!' groans Ruby, and everyone laughs.

When Erin and I go into the kitchen to make Gloria some hot tea, we both instantly notice the 'lemonade' bottle standing empty on the counter.

We're laughing about this, when Jed comes into the

kitchen. 'Poppy, you've got a visitor.'

'A visitor? Who?'

He smiles, although I notice it doesn't quite reach his eyes. 'It's Harrison.'

Chapter 27

*H*arrison?

But he's not meant to be flying back till New Year's Eve!

Cheeks flushed, heart beating fast, I brush past Jed, who's holding the door open for me, and go out to the hallway.

And there is Harrison.

His blond wavy hair is ruffled and his dark-rimmed glasses are needing a wipe because they're starting to steam up.

'Wow! What are you doing here?'

We hug and he says, 'I've been trying to contact you all day, Puss, to let you know I was flying home early. But your phone must be switched off.'

'Damn! I left it in the car. Sorry, I've been so busy.' I shrug, smiling, happy to see him.

'So your mum said.' He grins. 'I've got to hand it to you, Puss. This is some assignment you've landed. Not a bad start to your new career in catering.'

'Thank you,' I say modestly, delighted that he seems pleased. I thought he might disapprove, but apparently I was wrong. 'I can't believe you're here. Why the early flight?'

He frowns. 'Mum's been invited to join Rosa's dad on his yacht in the Med.'

'Oh.' I stare at him, startled. Mrs Ford has a new man? 'That's fabulous. She's definitely moving on, then. Good for her!' I frown. 'Erm, who's Rosa?'

A startled look crosses his face, as if he thought he'd already mentioned her. Then he smiles. 'She's our flamenco-dance teacher.'

'Oh. Right.' We're still standing in the hallway, so I pull him through to the living room and say, 'Everyone? This is my boyfriend, Harrison.'

'Your fiancé, you mean?' points out Ruby.

I glance at Harrison, expecting him to smile, but to my surprise, he looks a little uncomfortable.

'Drink, Harrison? We've got champagne?' offers Clemmy.

'Oh, no thanks. I – er – can't stay.'

I link his arm. 'Not even for a little while?' I'd like him to relax a bit and get to know everyone, but he's standing there so stiffly; the arm I'm grasping still ramrod straight at his side. He must feel uncomfortable because he doesn't know everyone like I do. My heart swells with love. I scan the room. Jed's not there. For some reason, that's very important in the light of what I'm about to say.

'I've been thinking hard during our cooling-off period. And what I want to say is: Harrison Ford, I would *love* to be your wife!' I grab his hand and beam at him.

A beat later, Ruby giggles. '*Harrison Ford*? Isn't he that ancient actor in those films? Indiana Jones? I'm hungry. Are there any more of those nibbles?'

Everyone politely ignores her, except Erin, who mutters, 'In the fridge.' And as Harrison still seems welded to the spot with embarrassment, I throw my arms around him to put him at his ease, and bury my face in his chest.

About five seconds later, I'm starting to realise it's a bit of a one-sided embrace. His arms are still firmly by his sides. It's a bit embarrassing, really, in front of all my new friends here who are pretending they haven't noticed.

I draw back and look him in the eye. 'Harrison? Is something wrong?'

He shakes his head. 'Nothing's wrong.' Then he pulls me behind the baby grand piano and whispers, 'It's just I've been doing a lot of probability work, and the thing is, Puss, there's really no easy way to tell you this, so I'll just come right out and say it. I don't think we're going to make it.'

There's a stunned silence in the room.

Harrison seems to think he's being discreet, but his whispers are more like loud stage whispers. Everyone can hear.

'Anyone else want a nibble?' asks Ruby, holding out a plate. 'Fridge Raiders of the Lost Ark?'

Ryan sniggers and Clemmy nudges him.

'Don't get me wrong,' says Harrison, in another urgent whisper, 'It was all looking very promising, but then you resigned and started this extremely risky new venture. Do you know how many small businesses go to the wall in their first year? I can provide you with heaps of stats.'

'No, no, it's fine.' My cheeks are scarlet. 'Look, shall we talk about this at home?'

A shifty look crosses his face. 'I'm – um – not going home tonight.'

'What?' I feel sick. 'So where *are* you going?'

'I'm staying at The Pretty Flamingo tonight.'

'Ha! Good one.' He's joking. He *must* be...

Ruby emerges from the kitchen, chewing. 'Did I miss anything?' She glares at Harrison. 'Don't you *want* to marry our Poppy, then?' she demands.

Harrison reddens. 'Well, I thought I did. But I've realised the odds are stacked against it.' That smug look comes over his face. The one that tells me he's limbering up for a quote. 'As I always say, there's no room for more than one ambitious person in a relationship!'

I truly can't believe I'm hearing all this.

'Hold on, so you're rejecting me because I want to *make* something of myself? Follow my dreams? Really, Harrison? Because that's a pretty dodgy reason for withdrawing a proposal of marriage!'

'Waaaaay!' Ruby starts clapping and Gloria slaps at her hands.

'It's honest, though, isn't it?' says Harrison. 'And surely honesty is the most important thing in a relationship?'

The mention of honesty brings a guilty flush to my cheeks. I'm not really in a position to be *too* high and mighty over this. But I'm still hurt and angry.

Ryan diplomatically puts some music on to drown out our discussion.

'So, while I was little meek and mild Poppy who wouldn't say boo to a goose and allowed herself to be walked all over, you were *attracted* to me? But now you're not? That's just perverse, Harrison.'

He shrugs. 'I'm still attracted to you, but ...'

'But I wouldn't have time to be your woman in the background, supporting you in your meteoric rise to success, is that it? I might – God forbid! – be a success in my own right, and you couldn't handle it?'

He shrugs, as if to say, *Sadly, you've got it in one*!

I can't believe I'm hearing this, although funnily enough, it doesn't really surprise me. I think I always knew Harrison had a coldly selfish streak. I just didn't want to see it.

He clears his throat. 'Rosa made a very good point. She said—'

'Rosa.' I glare at him.

'The dance teacher.'

'Yes. And is Rosa a mature lady in her seventies who, with the wisdom of age, can give you motherly advice?'

He blinks rapidly. 'No, she's twenty-eight and a former catalogue model. But that's beside the point.'

I swallow hard. 'Is it really? So you've been having discussions with a twenty-eight-year-old former catalogue model about *our relationship?*'

'Please leave Rosa out of this.'

I laugh bitterly. 'Leave Rosa out of this?' I yell, and everyone freezes.

I'm so hurt and angry, I want to push him in the lake. How could he do this to me? To *us?*

'Is this *Rosa* your new girlfriend, then, *Harrison Ford?*' demands Ruby, and I'm secretly hoping Gloria won't shush her because I'm actually quite glad of her support.

Gloria doesn't shush her.

'Ooh, did she brave the jungle with you and help you find your precious gem?'

'Ruby,' Ryan interjects sternly.

She frowns. 'Sorry, but it's not cool of him coming here to dump Poppy. Not when he's already asked her to marry him. I'm just saying what everyone else is thinking.'

'I know,' says Ryan calmly. 'I just meant you got it wrong. It wasn't *Raiders* when she helps him find the gem. It was *Temple of Doom*.'

'Oh.'

Harrison's face has flushed almost purple. He gets very tetchy when people make fun of his name like this. (I suggested he shorten it to Harry but he believes 'Harrison' has far more gravitas in the work arena.)

'So, have you slept with this Rosa?' I demand, not bothering to keep my voice down.

He's back to his shifty look.

I sigh. 'That's a yes, then. And have you worked out the probability of you and Rosa staying together?'

He shuffles his feet and stares at the ground. Then he says, 'It's looking quite good, yes.'

'But isn't she a dance teacher? Therefore by definition a career woman?'

'She says she'll give it up after—'

My legs start to shake. 'After you're *married*?'

'No!' He shakes his head vehemently and the heavy boulder inside me lightens just a little. 'After she comes over to live in England.' He hangs his head, finally having the grace to look apologetic. 'Sorry, Puss.'

'Er, there'll be no "Puss", thank you very much.'

Angry tears spring up. Actually, they're more to do

with hurt than anger. Hurt that he could find this other woman, Rosa, so quickly. Hurt that he cared so little, in the end, that he was swayed by mathematical probability! It feels as if our love was never even real.

I dash away the tears. Harrison has found himself a partner far more suited to his needs, leaving me feeling empty and deeply scared at the thought of all the years stretching ahead. Having to face the future alone, without Harrison's love and support, which I really thought I could rely on...

Chapter 28

I feel small and insubstantial. And terrified.

If I were a building, I'd be a shaky lean-to. Fragile, a bit of a wreck, and liable to fall apart at the first cold wind.

Ours might not have been the most passionate love in the world, but we had history, Harrison and I. We built a life together in our little terraced house and now, suddenly, it's all gone. I feel like my very foundations have been blasted to smithereens.

I've barely slept. I crept in last night, thankful Mum was already in bed because I really wasn't up to talking. Harrison dropped me off. In a further humiliation, I'd been forced to accept his offer of a lift home. Everyone else, including Erin, was well over the limit thanks to Erin pouring vodka 'lemonade' into the second lot of 'non-alcoholic' punch and mulled wine. There will be some sore heads in the cabin this morning.

And speaking of sore heads, I have the mother of all

migraines today. I'm curled up on my side, trying not to move because every time I do, the searing pain intensifies. The pressure in my head is almost unbearable. It feels as though it's trapped in a vice, which my torturer is screwing tighter and tighter with each passing minute. And that's quite apart from the red-hot poker that's drilling its way into my forehead, just above the right eye. This could go on for hours. Days, even.

I suppose there is a bright side. The emotional pain of thinking about Harrison with his Spanish-dancer lover is almost more bearable than this physical agony. Actually, I think they're inextricably linked. Because every time I find myself dwelling on the fact that Harrison doesn't want to be with me any more, the vice tightens to ever more excruciating levels.

Obviously, Mum knows there's something wrong – but she thinks it's 'just' a migraine. I'm happy to keep it that way. The very last thing I need when I feel like this is someone fussing around, asking every five minutes if I'm feeling any better. I know that sounds ungrateful, but when you've got a migraine, it's impossible to be charitable.

Clemmy phones me on my mobile and very quickly realises I'm not myself. I manage to utter the words 'migraine' and 'in bed' and bless her, she turns into exactly the sort of nurse I need. (The kind where not much replying is necessary so I don't have to move.)

'Stay in bed and don't even think about coming over to cook. We'll manage fine. I'm so sorry about Harrison. Remember, I'm here if you need to talk, although I know you've got Erin. It would be lovely to see you at New Year. Do the buffet if you want to – but if not, just come as my guest, okay?'

'Okay,' I croak. 'Thanks, Clemmy.'

'Take care, Poppy. Love you.'

Her words of comfort really make a difference. If only Ryan could see how great she is. I keep thinking of Clemmy's expression when Ryan had his arm round Erin, whispering something in her ear.

Relationships! Are we always doomed to fall for people who don't feel quite the same way about us? I'm thinking of Harrison, of course. But also Jed.

Thinking of Jed has the interesting effect of making the drill that's started attacking my right temple desist its tunnelling for a brief but blissful moment. Then I remember Katerina and how determined she apparently is to get Jed back, and the temple excavations step up with a vengeance.

Mum comes in at lunchtime with some soup but I feel too nauseous to even look at it. She sits on the side of the bed and strokes my tangled hair. I'd shout at her to leave me alone if only I could get up the strength. So I just lie there, feeling like I've been hurled to the bottom of a dark and smelly pit with no means of escape.

By teatime, the migraine is starting to ease. But that just means my poor hurting brain has regained the ability to think – and that's not a good thing right now. I start remembering how lovely Harrison used to be when I had a migraine. He'd come in and just sit quietly on the bed, reading one of his history books and holding my hand. Having Harrison there at those times, just silently holding my hand, was so wonderful. But I'll never have that again now...

Tears trickle down my face and soak into the pillow. That's the thing about migraines. They take you to a dark place, thinking dark thoughts and feeling totally alone. Not the best place to be when you've just been dumped from a great height by the man you were going to marry.

When I finally go downstairs, Mum's in the kitchen, doing some ironing. 'Feeling better, love?'

'A bit, thanks.'

'That's good. We've got to get you better for New Year, when Harrison comes back!'

She thinks she's cheering me up. She has no idea.

Her face crumples in horror when I start to cry. 'What's wrong, love? Tell me.'

But I can't stop crying long enough to tell her. I just keep blurting out 'Harrison' in between lots of snotty gulps and sniffs.

Mum's always been great at cuddles when I'm feeling

sad. She leads me through to the living room and we sort of subside together onto the sofa. And, with my tears giving her jumper a good soaking, she rubs my back gently and rhythmically, like she used to do when I was a child. At last, when I'm completely cried out and able to talk without hiccupping, I tell her all about Harrison leaving me for a Spanish dancer called Rosa.

She doesn't say he wasn't good enough for me. She just says calmly, 'Just remember, love, what's for you won't go by you. There's someone else out there for you, you'll see.'

She pours me some fresh orange juice, which is always what I crave after a migraine attack, and puts some eggs on to soft-boil. And now that the physical pain has receded and I'm starting to feel human again, it feels so good to be wrapped in motherly love and fed chucky eggs and buttered soldiers, as if I'm a kid again.

I will never condone what she did, keeping Alessandro and me apart, but I understand why she did it. She was frightened she'd lose me.

'Mum?'

'Yes, love?' She brings me a mug of sugary tea, which she claims will build my strength up and sits down opposite me at the kitchen table.

'What would you think if I tried to locate Alessandro?'

She smiles. 'I'd think it was probably high time you found your dad.'

'But how would you feel if I did?'

'I'd feel ... glad.' There are tears in her eyes. 'I've missed him all these years. It was terrible, leaving him in Italy, making the choice to return home and study for my medical degree, and bringing you up alone. But I promised myself I'd find you a dad and I did. Then after I married Martin and my ideal vision began to blur, I thought: well, I've made my bed so I have to lie in it. If I'd walked out on my marriage, it would have meant my sacrifice in leaving Alessandro in Italy was all for nothing and I couldn't bear that. So, I had to stay ...'

'Until Martin himself walked out.'

She nods. 'And that's when I finally realised it was all for nothing. I'd failed in my mission to find you the dad you deserved and I'd made the biggest mistake of my life in leaving Al. That's why I gave up on life.'

'And had a breakdown.' I look at her across the table, finally understanding what she must have gone through. All for my sake. 'One day, we'll find him, Mum.'

She nods and smiles at me, and the years roll away. She's that young girl again, falling in love for the very first time.

I lay my hand over hers. 'I know you don't like me asking questions, but ...'

'Ask away, love.'

'Okay.' My heart rate quickens. 'Tell me what it was like when you first met my dad in Italy.'

She smiles and stares out of the window, remembering. 'Well, I was having the most wonderful gap year imaginable. My school friend, Nancy, and I both had a thing about Italy. Possibly because our Italian teacher at school was tall, dark and dashing, just like the hero from a romantic novel.' She laughs, shaking her head. 'Talk about young and foolish! Anyway, neither of us had ever even been abroad, so when it came to deciding where we'd go for our gap year, the answer was obvious. Nancy had a cousin who'd just moved to Naples with her husband's new job, so we crashed at their house for a few months, then – once we'd found jobs in a local bar and café – we rented a room in an apartment and managed to get by quite nicely, topping up our wages with money we'd saved for our big adventure.' She smiles dreamily. 'We were having an amazing time – all on a shoe-string, really. I didn't think life could get any better. And then it did ...'

'You met my dad.'

She nods. 'I met your dad.'

'What was he like back then? He must have been really young.'

'Nineteen. And I was eighteen.' She draws in a deep breath and breathes out slowly. 'I thought he was incredible. Handsome and funny with a real zest for life. He came into the café where I was working and we just clicked straight away. His English wasn't perfect and my Italian was terrible, but that didn't seem to matter. He was working in the kitchens at a local hotel doing quite menial work, but I knew it wouldn't be long before he rose through the ranks because he had this real passion for food. I remember the first time I went to his apartment, he made me Spaghetti Napoli and I sat on a stool sipping a glass of wine, watching everything he did in total fascination. He talked to me about the origins of the dish in his lovely broken English, and even though the ingredients he tossed in were really quite simple – garlic, fresh tomatoes, olives – it was the most glorious food I'd ever tasted.' She smiles across at me. 'I suppose the fact that I was falling in love made it taste even better!'

'So was it love at first sight?'

She nods. 'I think it was. For both of us. The boys I knew back home talked about themselves all the time, but Alessandro was different. More mature. He was interested in me, wanting to know everything about my life back in England. We sort of 'got' each other, you know?'

I nod eagerly, drinking in every little detail, making up for all the years my questions went unanswered.

'Lots of kids our age were still wandering around a bit aimlessly, deciding what they wanted to do with their lives. But Alessandro already knew where he was going in life – just as I did.'

'So he knew even then that he was going to be a chef?' I murmur, not wanting to interrupt her recollections. 'Just like you knew you wanted to be a doctor?'

She nods. 'We were both so passionate about our careers. I suppose it was inevitable they'd end up getting in the way of our budding relationship. When I returned to England and found out I was pregnant, I was totally shell-shocked. It was never part of the career plan to have a child while I studied.'

'Gee, thanks, Mum.'

She laughs. 'Now, of course, I wouldn't change it for the world. But at the time, I had some serious decisions to make, which weren't easy, believe me. I was in love with Alessandro. I missed him every day. But I had my place at university to study medicine. I couldn't give that up. And Alessandro was just starting out on his own career path. A relationship spanning continents was never going to work. So I decided not to tell him about the pregnancy. I figured I was doing him a favour. He was far too young and ambitious to be tied down with a family to take care of.'

'So did you break all contact?'

She nods, her eyes glistening with emotion. 'I wrote him a letter saying I loved him but the distance between us was too great to sustain a proper relationship.'

'And did he just accept that?'

'No, no. Far from it. He kept writing and phoning.

And for a while, I even thought I might change my mind and give up my course to be with him.'

I swallow hard on the lump in my throat. 'But you didn't?'

She shakes her head sadly. 'Something happened that changed everything. I met Martin.'

I heave a sigh. 'And the rest is history.'

'When I told Al about Martin, he realised he had to let me go at last. I was moving on with my life in England. I guess he knew he had to do the same. So he wished me well and that was that.'

'But then he came over to England when I was twelve?'

She smiles. 'He actually came over to England for a conference a year earlier than that, although I didn't realise that until much later. Apparently he had no intention of raking up the past, but with a free day on his hands, the temptation was too great to hop on the train and look me up. We'd moved into Martin's house, which Al knew was next door to where I used to live. So he turned up, practically on the doorstep.'

My eyes open wide in astonishment. 'What on earth did Martin say?'

Mum shrugs. 'They never met. Al was standing in the street, apparently, and he saw you and me coming out of the house.'

A memory jolts my brain. 'I saw him, Mum! I knew

I'd seen him before. He was standing by a tree a little way from our gate, looking over!' *I'd thought I recognised him and it was true. I'd actually seen Alessandro that day – when he came looking for Mum!*

Tears spring to Mum's eyes and for a while, the emotion of the moment is too much and she can't speak. Then she puts her hand over mine and whispers, 'A few weeks later, in a letter, he told me that as soon as he saw you, he knew straight away.'

My heart starts beating very fast. 'Knew what?'

'That you were his child, not Martin's. There wasn't a single doubt in his mind. He just knew. You're so alike, you know. I see him in you all the time. He was dumbstruck, as you can imagine, and it stopped him from knocking on the door that day. He figured I'd made a little family unit and he wasn't about to threaten our happiness by just appearing back on the scene and have Martin realise you weren't his child.'

'So he just left?' My throat hurts. I can't believe how Alessandro must have felt at that moment, realising he had a daughter he never knew about. But having to just walk away from her!

Mum nods. 'When he wrote to me after that trip to England, he begged me to let him meet you just once. At first, I was determined that would never happen. But I felt such terrible guilt over keeping you from each other, so I eventually agreed that he could see you that

Christmas when Martin was working away. He promised that after that, he would leave us be. We decided it was best if you didn't know who he really was.'

'But then he changed his mind about staying away. He started to write those letters to me.'

She nods. 'When he came over that Christmas, he could tell things weren't great for you at home, with Martin. Just little things you said. So I guess that's when he realised you needed him after all. That you deserved a real dad who loved you to bits.'

I swallow hard. We're both crying now. 'You should have told me about him, Mum. A long time ago.' My heart feels unbearably heavy. 'I should have known as soon as I was old enough to understand.'

Tears spill down Mum's cheeks and she clings onto my hand. 'I know, Poppy, I know, my love. And you can't imagine how many times I've wished I'd taken a different path. Made different decisions. I did what I thought was right at the time, always with your welfare in mind. But now I realise it was the worst thing I could have done, keeping you and Alessandro apart. Not giving you the letters he sent.'

I scrape back my chair and go to hug her. She stands up and we cling to each other, both sobbing as if our hearts will break.

After a while, when we're all cried out, we break apart to wipe our snotty noses, and Mum says she'll put the kettle on because a cup of tea is the default rescue remedy of all time.

'Your mascara is on your chin,' she points out with a little exhausted smile.

'Oh, thanks, Mum,' I joke, feeling drained myself, but a thousand times better because we've finally talked. 'At least I've had my hair done this century. Unlike you.'

'Cheek! I thought grey was fashionable these days.'

I grin. 'Grey, maybe. Split ends, no. You'll look gorgeous with a trim and a colour.'

'It's not that bad, is it?' She looks in the mirror. 'Hmm, on second thoughts ...'

'I could call that mobile hairdresser you used to like.' I know I'm taking my life in my hands even suggesting this, but to my surprise she gives a cautious nod.

'Okay. Make me an appointment. But I claim the right to cancel at the last minute if I feel like it.'

I nod happily. It's a tiny step forward but that's fine by me.

Chapter 29

Erin left several messages on my mobile yesterday that I didn't pick up.

Feeling much better today – although still wiped out by the migraine – I give her a call and she's horrified by the whole Harrison story. But she's determined I should see the break-up as a brand-new start. 'You're on the threshold of something really exciting with this catering business.'

I groan. 'Except my first proper job has been a disaster.'

'No, it hasn't. It's just life getting in the way. You couldn't help your mum's bungalow catching fire, or you and Harrison breaking up. Bob understands, I'm sure. It doesn't take away from the fact that the meals you cooked were superb. Every last one of them.'

'Even the vegetarian ravioli?' I laugh, thinking how amazing it is that Erin always manages to make me look on the bright side. I guess I'll need her more than ever now that Harrison has gone from my life.

'*Especially* the ravioli. That lemon sauce was gorgeous.'

'Listen, can I come over for a quick chat when you get back from work? I know Mark is cooking you a special meal tonight but I'll be gone by the time he gets back home.'

'Of course you can come over. You don't have to ask.'

'Great. See you later.'

I'm determined to finally get to the bottom of Mark's weird behaviour. But first I need to get Erin out of the flat before Mark comes home so I can tackle him on my own. My plan is to look white-faced and miserable (I won't need to act much) so that she'll take pity on my plea for chocolate and leave the flat to buy some for me, at the exact time Mark is due home from work.

As it turns out, it all falls into place brilliantly.

'So, a dark-chocolate Bounty?' Erin sticks up her thumb. 'No problem. Shouldn't be long.'

'Take your time,' I call after her. 'And could you go to the takeaway on your way back and get me some chips?' *That will buy me more time.*

When she's gone, I pace nervously around her flat, rehearsing what I want to say to Mark. My hope, of course, is that he's completely innocent. I'd so love to be able to reassure Erin that Mark is here to stay, but it doesn't bode well, considering we've both had our individual suspicions.

360

I'm relying on the element of surprise to root out the truth. If I ask him outright if he's seeing someone else, I'm fairly sure I'll be able to judge from his reaction whether or not he's telling the truth. But I feel really sick at the thought of questioning him. Part of the problem – apart from my hatred of confrontation – is that I really like Mark. But I care about my best friend more, so it has to be done.

A car goes by in the street below, with some sort of classical music blasting out from its sound system. I wouldn't normally mind but it's so loud, I'm worried I might not hear Mark's key in the lock. Of course, it's typical that, far from passing by, the car seems to be parked right outside the flats, blaring what sounds like opera, and some man with a powerful baritone is singing his heart out like a poor man's Pavarotti. Oh God, it's probably some stunt for a council election. Or an advert for a theatre show. I'll never hear Mark's key over such a hullabaloo...

Then my heart nearly leaps out of my chest.

Someone is out there on the balcony! I can hear their footsteps on the wrought iron.

Oh my God, an opera-singing psycho has somehow managed to climb up onto Erin's first-floor balcony and is even now attempting to break in under cover of darkness!

What should I do? Flee? Phone the police? Shout for help?

My options are limited due to the fact that I'm frozen with terror to the spot. The drapes are drawn across, so I can't actually see onto the balcony but the doors will surely be locked.

Oh fuck, they're not. He's coming in! He's fumbling with the door handle. The opera singing is getting louder…

My heart is pumping, fit to explode in my chest. Glancing wildly around, I grab Mark's snooker cue that's propped against the wall in the corner, and I brandish it as fiercely as I can, raising it to shoulder height, poised for action.

As the warbling burglar fights with the curtains, I take aim and whack him hard with the stick. The singing stops and is replaced by a string of indignant expletives. And someone bursts through the gap in the curtains.

Mark?

I stare in bemusement. 'What the—?'

He glares at me, rubbing his arm. 'What the—?'

Erin bursts in with a bag of shopping. 'What the—?'

We all stare wide-eyed at each other.

It's Erin who breaks the gob-smacked silence. 'What's that cherry-picker truck doing outside our balcony?'

Mark groans. 'That would be mine.'

'*Yours?*'

'Well. Not mine exactly. It's hired. For the day.'

'Um … why?'

Mark sighs heavily. 'So I could climb up onto the

balcony with a bunch of flowers, sing some opera and ask you if you'll marry me.'

Erin claps her hands to her mouth. And my heart does a giant leap. Mark produces some rather squashed red roses from behind his back and snarls at me.

'Sadly your best mate here has just ruined the whole thing.'

*

It will no doubt go down in family folklore.

I turned a highly romantic proposal – inspired by Erin's favourite film, no less, and executed with mind-boggling attention to detail – into the biggest farce ever.

When I realised what Mark had set up, I couldn't believe I'd ruined it. He'd been planning it ever since he overheard Erin and me on the balcony that day, discussing how we'd like to be proposed to! I remember Erin saying she'd want it to be extra-special.

Mark is sitting on the sofa and Erin is lying with her head in his lap, gazing up at him adoringly.

'I still can't believe you dreamed all that up for me,' she says with a happy sigh.

'It didn't take too much imagination,' says Mark modestly. 'It had to be along the lines of that end scene from *Pretty Woman*, where he climbs up and rescues her and she rescues him right back.'

'Gosh, you're word perfect.' I giggle, feeling like the biggest gooseberry ever. 'How many times has she forced you to watch it?'

He grins and plucks a number out of the air. 'Seven-hundred and forty-two.'

His fiancée laughs delightedly and springs up off the sofa. 'Champagne! We need champagne!'

I feel exhausted.

To my enormous relief, when Erin arrived back with my chocolate and it finally dawned on her what was going on, she burst into peals of excited laughter. She gazed at Mark wide-eyed and then slightly hysterically threw her arms around his neck and said yes – around fifteen times.

I was going to sneak off and leave them to it, but they insisted I stay and celebrate. Mark graciously conceded that since I'd played such a pivotal role in the proposal, I deserved a glass of something at least.

'Who's the strawberry-blonde girl?' I ask, over-whelmed with relief that Mark isn't a bad guy after all.

'Louisa. Lovely girl. She's the employee assigned to my case. From Mariella's Matching Agency.' He whips a business card out of his pocket and hands it to me. 'The old-fashioned dating agency concept has appar-ently fallen on hard times. They were forced to diversify to survive. So they've branched out into organising marriage proposals for people.'

I suddenly remember something. 'Was it Louisa's frosted-pink lipstick, then? The one Erin found by the washbasin?'

He pulls a face. 'That was a close call. I was quite proud of myself for coming up with that nonsense about Erin tidying out her toiletries bag.'

I laugh. 'I was convinced you were up to no good. Was it Lousisa's idea to rent the cherry picker from the salvage yard so you could get up to the balcony?'

'Yeah.' He grins, then his face changes. 'How did you know about the salvage yard?'

'Ah. Er ... well, I just guessed.' I shrug, really not wanting him to know I was spying on them that day. 'I mean, where do you go if you need a cherry-picker truck? The salvage yard.'

He gives me an odd look but he's clearly too enamoured with his own brilliant plan to waste time thinking about it.

'I had to take operatic-singing lessons a few nights a week after work, and there was the hypnotist sessions as well, of course.'

'You've been going to a *hypnotist*?'

He shrugs. 'Fear of heights, remember? A bit of a bind if you want to get your leg over a first-floor balcony. Thankfully, he seems to have cured me.'

'Wow. You really went to town getting it right. That's so brilliant.'

He grins. 'She's worth it. And actually, I wanted to cure my fear of heights so I could go to the top of the Empire State Building when we're in New York.'

'Ooh, are you planning a trip there?'

'Yup. Another surprise for Erin. We leave tomorrow afternoon.'

Glancing towards the kitchen, I murmur, 'Oh my God, she'll be thrilled! Have you told her yet?'

'No. I'll – er – leave it till later.'

I smile apologetically. 'Until after I've gone, you mean. Don't worry. As soon as I've toasted you with some champagne, I'll be on my way.'

'Thanks, Poppy. And by the way, I plan to bear you no ill will whatsoever for cocking up the proposal so spectacularly. As long as you provide me with a lifetime of free chocolate cake.'

I nod, pretending to consider his terms. 'Done!' We solemnly shake hands on it.

'What's going on? More shocks?' giggles Erin, coming into the room with the champagne and three glasses.

'Wait and see,' says Mark mysteriously.

The champagne is lovely but I don't stick around. Walking home, I have a wistful smile on my face the whole way. Thank goodness it all ended well. I am so delighted for my best friend. She *so* deserves having the man she loves make such a fuss over her.

It's ironic, really. It should have been me planning

my wedding to Harrison. I take a big gulp of frosty air and resolutely bat the thought away. I'm trying to accept Mum's wisdom that what's for me won't go by me. Harrison did 'go by me' so he obviously wasn't the right one for me.

An image of Jed flashes into my mind but I give my head a little shake. Jed is probably with Katerina now. And anyway, it's going to take me a long time to properly recover from Harrison, and until then, there will be no romance. It wouldn't be healthy to bounce from one relationship to the next, so for the next year or so, I'm going to devote myself to establishing my new career. Luckily, I have some savings, so I'll be all right paying the rent and bills on my own for the first year. And by then, maybe I'll be earning money from the business.

But I won't have Harrison's support.

The nagging emptiness inside ratchets up a notch and a tear slides down my cheek. But a second later, I think to myself: Would I *really* have had Harrison's support for my new catering venture? I don't think so. He made that very clear when he broke up with me. No, this is something that I will do on my own. And I have a feeling it will be the making of me.

When I get back from Mark and Erin's, I'm feeling slightly better, so I phone Clemmy and tell her I'd be delighted to organise their New Year's celebration buffet. Clemmy's really pleased and we chat about everything.

I even ended up telling her all about Alessandro's letter and my desire to track him down, which, in true Clemmy-style, she finds terribly wonderful and romantic. She says Jed will be really pleased that I'll be there on New Year's Eve to do the food, and I somehow manage – with an enormous effort – to stop myself asking if he and Katerina are back together.

Not that it matters. Definitely no relationships – not even a chaste kiss – for at least a year. Possibly two.

Chapter 30

Saturday 31 December

This morning, Mum comes with me to buy the food for the buffet later on that night, and when we get back, the mobile hairdresser arrives.

'She's here. Do you want to do this?' I take her hand and squeeze it encouragingly.

I can tell she's nervous, but she forces a smile. 'Of course. Can you let her in? If you can be brave, then so can I!'

It's definitely a start...

I take a bit of time getting myself ready to go over to the Log Fire Cabin. Despite everything that's happened with the break-up, there's still a tiny flare of excitement in the pit of my stomach at the thought of seeing everyone again, and getting back to doing what I love: cooking.

I glance in the bedroom mirror before I leave. Skinny

jeans and sparkly top. Shiny dark hair tumbling down over my shoulders. I look thinner because I haven't eaten much since Harrison dropped his bombshell, but I could afford to lose a bit so that's no bad thing. My 'well-upholstered' days appear to be over for now. I frown, remembering Harrison's very dodgy 'compliment' that I tried so hard to see in a good light. Over the last few days there have been times I've wanted to kill him with my bare hands, so frowning is a definite improvement.

Popping into the kitchen to say cheerio to Mum, I find her chatting over tea and mince pies with Helen, whose nifty scissors and colouring magic have completely transformed her hair.

'You look amazing, Mum!'

She smiles at me modestly and runs a hand through her newly shiny chestnut locks. 'Hasn't Helen done a marvellous job?'

I smile at the hairdresser. 'You really have. She looks about fifteen years younger.'

'I was saying to your mum that next time we could try going a little lighter,' says Helen. 'Great mince pies, by the way.'

I smile, happier than I've felt in days. I like the sound of 'next time'.

When I arrive at the Log Fire Cabin soon after three, it's cold and crisp and already getting dark. When I ring the bell, the door is opened by Tom.

'Hey, Poppy! It's good to see you.' He's wearing drain-pipe black jeans and a cool turquoise shirt, and he seems to have matured since I last saw him.

'It's great to be back, Tom.' I smile, glancing around at the familiar hallway and the foliage and lights up the stairs that Jed and I put there together.

Tom comes through to the kitchen with me.

'This is Charlotte,' he says, as a pretty dark-haired girl gets up from the breakfast bar. She's wearing a cute cream dress and tan heels, and Tom puts his arm around her waist, looking proud as punch.

'I've heard all about your scrummy food,' she says shyly, as she follows Tom out of the kitchen, leaving me to get on.

A movement beyond the window catches my eye and I go over and glance out. Clemmy and Ryan are in the hot tub, bathed in candlelight, which I'm sure will have been Clemmy's idea. As I watch, Ryan leans over and kisses her full on the mouth. I draw back in case they see me, although they seem far too wrapped up in each other to be aware of anyone else. My heart lurches. Everyone is coupling up, which is lovely, but it all feels rather bittersweet to me. My stupid, hopeful heart was counting on Jed being here to welcome me, but he's nowhere in sight.

Ruby bounces through to the kitchen as I'm making

the mini smoked-salmon quiches. 'Tom told me you were here. Look at this, Poppy. Bob and I are going to do it next week.' She shows me a website on her brand-new phone. Apparently you pay money and you get to hang off a rock face, protected from a fall to your death hundreds of feet below by just a single rope.

'How sick will that be?' she says happily.

I grin at her. 'Sounds terrific. Where do I sign up?'

'You wouldn't dare!'

'You're right. I wouldn't. Is that the girl Tom phoned and asked out as a dare that night?'

'Charlotte, yes. Apparently she's always liked him, too, but she was too shy to do anything about it until he phoned.'

'She seems lovely.'

'Yeah, she's all right. She can windsurf.'

I nod. 'Praise indeed. I bet your mum's happier now that you and Bob are getting on.'

Ruby snorts. 'Yeah. They went off into Easingwold for lunch all smoochy-smoochy. Yuk!'

She grabs a tortilla chip and whisks out of the kitchen with a little wave.

I get on with preparing the evening's buffet, thinking how good it is to be back here among all these lovely people. A cold hand grasps my heart. But they're all leaving on the second of January. And after that, I'll never see Jed again...

The door opens and I look up expectantly. It's Clemmy, dressed in a silky, pale-blue robe, her hair twisted into a towel.

'Poppy! How lovely that you're back!'

'I've missed everyone.' I smile, and we hug. 'A lot seems to have happened in the few days since I was here last.' I give her an arch look and she reddens.

'Gosh, I know. Tom and Charlotte.'

'And you and Ryan. I saw you in the hot tub together.'

Clemmy beams, radiating pure happiness. 'I wore down his defences. He admitted he'd always secretly fancied me but didn't think I was his type, whatever that means.'

I laugh. 'Apparently he's changed his mind.'

She nods, her eyes shining.

'It seems strange to think that when Jed left that message on my phone inviting you for Christmas, I thought it was the two of you who were meant to be together.'

She sighs. 'Jed's lovely. I think he has a soft spot for you.'

'Really?' I turn away to mix the mayonnaise.

'Definitely. I've seen the way he looks at you when he thinks no one's watching.'

I swallow hard. 'But he's with Katerina, isn't he?'

She groans. 'Yes. Ry seems to think he's taken her to London. He heard Jed phoning a hotel there earlier in

373

the week, and they just seem to have taken off without a word.' She shrugs. 'It's a shame they'll miss the fireworks at midnight. It's taken Ryan ages to organise it.'

My heart, having flipped with joy when Clemmy said Jed liked me, is now plummeting down a lift shaft. I feel sick at the thought of Jed and Kat together in London.

'Hey, did you know I'd persuaded Ry to go and see his dad in France?' says Clemmy.

'You have? Oh God, that's brilliant, Clem. Will you go with him?'

She nods shyly. 'He said he'd spoken to you about him and you made him see the situation in a different light.'

'I'm so pleased. You only have one dad.'

I offer her a tortilla chip and she takes one, then says thoughtfully, 'You know, having you here, in this kitchen over Christmas, helped us all. We were at sixes and sevens when we arrived but it's as if everything has worked out as if by magic.'

'Magic?' I laugh. 'Well, I'm not sure I can lay claim to being a magician, but it's a lovely thought, Clem. Mind you, I've always believed in the healing warmth of a kitchen, as the heart of the house.'

She nods happily. 'You will stay for the fireworks? And have a drink and some food with us?'

'I'd love that. Thank you.'

We all gather in the living room, helping ourselves from the buffet I've laid out on the dining table. I'm driving so I stick to the fruit punch, having first established it doesn't contain any lemonade that might possibly be vodka!

At one point, I glance around, and it hits me how happy and relaxed everyone seems to be. A weight settles in my stomach. I've been telling myself that it doesn't matter if I see Jed or not because I'm not going to be acting on my feelings for him. And anyway, he's with Katerina. But finding him gone has made me feel as wobbly and lost as I felt when Harrison dropped me off and drove on to spend the night at the Pretty Flamingo Hotel.

I'm in love with Jed.

And there's nothing I can do about that, except wait it out and hope that one day, the feeling might fade. Emotion swells inside. I make an excuse and retreat to the kitchen, then I grab my coat and slip through the patio doors, standing just outside in the snow, looking out across the lake. It's very dark and I can't make out the cottage on the opposite bank, but the light flooding out from the cabin means that I can actually see a few yards in front of me.

I think about Harrison and how sad it is that we just couldn't work as a couple. Because I do realise that now. I've been thinking about practically nothing else since we broke up, and I know now that I was just kidding myself, wanting to believe that we could be happy together. I skated over the obvious signs that we were basically incompatible because I was so enamoured with the idea that I was loved. Martin had made me believe I didn't deserve love, but here was an attractive, intelligent man with a lot of caring ways telling me I actually *was* worthy. And that was everything to me.

But then things started to change in my life, which upset the fragile balance of our relationship and brought it crashing down.

I swallow hard as fresh tears well up.

I will get through this, though. I actually quite like myself now, which is a real revelation. I've been growing more confident and braver by the day, and the new business will throw up even more new challenges and adventures that I will have to rise to. And actually, it feels quite exciting, as well as a little nerve-racking. I couldn't have imagined doing something like this a year ago. Even six months ago...

'Aren't you cold out here?' A familiar voice reaches me from the shadows and when I turn, Jed is standing close by. My heart lurches painfully then starts beating at a million miles an hour.

I smile at him, sneaking a look behind him, wanting to know if he's brought Katerina. But there's no one else in sight. 'It was warm in the kitchen,' I say. 'I just wanted some air.'

He nods, standing several feet away from me as if he's keeping his distance. 'I was so sorry about Harrison ... the break-up. Are you okay?'

'Thank you. I'll be all right. I suppose it just takes time.'

'True. And when you're finally over it, you'll be amazed at how hopeful you feel about life.'

I smile shyly at him. He sounds as if he's talking from experience. 'How is Katerina?' I've got to know. I can't keep torturing myself, dreaming up all these possible scenarios – like I did with Mark.

He looks thoughtful. 'Katerina is ... fine. She'll be flying back to Australia tomorrow.'

'For good?' It's out before I can stop it.

'Er, well, I'm not sure about that.' His lips twitch. 'But she's taken another two-year contract. If that helps?'

I glance at him. Is he making fun of me? There's a definite glint in those gorgeous green eyes but it's frustratingly impossible to tell how he feels about me.

'It's good to see you,' he says.

'You, too.'

He moves as if to hug me, then he stops.

We lock eyes and my head starts to spin crazily as it always does when I'm close to Jed Turner.

'Listen,' he says, 'I know it's probably far too soon after your break-up for you to want to ...'

I nod, my heart drumming fast. 'Far too soon,' I murmur, transfixed by his mouth.

He nods. 'You'll have to get over Harrison first. Lay that relationship properly to rest. And I have absolutely no intention of being that transitional guy whose only function is to help you get over your heartbreak.'

His gaze drops to my lips and suddenly they feel all bee-stung and beautiful, which is weird. 'You could never be that transitional guy,' I tell him, astonished at my bravery. *What happened to meek and mild Poppy?*

'Maybe.' He shrugs but I can tell he's secretly pleased. 'All I'm saying is I'll wait. Until you're ready. Am I being too presumptuous?'

My knees are so weak I think I might have to sit down. I shake my head and murmur, 'Not at all.'

I love Jed Turner. I really, really love him! I can see it so clearly now that Harrison is no longer in my life. I think I was a goner the instant I spotted him at the station that time. Or maybe I fell in love with his glorious voice, who knows? All I do know is that he seems to have feelings for me, and that's just the most incredible thing ever.

I'm not sure how I feel about him 'waiting', though. Although I suppose it's probably for the best.

'We could always date.'

He frowns. 'Sorry?'

I shrug. 'We could go on dates because that's not being in a proper relationship, is it? Then I'd be able to – you know – get over the break-up in my own time.'

'While casually dating.' He weighs it up. 'You know, you might be on to something there, Poppy.'

'Glad you think so.'

'I do.'

Oh God, we're moving closer to one another. He's *so* within grabbing distance. We could do all sorts of things if we were 'just dating'.

He runs a hand through his hair and gives me one of his slow, heart-stopping smiles. 'What are you doing to me, Poppy Ainsworth? Are you saying we can definitely see each other? Because this distance between us here feels as wide as the English Channel.'

'If we're going to "date", it would be really weird if we didn't get very close now and again,' I say slowly, looking into his eyes.

'Like this, you mean?' He bridges the gap and slides his hands around my waist, then kisses the tip of my nose.

A delicious shiver runs through my entire body. Heart hammering, I pretend to consider. 'Maybe you should be a bit more *decisive* than that.'

He pulls me against him with a low groan. 'Better?'

'Much better.' My voice comes out as a squeak. 'I like this dating business.'

'Me, too,' he says, a second before he brings his mouth down hard on mine.

We kiss like we're never going to let go, and somehow

I end up pressed against the wall of the cabin, feeling all of Jed Turner's delicious weight against me. I think just once of Harrison, hoping he's happy with his Spanish dancer, then I abandon myself to Jed's touch, aware of nothing else in the world.

When we come up for air, we smile at each other rather bashfully and I lean against his beautiful chest with a little blissed-out sigh. Something wet lands on my nose and I look up at the night sky. It's started to snow again. A few flakes drifting down, just in time for New Year.

I smile up at Jed. 'So you were in London today?'

'Yes.'

'Business or pleasure?'

'Neither, really. I was looking for someone.'

'Really?' I pull away so I can look at him.

'Yes. You know him, actually. I took a photo.' He pulls out his phone and starts searching.

I stare at him, a strange feeling in the pit of my stomach.

He passes me the phone and I stare at the picture of a man.

He has olive skin and hair that's almost black, just like mine. Except that his is brushed with grey at the temples. But it's the eyes that I remember. Warm, smiling, the same dark brown as mine.

I look up at Jed in wonder. 'My dad.'

He nods.

'But how ...?' My head is whirling with questions but I can't seem to form the words.

'How did I find him?'

I nod, desperate to learn everything Jed can tell me. This amazing new development is truly like the icing on the cake of my day!

Jed smiles at me, his eyes full of warmth. 'After you told me about your real dad that time, I kept thinking about your situation. It's pretty similar to Ryan's, really, and I know what it meant to him to meet his biological dad.' He shrugs. 'I can speak a little Italian. Just enough to make myself understood. So I phoned round the big five-star hotels in Naples, hoping I might strike lucky.'

'Wow! What did you say?'

'That a family member was trying to track down an Alessandro Bianchi, who used to work in the kitchens there.'

'Did anyone remember him?'

He shakes his head. 'It was so long ago ... but I left my name and number just in case. And then a few days ago, I got a call from the head chef at one of the hotels, saying he worked alongside Alessandro when they were just starting out in their careers. He remembered that Al, as he called him, was always talking about moving to England when the opportunity arose.'

'Really?' *He'd wanted to live in England!*

'The guy gave me the name of a five-star hotel in Florence where your dad went to work as a chef de partie after he left Naples.'

'And you phoned the Florence hotel?' My heart is beating so fast, I feel like I might faint.

Sensing I'm overwhelmed, Jed steers me gently over to a stone bench and I snuggle against him in the cold night air, loving the protective feel of his arm around me.

'Yes, so the receptionist at the Florence hotel remembered him straight away. She said he'd moved to England a year earlier to take up a new job as a head chef – and she gave me the name of the hotel in London.'

'Oh my God.' My voice is barely above a whisper. 'So he's actually living in England now.'

Jed rubs a hand over his face. 'Listen, Poppy, I hope you don't mind that I did all this?'

'No, of course I don't. I couldn't be happier.'

'Good. I would have involved you earlier – I was just afraid my search might lead up a blind alley and I didn't want you having your hopes built up, only to be dashed all over again.'

'So, is that why you went to London yesterday? To find him and talk to him?' I need to know, but part of me dreads hearing something bad. I didn't reply to any of the letters Alessandro sent me. What if he doesn't want to know me any more?

Jed nods. 'He's a great guy. We had a good long chat. And when I told him you were desperate to contact him again, his face lit up and he didn't stop smiling for the rest of our conversation.'

'So ... he actually wants to see me?'

'Of course he wants to see you.' Jed smiles, gently brushing my face with his thumb to wipe away a tear. 'You're his daughter and he's never stopped thinking about you. And your mum.'

'She'd like to see him too. I'm sure of it.' I gaze up at him. 'Thank you so much for this. I can hardly believe it.'

Jed pulls me into a hug, and the emotion that was choking me up starts to spill out. I weep happy (and copious) tears into Jed's jacket, but he doesn't seem to mind at all. He just holds me closer. And being crushed against him feels just as incredible as finding my real dad at last.

Finally, I pull away and look up at him. 'So is he ... is my dad coming here?'

Jed nods. 'He's got a few days off after New Year and he wants to see you.' He fishes something out of his pocket. 'He asked me to give you this. He's kept it all this time.'

I take it. It's a small, square Christmas card, hand-made, with a child's drawing of two people having a snowball fight and 'Happy Xmas!' emblazoned across the top in red glitter. Over the years, the glitter has grown somewhat sparse. I hold the card in my hands as if it's a precious, ancient manuscript. Opening it, I read the words, '*Love from Poppy*.'

I gasp. 'I made this for him when he was here that Christmas! I can't believe he's held onto it for all these years.'

Jed grins. 'He asked if we had snow here.'

'He did? Why?'

'He said he'd very much like to have another snowball fight, although he accepts that you might have honed your snowball-throwing skills just a little since you were twelve!'

I laugh in delight. 'He remembers that snowball fight?'

Jed smiles, looking equally delighted, and then leans down for another kiss.

When we finally draw apart, I gaze up at him coyly. 'Are we on a date, then?'

'A date? Oh, yes.' Jed nods solemnly. 'Which means I get to kiss you very thoroughly at midnight.'

Just as he says the words, there's a loud crack and then fireworks begin sizzling and exploding overhead. Nestled in the crook of Jed's arm, I gaze upwards, laughing as Ryan and Clemmy's glorious display lights up the entire night sky.

'Forgot to tell you,' murmurs Jed close to my ear, 'Bob

likes your food so much, he wants to hire you.'

'He *does*? Oh my God, can this day possibly get any better?'

'My feelings exactly.'

Jed pulls me against him once more. And as the snowflakes drift down around us, I mould myself against him, revelling in the heat and solidity of his body and sinking ever deeper into his kiss. The technicolour explosions going off around us really are the perfect reflection of how I'm feeling inside.

This could very well turn out to be my best year yet...

Acknowledgements

Huge thanks as always to Heather Holden-Brown, my wonderful agent. Heather, your unfailing enthusiasm for my books has hauled me out of several pits of self-doubt, so thank you!

A million thanks also to the incredible team at Avon, particularly my lovely, super-talented and endlessly patient editor, Phoebe Morgan.

And of course, my family and friends. Your love and encouragement make this publishing adventure of mine even more rewarding and exciting than it already is. I couldn't have achieved my dream without you!

Some secrets can't stay in the past for too long...

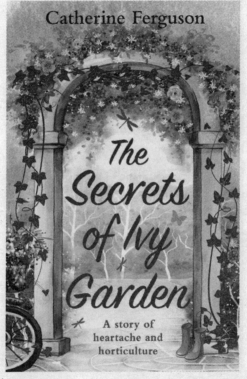

Heartache and horticulture from the ebook bestseller

Wedding season isn't always smooth sailing...

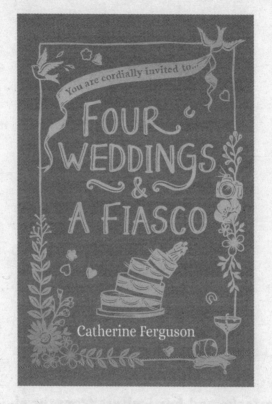

A funny, feel-good read about weddings gone wrong...

Lola Plumpton can't believe her luck. Until, of course, her luck runs out…

A warm and cosy festive tale you won't be able to put down.

Can Izzy sort the wheat from the chaff and the men from the boys?

When Izzy Fraser's long-term boyfriend walks out on her, she decides to take matters into her own hands...with unexpected consequences!

Two ex-friends. One Christmas to remember…

A funny, heartwarming read - the perfect book for fans of Jenny Colgan and Lucy Diamond.